Gabriel Bergmoser is an award-winning Melbourne-based author and playwright. He won the prestigious Sir Peter Ustinov Television Scriptwriting Award in 2015 and was nominated for the 2017 Kenneth Branagh Award for New Drama Writing. In 2016 his first young adult novel, *Boone Shepard*, was shortlisted for the Readings Young Adult Prize. His first novel for adults, *The Hunted* (HarperCollins, 2020), is a bestseller, and a film adaptation is currently being developed. His 2022 Audible Original novella, *The Hitchhiker*, spent a month at number one in Audible's bestseller chart.

Praise for *The Hunted*

'An original and high-octane read, it makes *Deliverance* look like *Picnic at Hanging Rock*' – *The Times/Sunday Times* Crime Club

'This slice of outback noir is ... at once exhilarating, gleefully vicious and totally, race-to-the-finish-line unputdownable' – *The Observer*

'An audacious walk on the wildest side of outback noir ... a vivid thriller' – *Sydney Morning Herald*

'A perfectly paced, thrilling read with an unrelenting sense of dread and menace ... building suspense at every turn of the page. Crime and thriller readers will love this savage Rottweiler of a novel that will clamp its jaws around their throat and shake them to the end' – *Bookseller+Publisher*

'Tough, violent, suspenseful and peopled with great characters, *The Hunted* could well be the Australian thriller of the year. This is Jack Reacher for adults' – *Canberra Weekly*

Praise for *The Inheritance*

'More turns than a winding road and more twists than a roller-coaster' – *Herald Sun*

'Swiftly builds to an explosive climax. A ferocious tale' – *Canberra Weekly*

'Australian outback noir at its finest ... featuring a heroine who lingers long in the memory' – *Daily Mail*

'Energy and cinematic panache ... compelling' – *The Times*

'*The Inheritance* can be enjoyed by any reader with a taste for straight-ahead, no holds barred brutal crime thrillers that have an Australian feral tang' – *The Australian*

'Maggie is an engaging psychopath, latter-day Fury, agent of retribution ... The momentum rarely stalls ... the twists and turns kept me in page-turner mode' – *Good Reading Magazine*

'As far as action heroines go, Maggie is up there with the best of them' – Better Reading

'Stands out for its quality character development, its page-turning action and its literary quality' – NZ Book Lovers

'Heart-in-mouth reading' – Queensland Reviewer's Collective

'A terrific thriller that deserves to be read in a single sitting' – Murder & Mayhem

'A thrill-a-minute ride that keeps up the reading momentum throughout, packed with Aussie chutzpa and hugely entertaining' – Crime Fiction Lover

GABRIEL BERGMOSER

THE CARETAKER

HarperCollins*Publishers*

HarperCollins*Publishers*
Australia • Brazil • Canada • France • Germany • Holland • India
Italy • Japan • Mexico • New Zealand • Poland • Spain • Sweden
Switzerland • United Kingdom • United States of America

HarperCollins acknowledges the Traditional Custodians
of the land upon which we live and work, and pays respect
to Elders past and present.

First published in Australia in 2023
by HarperCollins*Publishers* Australia Pty Limited
Gadigal Country
Level 19, 201 Elizabeth Street, Sydney NSW 2000
ABN 36 009 913 517
harpercollins.com.au

A catalogue record for this book is available from the National Library of Australia

ISBN 978 1 4607 6313 1 (paperback)
ISBN 978 1 4607 1571 0 (ebook)
ISBN 978 1 4607 4909 8 (audiobook)

Cover design by Alex Ross
Cover images by istockphoto.com and shutterstock.com
Author photograph by Sean Carney
Typeset in Sabon LT Std by Kirby Jones
Printed and bound in Australia by McPherson's Printing Group

PROLOGUE

And there she was. Getting out of a dust-strewn sedan, dark sunglasses on despite the overcast day, shoulders slightly hunched as she checked her surrounds. Something fearful about that look, something that caught his attention.

She'd taken steps to conceal herself. In all the photos he'd seen, she was blonde, hair immaculate and makeup perfect. She wasn't especially pretty, but in those photos she looked like she belonged on a red carpet. Not here in this nothing town, scared and skinny and alone, hoping a hoodie and a dye job would be enough to disguise her.

Maybe, until now, they had been. Months on the run and he guessed he was the first to recognise her, given she was still alive. A lot of people wanted a lot of things from that woman. She could be a career-maker if you were a cop or a mobster. A giant payday if you sold her to the right buyer.

Some people had no imagination.

She hadn't noticed him. He was very good at going unnoticed. She was crossing the road. He watched her from his spot beside the post office and considered how best to make his approach. He bit his lip.

He took a coin from his pocket and flipped it.

CHAPTER ONE

Now

Charlotte Laurent stepped out of the car, quickly and carefully scanning her surrounds. She didn't expect to see anything out of place. But then, expectations and reality did not always align.

Burnley. One of those country towns that looked to have sprung up almost by accident – a few hardy settlers deciding to build houses between the gum trees and scrubby hills around the same time, their descendants trying to claim those rundown old buildings somehow made the place historically significant. In reality, Burnley only held on because you had to drive through it to get to a ski resort. Not a good ski resort or even an especially close one – it was almost three hours from here to the top of Mount Skillion, with nothing but black ice and hairpin bends and trees in between. Charlotte, slow and cautious and watchful, had done it in four the first time. She'd passed nobody on the way. It was spring and the snow was gone.

Charlotte crossed fast to the faded supermarket. This was the second supply run she'd made since taking the job. On the first she clearly hadn't bought enough; that had only been three weeks ago. She could allow herself one mistake. She couldn't afford a second.

She still instinctively checked her reflection in every window or mirror she passed. She wasn't sure why. Short of plastic surgery or a mask, she'd gone about as far as she could in changing her appearance. She knew her wide blue eyes were distinctive, so she almost always wore sunglasses. Her wavy blonde hair was now dark, cut shorter than it had ever been in those photos on the news. She would always be tall, but she'd taken to hunching where possible, and tried to wear bulky jackets and cargo pants that hid how thin she was. Whether it was enough was unclear. Charlotte was no expert at this; she'd been improvising for months now.

The automatic door groaned as she stepped inside, doing her best not to flinch at the sound of the bell. Squat, balding Barry beamed at her from behind the counter.

'Katie! Back already, eh? How's the mountain – gone crazy yet?'

It was impossible to stop news spreading in Burnley, even news as boring as her job.

'Compared to the wild metropolitan life down here? It's paradise.'

Barry chuckled. 'Got a warped idea of paradise, but to each their own. Need some boxes?'

She grabbed a trolley and started collecting supplies. Canned food, toilet paper, bottles of water.

She was halfway through her third round of the shelves when she noticed she wasn't alone in the cramped aisle. A very tall, thin man, maybe in his forties, was examining a can of soup. He stood out immediately; blond hair, light blue eyes and a face that might have been handsome in a rough-hewn sort of way if it wasn't for an intense focus that made her heart pick up.

She grabbed some two-minute noodles from the shelf, trying to move fast enough to disguise the unsteadiness of her hands. She dropped a packet.

The man was there in seconds. He handed it to her. She gave him a tight smile. He didn't look away.

'These' – he nodded to the noodles – 'they're good?'

He had a slight accent, something Scandinavian.

'They're two-minute noodles.'

Was she imagining it, or had that focused look tightened as he searched her face? The changes to her appearance were supposed to offset a glance, but this man was giving her more than a glance.

'You are local?' he asked.

'Just passing through.'

He looked towards the front of the shop, where the boxes waited by the counter.

Her mouth was dry. Telling him she was staying somewhere remote was too close to the truth. If he was inclined to dig, it wouldn't take him long to work out where she had to be. But there weren't many other decent excuses for the way she was stocking up.

'I'm meeting some friends,' she said. 'Week away, you know? I drew the short straw. Gotta get the supplies.'

'A lot of supplies for a week.'

'A lot of friends.'

'How lucky.'

A moment of silence. He still wasn't looking away.

'I'd better go,' she said.

'What is your name?'

She blinked. The question was so abrupt, so strange – who just asked someone in the supermarket that? Her hands were sweaty, she couldn't draw enough breath, she—

No. *No.* She was ready for this.

'Katie,' she said. 'You?'

'I am Anders.'

She raised an eyebrow, going for bemused and praying she got it. 'Well, uh, see you round, Anders.'

She returned to the front, steadying herself on the counter as Barry added the noodles to one of the boxes. Anders was still watching her.

'Need some help getting these to the car?' Barry asked.

'Um ... actually, I was just thinking I might have to quickly run another couple of errands for Liam. Could you hold these behind the counter for me?'

She helped him shift the boxes, making a point to push them to the furthest, least accessible corner. Then she thanked Barry and, doing everything she could not to look back, stepped out into the cool air. It was afternoon but with the cloud cover and low light it might as well have been evening. She made it a few metres down the street before the shaking overcame her and she had to lean against a wall. Focusing everything she had on keeping her hand doing what she needed it to, she withdrew her old flip phone, a burner, from her pocket and concentrated on it, as if sending a message. She listened for footsteps. None. She breathed. Four beats in. Four beats hold. Four beats out. Four beats nothing. She repeated until she felt steady enough to continue. She chanced a look over her shoulder.

No-one.

* * *

She had arrived in Burnley for the first time a month ago. By then she'd already taken pains to change her appearance, but still she had kept her head down as she walked through the tiny town, taking note of all the shops and where the few security cameras were. She had eaten a burger in a little park behind the main street, watching for the occasional breaks in the overcast, late-winter sky, the moments she could see the distant undulating roll of the mountains beyond. So much land, thick with trees and rocks, and only the tiniest pockets of civilisation. One of those pockets was now closing up as the season ended. If all went well, after months of living in constant fear, that pocket would be her sanctuary.

She'd met Liam in a large, brightly lit café that had made her uncomfortable for the half an hour she waited, eyes on every dining family or elderly couple. When he arrived he spent a few seconds standing in the middle of the floor scowling until Charlotte, deciding to chance this being him, waved him over. The flash of surprise in his ruddy face almost sent her running for the door.

'Katie?' he asked.

She nodded, not trusting herself to lift her coffee to her lips.

'Not what I was expecting.' Liam was gruff, heavyset and maybe in his late thirties, with a broad, stern face and a goatee. Charlotte did not like the way his brow furrowed as he watched her.

'Everything okay?' she asked.

'Course,' he said. 'I mean, just ... how old are you?'

She gestured to the papers in front of her. 'Thirty-one. It's in my résumé.'

He made no move to pick it up. 'You look young for thirty-one.'

She might have to amend that for future applications. If she made it that long. She did her best to smile but didn't hold it too long. Any discomfort would make him look closer.

'Right then,' Liam said. 'The job. You read the ad properly?'

She nodded.

'You sure?' Liam pushed. 'I only ask 'cos we've had applicants in the past who thought it'd be like winter. A big nonstop party. Mount Skillion's not like that in the off-season. There's no-one else up there. National Parks might stop by occasionally. If we're really lucky, somebody'll book a lodge. Had a footy team do a buck's party there last year, no idea why until I saw the damage. Figured nobody would call the cops on 'em. But bookings like that are rare. Chances are, it'll be you by yourself from now until autumn. You clear on that?'

The whole reason she had applied for the job would, to just about anyone else, be reason to stay the hell away from it. But at least Liam's surprise seemed more to do with seeing a skinny young woman applying rather than him having recognised her.

'Yeah,' she said. 'I'm actually, um ...'

Use as much reality as you can afford to make the lie ring true.

'I'm kind of an aspiring writer and like, the isolation is what I need, you know? No distractions?'

Liam didn't bother to hide his eyeroll. 'Right. Whatever. Well, as long as you don't let the great Australian novel get in the way of your job, I couldn't care less what you do up there. I'll put it all in an email for you, but it's not rocket science, especially if no-one else is around, which so far no-one else will be. Keep an eye on the lodges. Keep 'em tidy. Most of them are pretty well insulated but every now and then there's some wear and tear we miss and mildew starts happening. Keep on top of that, the smell can be a prick to get out once winter starts, and guests get complaining. Watch the windows too – sometimes idiot birds fly into them and smash them, and if it rains or there's an unseasonal snowfall with no-one there to check, it can be a killer. There're only six lodges on Skillion – take one out of commission and that's a big fucking blow to the profits. That happens, board the window up, call me.'

'Do you live down here?' Charlotte asked.

Liam scoffed. 'Shit no. Couldn't pay me to live here. Skillion's alright during winter, rest of the time it's, well, you'll see. Burnley isn't even good in the winter. Nah, I'm over in Stratton, but I'll still be managing the emails and the admin and shit. Anyone books a lodge, I'll give you the heads up and you can make sure it's good for them. All the lodges have combinations so no need for 'em to bother you for keys or anything. Now, you get into any trouble up there—'

Charlotte did her best to maintain a neutral expression.

'Well, my advice is, don't.' Liam sipped his coffee.

'But if I do?'

'It's a three-hour drive from Burnley to Skillion,' Liam said. 'The road is winding as fuck and the conditions can be garbage at the best of times. Mobile reception is dogshit. There's an internet connection in Snowhaven, but it's not reliable. There's a radio in the parking booth, but again it won't do you much good unless a ranger is in the area. If you can get to the landline, you might get a chopper up in a total emergency. But honestly, I doubt it. Snakebite's the worst that can happen unless you go fucking around on the cliffs, and it tends to be too cold for snakes up there. Don't be an idiot and you'll be right.'

Charlotte made a show of considering her papers. Privately though, her mind was racing. Months on the run, always looking over her shoulder, analysing every too-long stare that came her way. But up there, alone, it was unlikely anyone would find her, cops or the others. It also meant that if they did, she was screwed.

But what was the alternative? Keep bouncing from town to town, waiting for the click of a cocked gun or a shriek of sirens? Her face had been on the news and she knew her picture would be doing the rounds through less legitimate channels as well.

Wanted for questioning about the murder of—

'You right?' Liam asked.

Charlotte's head snapped up, too fast.

'Look,' Liam said. 'I really need to know if you're gonna get cold feet, 'cos the owners won't accept another summer without a caretaker and we're pressed for time and—'

'No, it's okay,' Charlotte said. 'I'll do it.'

Liam took her through a few more details that Charlotte barely listened to. It would all be in his email anyway. Finally he slipped her an envelope containing the combinations to get into all the lodges.

'Take your pick of where to stay,' he said. 'Just don't lodge hop. It's fucking annoying if one gets booked out.'

She nodded and pocketed the envelope. Liam was fidgeting, impatient. She wondered if he had a family to go home to. The thought gave her such a stab of savage, unexpected loneliness that she almost crumpled in on herself.

'Right well, that's about it,' Liam said. 'You got my number. You've got the business card for supplies. I'll be watching the accounts so don't spend on anything stupid. Also, I hate to have to say this, but if you're looking to rob the lodges—'

'I'm not.'

'Great, but if you are, I'm telling you now there's nothing valuable in any of them. They're empty buildings that will be worth jack shit if the snow ever stops. So if you're a criminal, you're out of luck.'

Liam, for the first time, grinned. Charlotte tried to match it.

'Well?' he said. 'You a criminal?'

She couldn't stop her smile faltering. 'No. Of course not.'

* * *

Once she could breathe again, she let her thoughts turn to Anders.

She played out the conversation, trying to look at it as clinically as possible, trying to identify a point where she might have screwed up. Not that the best performance in the world would have mattered if he had recognised her. But then, there was very little reason to think that he would. She had been beyond careful these past months. She had covered her tracks. She had doubled back from every place she stopped, taking routes so convoluted and absurd nobody could figure out her direction. She had found her job via public computers and only met Liam once. If he'd been suspicious, well, he knew where to send the cops. They'd never arrived.

She took the long way back to the supermarket. There was no-one else on the street. Telling Barry she'd forgotten something, she did a round of the shelves and grabbed a box of biscuits. No-one else there. She returned to the counter and handed it to Barry.

'That guy, before,' she said.

'The Swedish one?'

'Yeah. He say anything to you?'

'What do you mean?'

She forced a smile. 'I guess he just gave me a weird vibe. He didn't ask anything about me?'

The expression of dumb incomprehension on Barry's face almost made her wince. The one thing she could not afford to be was memorable, and paranoia was always memorable.

'Don't think so. If he gave you the heebie-jeebies, I could always call Herb down at the station and—'

'No,' Charlotte said, harder than she'd meant to. 'No, it's fine. Just wanted your read, I guess. All good.'

She drove slowly through town, in the opposite direction to the mountain, passing the poky Town Hall with the uneven roof, the one servo and the tiny hospital. She chanced looks to either side, then in the rear-view mirror. No car behind her, no watching eyes. Houses thinned, then it was trees and paddocks again. She kept driving until a dirt road neared on the left. Checked the rear-view again. She turned on to the dirt road. Drove a way down it and stopped. She got out and ran her hands inside the wheel wells. She checked under the fuel door, then popped the boot and carefully went through the boxes, feeling around the sides, checking each packet for any sign of having been opened. Finally she took a torch from her glovebox, lay down on the cold ground, and looked under the car.

She got back in the front seat. She kept her eyes on the mirror. Fifteen minutes passed. She started the engine.

It took her nearly half an hour to get back onto the main road via this lengthy detour and even then her eyes kept moving to the mirror. When the trees grew thick around her and the road started getting steeper, her focus turned forward. If Anders had figured it out, he might have got a head start. She couldn't discount any possibilities here, even the ones that seemed absurdly paranoid.

Her hands tightened on the steering wheel. Sometimes, when the fear receded, what she was left with was anger. A snarling, grit-teethed fury at the injustice of it all.

She blamed herself for a lot. But sometimes, it was far easier to blame Leo Grey.

CHAPTER TWO

Then

Twenty-one years old and terrified, Charlotte Laurent watched the doors to the lecture hall. Her palms were sweaty and her heart was in her throat. She glanced around the foyer. Everybody else had gone. So much for a committed, curious creative writing class.

Her phone buzzed again. She didn't need to check to know that would be Mel, sending another guilt-tripping message. *We haven't hung out in ages, Charli. What's happened to us? Do you really want me going out alone?* By now Charlotte could predict it all, just as she could predict the long-since ingrained instinct to apologise and line up a time.

But not today.

The doors opened. Charlotte flinched, backing away as Leo Grey emerged, leather bag over his shoulder.

He didn't spare her a look. Everything from his sweeping blond hair to his angular face and blue eyes and perfectly fitting designer coat made him seem out of place on campus, the last person who should be wasting his time speaking to talentless uni students.

He was making for the exit. Charlotte tried to speak. Managed a rasp. He was almost at the door.

'Mr Grey!' she squeaked.

He turned. Saw her.

She just stared.

'Can I help you?' he asked, polite and friendly.

Say no. Apologise and say no and leave him alone and go home and hide and never come out again.

'Um ... I just wanted to say how great the talk was.'

He smiled. 'You sure? I reckon I put a few of your classmates to sleep.'

'They're idiots,' she said before she could stop herself.

Leo Grey raised an eyebrow. 'I thought they were the cream of the educational crop here. You know, when I went here there was a guy in my class who told me he could write a better book than me if he wanted to. Clearly he didn't want to, because he still hasn't.'

'But you ... you'd already sold a manuscript by then, right?'

'Yeah but obviously that was just a fluke,' Leo said. 'Don't you know? The *real* writers are the ones who tell everyone they're writers while mocking anyone who says the same and desperately masturbating over David Foster Wallace instead of ever, you know, writing.'

Charlotte couldn't help her blush.

'Oh God.' Leo winced. 'That was crass. Sorry, yuck. And you were being so nice about the talk.'

Charlotte grinned. Leo, realising he hadn't offended her, gave an apologetic laugh.

This. This was a moment. She had him. *Don't let it pass, don't—*

'Can I buy you a coffee?' she asked.

She'd been in school when Leo Grey's first novel had come out. At the time, it had been the kind of news story that Charlotte assumed everyone knew about, only to quickly learn nobody cared.

'Probably got his mum to write it for him,' Mel had said when Charlotte, clutching her copy of *Duality*, had told her he was only a few years older than them and already had a book on the shelves and another on the way.

But to Charlotte it had been proof of what was possible. There was a certain look you got from people when you told them you wanted to be a writer, a weird kind of scepticism borne from the vague sense that you needed to be someone *special* to pull that off. Like authors emerged fully formed and didn't start out as awkward high school students tapping away on barely functional laptops in their spare time.

To be fair, the few friends Charlotte had convinced to read her stuff hadn't been all that impressed. Some told her with false enthusiasm how much they'd loved it, then got vague when she pressed them for any details at all. Occasionally Charlotte would ask them about a non-existent plot point only for the inevitable reaction of 'Oh yeah, that was great.'

Only Uncle Mac had ever been honest with her.

'Look, it's bloody impressive,' he'd told her on the phone when she was thirteen. 'But I'm not sure it's my thing, love. Bit too much kissing and romance and mooning over boys. You sure you're writing what you know?'

From anybody else that might have hurt, but from Uncle Mac it came across as a good point. Charlotte's early high school attempts at swoony love stories were more based on other stuff she'd read and what she'd *liked* to have experienced than anything real. The problem was, the real stuff was boring.

Coming into her creative writing degree at uni, she'd tried to look at things differently. She'd had a couple of brief and awkward relationships by then, but it was hardly the stuff of starry-eyed romance. Instead, she tried to go more literary, to focus on slice-of-life stories that were more about making the minutiae interesting and beautiful than keeping the pages turning.

'I just don't think it's all that authentic,' her toad-like first year tutor had told her with that slack, lazy-eyed smile she hated so much. 'I mean, that line about your distorted reflection in the side of a toaster capturing your fractured sense of identity – have you ever actually *thought* that, or did you just reckon it sounded impressive?'

Face burning, Charlotte had said nothing for fear of crying. He was right, of course, but it didn't leave her with much of a clear path forward or an idea of what she *should* be writing. If what she knew was boring and what she didn't was inauthentic, what else was left?

So that had been uni. Doing the exercises, struggling through the readings, occasionally going for drinks with other writing students who were a mix of uncaring and insufferable, and starting to wonder if she was really all that different. She wanted to write. It was the only thing she'd ever wanted to do, apart from a brief primary school dalliance with dance that was more her mother's idea than hers.

And all the while her vague dreams of a life better than high school had begun to sputter and die. She was still hanging out with Mel. She was still living with her dad, who had been gruff and distant and not especially interested in anything she did for a while now.

So when she'd first seen that Leo Grey was coming to give a lecture at his onetime uni, she'd jumped at the opportunity to remind herself of why she was here. Other students might have seen him as a mainstream hack incapable of saying anything halfway profound, but Charlotte hadn't felt that way reading his first book as a teenager, and she didn't feel that way listening to him now from the back of the hall. Leo Grey, whip-thin with an easy smile, was so far above all the mutters and the judgement and the barely veiled jealousy of every wannabe in that room. Yet he didn't seem to think that. He was self-deprecating. He called his debut 'a cosmic-scale fluke' and his even more successful follow-up 'fate fucking you over by doing the same thing again and leaving you wondering how the hell you're supposed to pull it off a third time'.

At one point he claimed his books were 'predominantly enjoyed by parents who force their teenagers to read them, and despised by the teenagers forced to read them'. Charlotte disagreed with that, but she'd still laughed along and as she had, a mad idea occurred to her. Did she have it in her to *talk* to him? She'd never done that before, hadn't even raised her hand to ask a question of a guest lecturer. But this felt different somehow. This moment was a chance she couldn't let slip. This was a gift, and if she got scared and didn't at least *try*, she'd regret it forever. Because she had the sense, the sense you only sometimes get but know intimately when you do, that this moment could change the course of her life.

She took Leo to a small, outdoor café, in a gap between uni buildings, with umbrellas over tables made from pallets. It wasn't the type of place she normally went, but it felt boutiquey and cool enough to make her seem relatively tasteful while also being out of the way, lowering the likelihood of him being recognised. Although, seeing the ease with which he walked, like a *normal* person, Charlotte did start to wonder whether she had overestimated how instantly recognisable authors were.

Charlotte bought the coffees – a latte for herself, long black for Leo. For his part he sat at their table, smiling easily as he watched chatting students pass. None looked twice at him.

'So what do you write?' he asked.

Charlotte had dreaded this question even as she'd known it was the kind of thing she should *want* him to ask, a chance to pitch herself, to make him take notice. The problem was, she didn't have a tonne of confidence in the pitch.

She figured being upfront about the fact was her best bet.

'That's kind of the problem,' she said. 'I mean, I've done a mix of stuff, or at least *tried* a mix of stuff. But what I started out writing was, I dunno, not *authentic* and then when I tried to go authentic it was boring or pretentious or ...' She shrugged. 'So I don't know. I don't know what I'm supposed to do.'

'And I take it it's your tutors and other students telling you those things?'

Charlotte nodded.

'Do you like what *they* write?'

'No, but—'

'Okay, look.' Leo leaned forward. 'This is a guess. Could be a wrong one but I went to this same uni and I suspect I dealt with the same type of wankers. A lot of people? They love the *idea* of writing, not writing itself. They don't want to tell stories because they're burning to; they want to tell them because they think it makes them seem cool and special. Which is why they've never once interrogated what actually draws them to writing. So they see someone like me, who makes money doing it but writes the kind of stuff they wouldn't think was good enough to use as toilet paper, and they make a big show of rolling their eyes and looking bored and they think I'm too dumb to notice.'

'Does it bother you?' Charlotte asked.

'It did,' Leo said. 'Until I realised that I'm successful and they're not, so why worry? That's not ego talking, by the way, it's experience. I've met plenty of impressive literary authors and none of them have ever looked down their nose at me. Because they're real writers and they know how hard it is. That's the difference.'

Charlotte didn't want to admit to being confused, but she had the sense Leo was letting her into his confidences and it seemed being open with him was achieving that. So she said, 'I'm not quite sure what you mean.'

'I'm babbling,' he said with a laugh. 'Sorry, brevity was never my strong suit. What I mean is, there is absolutely no point in writing anything that you don't want to write. The reason you can't stand what your classmates do is because it's hollow. A facsimile of authors they think are impressive. It's not *them*. Writing what you know doesn't mean writing what you've explicitly experienced; it means writing what *matters* to you. Using as much reality as you can afford to make the lie ring true.'

'But what if I'm the fake one? What if they're right and—'

'You know how I know they're not?'

Charlotte shook her head.

'Because you're the one asking that question. Listen. I know, all too well, how overwhelming that insecurity can be. The need for validation. To be taken seriously. The fear that because you're not *yet*, you won't ever be. But if I can give you one piece of advice, it's this. You can't control your circumstances. You can't control what happens to you. If a car swings out of nowhere and runs you down, if a crazed mugger decides to shoot you, if a bolt of lightning hits you, whatever, you have no say in that. You are at the mercy of the world. What you don't *need* to be at the mercy of is yourself. Your own insecurities, fears, doubts, whatever. Now don't get me wrong; this isn't some self-help bullshit. You don't control your fate any more than you control the weather. But you can control what *you* do and feel. There's no big secret to being a writer, Charlotte. The secret is that you write and you love it and if you keep at it, you'll get better and eventually you'll get noticed. And I can promise your chances of success are a lot better if your self-worth isn't tied to what somebody else thinks of you.'

He spoke as if it was all so easy. Charlotte sipped her coffee and didn't reply.

Leo took her hand. Squeezed once and let go. He was smiling again.

'You're doing everything right. Keep doing it, yeah?'

* * *

She stayed put for a while after Leo left. Her coffee was finished and the staff were packing up around her. She sat and stared into space and it took her far longer than it should have to realise that what she was feeling was a thrum of steadily building exhilaration.

Holy shit. Holy shit, holy shit, holy *shit*. Did that actually just happen? Had she bought Leo Grey a coffee, had he smiled and told her he thought she was doing everything right, implied that he saw her as belonging almost to the same kind of class as him? Leo Grey, whose first book she'd obsessed over in school, whose every interview she had scoured from top to bottom.

Leo Grey had told her she was doing everything right.

She could dance, she could sing, she could run around this campus hugging everyone she saw and telling them that it was okay, that she wasn't a fraud or a failure, that *Leo Grey* thought she was doing everything right.

She stood. She was vibrating. She couldn't contain her grin.

She had to do something with this energy. She had to celebrate. She had to enjoy the moment. She couldn't just go home and watch TV and go to bed. No, today was special, she knew it. Everything was going to change after today. She had to do something to mark the occasion.

Her phone buzzed again. She took it from her pocket. Mel. Still at her to come out tonight.

She didn't put it away. She considered.

She typed a reply, hit send and went home to change.

CHAPTER THREE

Now

Halfway back up to Mount Skillion, she again got the feeling someone was watching her. The road through the foothills was narrow and never stayed straight or level for more than a hundred metres at a time. Towering grey ghost gums grew on either side, the canopy meeting above and turning the bitumen dappled dark. It was late afternoon and the sharp turns had made her stomach churn. She slowed right down as the trees to the right shrank away where the mountain began to slope – gradually at first then, as the road reached its windiest point, sharply, suddenly, as though the ground had just been cut away. She was moving at a crawl when she felt the prickle on the back of her neck.

She stopped the car in the middle of the road. Didn't let go of the wheel. She looked to her left, into the trees. She could see through them at first. Deeper, the shadows took over.

Breathe in. Out. Stay calm.

Isolation was fertile ground for fear. Charlotte knew how easy it was to see tree branches as hands reaching for you, pinpoints of light in shadow as watchful eyes. She also knew how hard it was to pull out of a panic when it had you in full grip, how logic and reason and even the truth that was right in front of you stopped meaning much at all.

She cleared her mind. Kept breathing, focused on nothing.

She got out of the car. Already the cold had her pulling her jacket tighter around herself. The sky was overcast. She approached the trees. Wind rustled grey leaves. Peeling curls of gum tree bark waved gently. Twigs cracked under her feet. She stood and faced the dark and listened.

She knew from her first drive up that there was nowhere along this road to conceal a car, no convenient rest areas or side paths. Not until you reached the resort proper. Nobody looking for her would come up on foot. Nor would they leave their car up ahead then walk back to hide in the trees.

The mountain air pierced her lungs. The smell of eucalyptus and distant snow was strong. She crossed to the other side of the road and looked over the flimsy steel guard rail. Her head spun. The ground dropped away sharply. Rocks, then treetops, levelling out and spreading over a valley to further distant hills.

Breathe in. Out.

She looked back at the shadows. No sound or movement. She returned to the car.

Even by Australian standards, Mount Skillion was a tiny resort – the smallest in Victoria. Only four runs and six lodges to choose from if you wanted to stay. It brought enough passing business to keep Burnley afloat, but compared to other ski resorts Skillion was beyond humble. Nor did it have any real off-season incentive to visit. The surrounding bush was too dense and rough to be much good to all but the most ambitious hikers, and unlike somewhere like Thredbo there were no pleasant bike trails.

On her arrival she had felt an unwinding relief as she'd passed the abandoned ticket booth and pulled into the empty carpark that fronted the Mount Skillion 'village'. But not today. Her mind was still back with the man in the supermarket and that strange moment on the drive up. Maybe nothing. Maybe warnings she couldn't afford to ignore.

She drove past the tiny, one-pump service station that doubled as a maintenance shed and only opened in winter, the low-slung pub with its jutting tiled roof and drawn blinds behind dirty windows, the single restaurant and the boxy, dark-grey lodges that lined the lone, cracked street leading to what, in winter, were ski slopes but in any other season were just gently tilting expanses of overgrown grass and speckled rock. Behind the lodges on her right the trees encroached dark and thick. On the left, the ground sloped upwards, dotted with lift towers, abandoned for the season. At the crest of the hill, the trees started again. Bush hemmed the village in on all sides. The Burnley road was the only way out. A veil of mist hung over all of it, turning the trees faint and ghostly. Even between the lodges, wispy tendrils blew between the quiet, still buildings. The sky was grey.

Charlotte parked outside Snowhaven, the biggest lodge on the mountain and to all intents and purposes her home – high windows below a sharply sloping roof and towering chimney, metal staircases up the side, and a rocky foundation going some way to making it look less industrial. She didn't get out of the car. She sank low and watched the rear-view. She could make out, back past the rows of buildings, the expanse of the park and the cord of dark that was the road behind her.

Her stomach growled. Three hours since Burnley. More than twice that since she'd last eaten. Light-headedness was coming on.

She didn't move. She barely blinked. She watched until the carpark was bathed orange and the trees at the mouth of the road glowed briefly gold in the setting sun. Only when the night claimed them did Charlotte get out of the car, her footsteps small and echoing and alone.

The first thing Charlotte did, every time she set foot in the lodge, was check the fine, thin thread that crossed the hall just past the front door. In the gloom it was impossible to see. If you walked through and broke it, you wouldn't notice.

But Charlotte would. Today, as usual, the thread was intact. She went upstairs.

Snowhaven was not the most luxurious of the lodges. The beds were all jammed-together bunks with the rough comfort level of slightly damp wood. But aside from being the only lodge on the mountain with internet, it was the biggest and that had benefits. There were several ways out. It would be hard for a pursuer to corner her. And the central communal area with its large fireplace, couches you could sink into, adjacent kitchen and vast window overlooking what in winter would be white slopes, was not a bad place to spend her ample free time. The warmth of the fire kept away the slight musty smell of disuse that permeated the other lodges. And there were several shelves of old books, mostly falling apart, at least a third of which Charlotte had already read.

She boiled the kettle in the kitchen, which reminded her of too many school camps in dingy dorms, and made a large cup of tea, then two packets of noodles.

She took a spot in her favourite armchair, facing the window and the view beyond. At this time there wasn't a lot to see. Just the mass of black forest and the bright stars above it. The clouds, for now, were gone. She ate and watched the night and listened and still the tightness in her muscles and clench in her stomach remained.

* * *

Her first night here had been the worst. With her emailed instructions from Liam, she'd driven slowly and carefully up the road. There was more snow then, big clumps of white still visible through the trees, stubbornly hanging on as winter died.

The empty village had seemed almost post-apocalyptic. Maybe it was the fact that up until recently these lodges would have been full of families, the pub bustling and alive, the slopes colourful with skiers, music blaring from the speakers on the poles. Somehow, getting out of her car in the otherwise empty park, Charlotte could feel all of that – or maybe more pertinently, feel its absence, like the cool tenderness of skin after ripping off a band-aid. Walking into the village, her breathing and footsteps filled the place. She slowed, eyes moving between the dark windows.

She had checked each of the lodges. The first, her mouth was dry and palms sweaty. By the last, there were tears in her eyes as her heart galloped. It had taken everything she had to open each door. Momentary relief burned away by the renewed fear of checking the next.

And she knew, she fucking *knew* she was okay. She knew nothing would be waiting for her. But that was the worst part. Fear so poisonous you could no longer distinguish between the real threats and the imagined.

Snowhaven was the last lodge she checked. Not wanting to go back, she had turned on every light and brought in her bag. She had struggled to pass the darkened doorways. She left them all open. She made tea and she wished for wine and she watched the night out the window and *still* fear coursed through her. It was dark and the village was silent and she was alone and *they could be out there waiting in any of the other lodges, ready to pounce and—*

She didn't sleep.

She remembered, the next morning, one of the fishing trips with Uncle Mac. She didn't like thinking about them anymore. But on that day the memory had appeared clear and unbidden. Uncle Mac lashing sticks together, making an underwater cage, boasting that this was the best way to catch fish.

'I'm telling you love, there's nothing like a well-placed trap,' he said. 'And sticks are the best for it because to the fish they look natural. Swims in to get a treat, door shuts, that's our dinner sorted.'

The traps never worked. It was almost always Charlotte's father who caught the dinner.

She'd got good at improvising in the past months. Squeaky dog toys hidden under the doormats of the cheap motel rooms she sometimes stayed in, a chair beneath the handle and a knife in her pocket. Whenever she slept in her car, always somewhere grassy and off the road, she would sling rope around sticks driven into dirt in a wide perimeter, so that anyone approaching might trip and fall into the nail-lined planks she would place in the grass, if she was lucky. Simple, temporary measures, with no guarantees. But if she was going to be here long term, she'd need more. Several traps, better traps, hidden in different locations – some far out enough that, if it came to a chase, she could lead someone into them. That first day on Mount Skillion, she set out to find some sticks.

* * *

She woke early, before dawn. She rolled out of bed, removed the chair from under the door handle and headed through the chilly, dim lodge into the kitchen. Last night's embers remained in the fireplace but she couldn't feel any heat from there. She made a coffee, checked the thread was still intact, then headed into the freezing morning. There was something pleasant about the cold, something that always sharpened her focus. She walked up to the still-dark slope and took a seat on a flat rock, like ice on her bum. She drank her coffee and watched the sun rise. It started slow, touching the tops of the trees with gold glimmers that crept down the slopes and made the valleys shine before the sky became flame chased away by blue. It was going to be a nice day.

In the mornings, the village seemed to emerge from the fog, blurred lines hardening, forms taking shape as the dangerous cold of the night retreated. She kept her jacket wrapped tight and hard until the first touch of warmth on the skin of her face. She breathed it all in, eyes closed, and for just that second tried to banish the ever-present whisper of fearful reminders. She was alive. She was alone. She would never go as far as to assume she was safe, but at least up here she could, for a moment, embrace the illusion.

Charlotte let herself into each of the lodges, checking all the rooms with her torch. She knew the spots to avoid. A thin layer of dust over everything but she didn't bother cleaning. Her first week here she'd scrubbed every lodge from top to bottom, wiping surfaces and removing the rubbish from the previous season's visitors, then found the rooms stale again within a week. There would be no point in doing another big clean until right before the season started, unless somebody did decide to hire a lodge in the next few months.

She was done by noon with no sign of intruders and nothing she had to seriously attend to apart from a busted lightbulb in one of the bathrooms of Andrew's Alpine Escape, the closest lodge to the carpark and the one likely named by somebody with an imperfect grasp of alliteration. She returned to Snowhaven, made some soup for lunch, and ate watching out the window. She gave herself an hour to read a little more of her book (the wealthy Lady was torn between the thought of her impending marriage to the stable yet boring local duke and her inability to stay away from the temperamental yet strangely enticing blacksmith). By one o'clock, she figured it was too nice a day to waste and she might as well go for a walk. After a moment's consideration, she brought her notebook with her.

Back in primary school, Charlotte had listened with disbelief to other kids going on about beach holidays. She'd never understood why people liked the beach, especially in Melbourne; all that sticky sand and smelly water and the need for a shower afterwards. To her, it had always seemed more trouble than it was worth.

The mountains were a different story. And when Charlotte spoke about those trips to Thredbo with her father and Uncle Mac, it was the other kids' turn to be confused. What was the point, they'd ask, of going to the mountains when there was no snow?

It wasn't as though Charlotte had an answer, at least not one she could entirely articulate as a child. To her, it was so many things. The way the lodges all seemed piled on top of each other up the hilly drives of the town. The muted colours and the vast, sparse slopes surrounding her, gouged with bike tracks and peppered with lift stations abandoned until winter returned. The way that even in summer it was cool and windy with a fresh smell on the air that suggested snow might not be so far away. Charlotte had loved the burbling rivers among the bent grey gums, the wiry bushes and the sense that she was somewhere distant and far away on an adventure all her own.

Maybe that was what had drawn her to Mount Skillion. It was no Thredbo – Skillion was in every way a budget resort. But there was a similarity to all Australian mountain towns. Skillion was denser, lonelier, more isolated. But the smells and the winds and the cold, cleansing air; all of that was familiar in a way that was, if not comforting, then at least some kind of touchstone that made Charlotte feel a little less like a half-forgotten ghost drifting through an empty purgatory.

There was something perfunctory about the way only certain sections of the trail had been cleared, and narrow ones at that. Her guess was that somebody had once tried to make the mountain a hiking destination to bring in a little money during the summer, but Skillion wasn't high enough for any decent lookouts and the trees were too dense, the rocks too frequent, the location too remote. She liked the way the forest closed in around her, killing any sound that wasn't the rustle of a wombat or a roo. Colours looked to have been leached out of the surrounds; the only grass and trees and bush that survived the snow were hardy, more grey than green. She'd found the ghostliness a little creepy at first but had come to appreciate it. The vegetation up here might not be pretty, but it survived.

Sometimes, walking alone through the drab and faded trees, too far from the village to see any sign of it, in deep where the path barely existed, the sense of unreality mounted. What brief human interactions she had these days felt false somehow, like overacted scenes from a bad play. She went days without saying a word. In among the trees, she would stop and look at flat rocks covered in large, lazy skinks, entirely still until a cracking twig sent them vanishing into the undergrowth. She wondered how they survived up here in the cold. She supposed they'd been designed that way. No skinks she'd ever seen in the city had grown to those sizes.

About fifteen minutes' walk from the village was a small clearing; a couple of square metres of rocky dirt. Charlotte sat against a tree and opened her notebook. All the pages were blank, as they had been since she bought it months ago. She rested her pen against it. Looked around at the trees, the fractured, weak sunlight splintering through them, lighting slivers of white among the grey. Thought about Anders, about that feeling on the road. Thought about putting it all into words.

She pocketed her notebook, stood and kept walking.

Once, she'd been shocked by how abruptly the trees changed. One moment they were alive, if colourless. The next, bone white and leafless, dead branches like jagged claws. A wooden graveyard. She continued until the dead trees were all she could see, a bone forest stretching up to a blue sky that seemed so incongruous past those sharp, bleached branches.

Even now she still felt a little unsettled walking through the dead trees – the result of a beetle infestation, she'd learned – but over time she had come to find a strange beauty in them. There was no sound in the bone forest. No sign of life. Just Charlotte, alone. And maybe that was why she liked it so much.

She kept walking until she reached the spot that had scared the hell out of her the first time she'd come here. The point where the trees suddenly stopped. Beyond were maybe two metres of slanting dirt then a sheer, sudden drop. Charlotte stopped just past the treeline. She took care to stay well clear of one tree jutting out almost horizontal over the edge. She could see the trailing rope from here. Still in place, at least.

She glanced over her shoulder. Just the dead white trees. She returned her attention to the view over the cliff. The rolling expanses of grey-green. The ruggedly forested mountain ranges far away. Nothing out there but trees and bushes and animals. She inhaled mountain air, fresh, bracing. Dared to close her eyes for a moment. Imagined stepping out into space. Imagined vanishing into the wilds, living like a hermit among the trees.

She walked slowly back to the village. She didn't know how long she'd been away.

The trees were parting and she could see the lodges. She felt lighter. The man from yesterday had faded from her thoughts.

It was only when she moved through the gap between Snowhaven and Bushmill next door that she saw the unfamiliar car.

CHAPTER FOUR

Then

Mel was annoyed at Charlotte for being late, which was a bit rich given it had only been an hour and a half since she'd agreed to come. But while Charlotte would usually have apologised just to keep the peace, today she was flying too high.

She paced back and forth in Mel's studio apartment while Mel, in the bathroom, checked her makeup.

'And you know, it was such a relief. Like, he told me I was doing everything right which like, I know it *sounds* kind of easy and everything, but honestly so much of the time I wonder if there's some secret cheat code to being a writer, like something I'm missing, but Mel, he was so down to earth, so friendly and normal and I dunno, I just feel like, for the first time in ages, it's kind of achievable, you know?'

Mel didn't reply straight away. When she did, there was a playful edge to her voice.

'So did you get his number?'

'What? No, it wasn't like that, it was—'

'Charli!' She burst out of the bathroom. 'Why not?'

'Because! It wasn't a date or anything, it wasn't ...'

She trailed off. She hated that knowing smile, the one Mel always got when she was about to dole out some worldly wisdom that sounded more like condescension.

'Charli, come on. A young author does a campus talk – don't you think a perk of the job is getting to pick up uni girls who idolise him?'

Mel was wrong, that was stupid, but already Charlotte could feel the bubble of excitement starting to deflate. She fought to keep it.

'It wasn't like that,' Charlotte said again. 'I didn't once feel like he was trying to ... I mean he was nice and he didn't ask for my number and—'

'He probably didn't think he *had* to,' Mel said. 'He probably thought that it was a lock. Honestly, you're so naïve, Charli. I'll bet he was completely confused when you left without suggesting a drink or a duck behind the dumpster.'

'Don't be disgusting,' Charlotte said, but a flicker of doubt took the heat out of her words.

Maybe she'd missed the signs. Maybe she'd been too caught up in the fact that he was talking to her, too willing to believe she was somehow special.

'Oh Charli,' Mel said softly. 'I'm sorry. See, this is why you need me around. Don't worry. We'll find you someone pretty tonight, get you looked after.'

She retreated to the bathroom again. Charlotte stayed where she was.

'By the way,' Mel called back. 'You sure you want to wear that?'

* * *

Charlotte and Mel had met on the first day of high school. Charlotte, alone in the courtyard with a book under her arm, had been quickly bailed up by Mel and spent the rest of the day being dragged around behind her. She didn't remember saying a single word that whole week.

In some ways nothing really changed in the following years. For a long time Charlotte hadn't minded. She'd always been on the shy and awkward side, and Mel not only made up the difference but pushed Charlotte in ways she'd later appreciated. The first time she kissed a boy in a game of spin-the-bottle, her first shots at a party she'd never have been invited to alone, the first gig she snuck out for. Without Mel, none of that would have happened.

But Charlotte would be lying if she said that the end of high school hadn't brought with it a sense of relief. As she'd got older, she'd started to chafe at the idea of this dynamic continuing into adulthood.

Maybe Mel sensed that. All through Charlotte's first year, Mel seemed to seize every possible excuse to hang out, more often than not happening to be 'in the area' near the end of classes, whisking Charlotte away just as the other students were going for drinks. It took Charlotte a while to realise that the simmering feeling she got every time Mel called was resentment.

Now, hemmed in by a wall of music and neon and a strange perfumey smell that couldn't quite cover up the sweat, that feeling was back.

They waited at the island bar in a line that felt almost as long as the line outside, before paying a painful amount for cocktails that they drank way too fast. Then a fit blond guy in a too-tight shirt with a slightly bullish face was there, offering to buy Mel a drink, and Mel was off with him, leaving Charlotte alone. Fingernails digging into her palms, she eyed the exit. Would Leo Grey put up with this, or would he be at home writing? She started to move.

A deep voice from beside her, somehow audible despite not yelling, asked, 'What are you having?'

A man was leaning against the bar. And, Charlotte was surprised to realise, he *was* a man, not a boy just out of school. He wore a suit jacket over a white, buttoned shirt. He had dark hair. His face was practically chiselled; a strong jaw, sharp cheekbones, dark eyes under thick black hair. He was maybe in his late twenties, but there was an ageless quality to him, like he was outside time. He was handsome – no, handsome didn't do him justice. Despite the low lights and the dancing and all the distractions, it was like he was the only one in the room, like he exuded this force that drew all your attention to him. As all of this raced through Charlotte's head, she realised she had been staring without replying.

'Oh. Um. A … a vodka lemonade. Please.'

What was she doing? She knew not to accept a drink from a stranger. But the man raised a hand and the bartender was there in an instant, making the drink which he slid straight to Charlotte. The man raised his own glass – it looked like a straight whisky – then smiled as he sipped it and Charlotte tried to do the same even though she could not take her eyes off him.

'I'm Dominic,' he said.

'I'm ... I'm Charlotte.'

'What brings you here, Charlotte?'

'I'm with, um ...' She gestured towards the dance floor. 'A friend. But I, uh, I think she's abandoned me.'

'Not much of a friend then.'

'No, she's okay, she just ... she met a guy.'

Dominic drank. His eyes held hers, made it next to impossible to look away. Not that she wanted to, even if that gaze was making her heart race, sapping the breath from her.

'What, um, what about you?' she asked, because she didn't know what else to.

'What about me?'

'Why are you here?'

'What, in this winning establishment?'

Charlotte laughed.

Dominic smiled. 'A business meeting ended up here. Truth be told, I hate the place.'

'Business?'

'Fittingly, nightclubs. Way more boring than you'd think, behind the scenes. Anyway, that's why I'm at the bar trying to pretend this is the kind of place where you enjoy a peaceful scotch and not where the peaceful scotch ends up all over you. How about you? This the kind of place you like?'

'Not really.'

Dominic swirled his scotch in the glass. 'Here's a question then. If I don't like this place, and if your friend has abandoned you, why are we staying?'

We.

This wasn't happening. No way was this happening. It was some ugly prank someone had set up, some trick. Because a guy like this, a guy so handsome and charming and *adult* was not the kind of guy who turned up at a club and swept Charlotte Laurent, of all people, off her feet.

As she fumbled for a polite way to tell him no, she saw, over his shoulder, Mel. Watching, mouth slightly open in a look of surprise that caused something hissing and spiteful to rise in Charlotte's chest.

'No idea,' she told Dominic. 'Let's go.'

They finished their drinks and left. The whole way Charlotte could feel Mel's eyes on her. As they stepped outside, she could barely contain her grin.

They walked together through the city crowds until they neared Flinders Steet Station, which was lit up bright and golden. It was quieter here, especially once they took a turn down a staircase and onto the path running along Southbank, the slow river twinkling in the lights from restaurants and bars.

'Are you studying?' Dominic asked.

'I am, yeah.'

'What?'

Instinct told Charlotte to lie. Creative writing, to most people, was a fancy way of saying 'Bachelor of Arts', and 'Arts degree' was a fancy way of saying 'pointless money sink'. That afternoon, with Leo, she'd felt vindicated about her choice. Now she wasn't sure. She wanted to seem mature and level-headed and realistic to this guy, but it was hard to tell how he'd react to the truth. What it would say about her.

'Creative writing.' She glanced sideways at Dominic as she said it. His expression gave nothing away and that sent worry spinning through her thoughts. 'I know, cliché.'

'Is it?'

'I mean ... kind of.'

'I guess it depends on why you're doing it. I'm going to guess you take it seriously.'

'I do,' Charlotte said. Her clarity and certainty surprised her.

Dominic nodded. 'Does your friend?'

Charlotte didn't reply.

'You care what she thinks, huh?'

'Is that a bad thing?'

'You tell me.'

Again, Charlotte didn't reply. She saw a hint of a knowing smile that made her feel strangely defensive.

'She's a good person. When you get to know her.'

'I don't have to know her.' Dominic guided Charlotte towards a small, bronze-edged bar with low amber lights. Inside it was warm and smelled like lavender. They took a corner booth. A waiter was there in moments – Dominic ordered a bottle of wine that sounded specific and expensive.

'I don't have to know her,' Dominic repeated, once the waiter had left. 'Because I know her type. People who are so insecure about themselves that they try and control others.'

'Hang on,' Charlotte said. 'Mel isn't insecure and she doesn't *control* ...'

Dominic just watched her.

'Okay so maybe she controls me a little.'

'Can I be brutally honest?' Dominic asked. When Charlotte nodded he said, 'I'm going to guess you've been trying to pull away from her for a long time. Probably since the end of high school. And she's been hanging on to you, right? Not making new friends?'

Charlotte nodded.

'The reason she does that,' Dominic said, 'is because she's used to you making her feel big. Now you've got your own interests and your own life and that's a threat to her. Because she's probably known all along that you're the more interesting one and her entire sense of self relies on convincing you otherwise.'

The wine arrived.

Charlotte looked away.

'I'm sorry,' Dominic said. 'Was that too far?'

'No.' She met his gaze again. 'No, I guess it's just ... it's just weird to hear out loud.'

'See?' Dominic raised a glass. 'Not a cliché at all.'

Charlotte laughed.

And like that, the whole night shifted. Thoughts of Mel evaporated. Her own nervousness was dissolved by the wine, which was ridiculously good. And while that faint sense of unreality at this whole situation lingered, it didn't matter. None of it mattered because Dominic was here, with her, and he was keeping the conversation going with question after question, and she was finding she had so much to say. Every time she thought she might be boring him, she slowed, ready to laugh it all off, only to see that he was still smiling, still watching her like she was the only thing in the world that mattered. In this light he looked like something from a dream, hazy and not quite there but warm and safe and hers alone.

It got late. The bar was closing up. Dominic paid their tab (Charlotte didn't put up a fight – no guy had ever done that for her before) then they stepped out into the icy air. Dominic draped his jacket over her shoulders, something that might have seemed corny if he hadn't done it with such matter-of-fact ease.

He looked towards the distant train station. 'I'll walk you to the cabs, make sure you get home safe.'

Charlotte said nothing.

Dominic looked back at her. For a moment, a moment that lasted all too long and not long enough, they held each other's gaze.

And then Charlotte kissed him. She worried he would laugh at her, turn pitying. But he kissed her back, wrapping those arms tight around her, and Charlotte almost ran laughing and whooping into the night.

CHAPTER FIVE

Now

She was frozen to the spot. It had happened. Finally, it had happened. After all her caution, all her care, somebody had found her.

How could she have been so stupid? *Of course* Anders knew who she was. Of course the way he had behaved in the supermarket was a gigantic warning sign. He knew she had nowhere to run. He had taken his time, made sure of her hiding place. And now he was here.

She stepped back, slipping between the buildings, thoughts tumbling over themselves as she tried to work out a plan, a way clear, a trap to lead him into, anything—

'Hi there!'

She jumped. Somebody was emerging from the direction of White Republic, the lodge that sat opposite Snowhaven. It took her a second to realise it was not Anders. This man was about medium height, middle-aged and a little pudgy with greying hair, a moustache and a big smile. He was dressed in a thick knitted jumper, plain trousers and shoes that were entirely wrong for a mountain.

Charlotte said nothing.

He came to a halt a couple of metres from her. 'Sorry if I gave you a fright there! I was just looking around for the caretaker. The man, darn it, what was his name? Liam! That's right. Anyway, he said you'd be here. He gave me the combination so I was good to just let myself in, but I didn't want to scare anyone.'

She couldn't catch up, couldn't reconcile what he was saying with the racing, paralysing panic she'd felt just seconds before. So she asked the only question she could think of, the only one that mattered. 'Who are you?'

The man smacked himself on the head. 'Pretty rude not to start with that! I'm John. Did Liam not send an email or anything?'

Charlotte shook her head.

John winced. 'Look, I can't say I'm surprised. The bloke seemed a bit like this was the bottom of his priority list! But hey, who knows what he had on. Anyway, I'm, um ...' He glanced around. 'I'm sorry, there's really no way to say this without sounding like a total numpty. I'm working on a book. But sitting on my bum in a suburban office trying to imagine all this stuff I never get to see, when there's all this only a few hours away?' He gestured around. 'Crazy! So I figured, what the hey! Deadline's looming, don't want to get in trouble this early in the game, so I decided to go bush, get away.'

Charlotte swallowed. 'Why here?'

The man – John – clapped. 'That's just it – why not? No, honestly, it was me being a big old sook. The whole isolated cabin in the woods, drop dunnies and no hot water thing – I like my creature comforts a little too much for all that!

Plus, heat and I don't get along so it had to be somewhere a bit milder but somewhere without any distractions. So I gave it a think and it hit me – a mountain resort! But most of them are still pretty busy in the off-season so a little internet digging and hey presto. Liam gave me a good deal – by which I mean he probably ripped me off but how should I know – and here I am.' He finished with a flourish and a beam.

Charlotte's mind was spinning. She had been so sure it was the stranger from the supermarket, here either to kill her or, worse, bring her home. She knew she had to be careful, but looking at this man, all soft edges and giddy energy and careful dodging of anything close to a swearword, it was hard to imagine him as any sort of threat. And she could not deny a slight tug of yearning when he mentioned working on a book. Yearning and curiosity.

But that could not be a factor.

'Right,' she said. 'Well, I'm Katie. The caretaker. You mind if I give Liam a quick call, just to confirm it? I didn't hear anything from him.'

'Be my guest,' John said. 'Then I can be yours!'

Muscles corded, she moved past John to the door to Snowhaven. She unlocked it, taking care to cover the combination. Inside, she gave herself a moment to lean against the wall, let the shakes do their thing, catch her breath. She checked the thread. Still intact.

She hurried up the stairs and down the hall to the office. She dialled Liam's number. Through the window she could see John below, rubbing his arms as he paced around his car, taking in the village with a look of delighted fascination.

The phone rang out. She tried again. Still nothing. She dropped it, leaning back in her seat.

She didn't like this. She was here for solitude, for quiet and safety. Not to deal with this guy bumbling around the place. But then, if Liam *had* approved him for the lodge then Charlotte was in no position to refuse.

She tried Liam one last time. Nothing. She put the phone down and watched John, who had stopped to shiver against his car.

She opened her email. And there it was. One new message from the day before.

Katie,
Heads up, bloke by the name of John has booked White Republic for two weeks. Writer or something. Nothing you need to do except make sure the lodge is in decent shape for him. Still, a clean once he's gone would be good. Give me a shout if you need anything.
L

Charlotte closed her eyes. She exhaled. Placed both hands on the desk and pushed herself up, then returned downstairs.

She opened the door and forced a smile. 'All good,' she said. 'Liam emailed me yesterday. You're over in White Republic. Let me just clean up a couple of things inside then it's all yours.'

'Oh, I don't mind,' John said. 'I'm happy to head straight in – I'm not super worried about a little mess and mustiness.'

'Just, um, indulge me,' Charlotte said. 'Pride in the job and all that. Happy to wait out here for five minutes?'

Entering White Republic, she almost locked the door again behind her, but figured that would seem strange. She checked through the window next to the door. John was pulling bags out of his car while singing something to himself.

She moved quickly into the living area. White Republic was creaky and rundown with a dismal heating system and apparently undiscoverable gaps letting cold air leak through. Charlotte had done her best to keep it tidy, but there wasn't a lot she could do about the rotting wood panels in the walls or the discoloured kitchen.

She found the first familiar spot in the living room then, using her car keys, jimmied up one of the floorboards. The moment it was out it fell in half – the break was almost indiscernible with the two pieces jammed together, but if you stepped on it you'd go right through.

She put the two pieces aside and reached through, taking care as she removed the block of wood through which she'd stuck several long nails, pointing upwards. She put it with the broken floorboard then, moving fast, found the three other spots where she'd done the same thing. A half-hearted renovation had replaced some of the older floorboards and left a lot of the material in a storage cupboard, which Charlotte had taken advantage of. Naturally she would have fixed everything up before the season started, but the only person who was supposed to be in these lodges was Charlotte – at least until now. The traps were in place for anybody who *wasn't* supposed to be there.

She retrieved the intact floorboards from the cupboard, along with a canvas bag with which she wrapped the nail bars and the broken floorboard pieces. She replaced the right ones, stomping hard on them to ensure they looked flush with each other and were solid against the crossbeams, then stepped back and cast an eye over the room, mentally checking that she'd removed all of them. Of course she had. You didn't forget where you'd left traps.

The canvas bundle under her arm, she returned to John and invited him in.

'So much character!' He ran a pudgy hand over the wooden walls.

Charlotte winced, expecting splinters.

'Honestly, it's perfect,' John said. 'I wasn't going for full wilderness or anything, and you know, the lap of luxury didn't suit either. But this.' He tapped a rough-hewn table. 'This strikes just the right balance.'

Charlotte wasn't sure how to respond to that so she didn't. 'Bedding is all in the hallway cupboard.' She pointed. 'The drying room is a bit draughty, so I'd keep the door there shut. I'll switch on the boiler before I go, so you'll have hot water by tonight. Sorry, if I'd known you were coming ...'

She should have known. She should have checked her emails last night. Instead she had been too busy fretting about Anders.

'No worries, no worries,' John said. 'I'm not so pampered that I can't put up with a little cold.'

'Anyway,' Charlotte said. 'If you need anything else, let me know.'

She headed for the door.

'Sorry ... Katie?'

She looked back. *Had he recognised her, had he—*

'Nothing important,' John said. 'I just wanted to clarify – I'm not here to step on any toes. I'm just going to lock myself away, get this book done, maybe take the occasional walk. You know, the not-so-difficult paths.' A smile. 'Anyway. Point is, I'll be totally out of your hair while I'm here. Just ignore me and I'll do everything I can to be totally ignorable.'

Again, she wasn't sure what to say to that. *Thank you, paying customer? No, that's fine, please be obtrusive?* So she just nodded.

Back in the office, she positioned herself behind the computer and watched. The lights were all on in White Republic. After about half an hour, John headed out and continued unpacking his car. He seemed to be whistling. He only had a suitcase and a couple of cardboard boxes, presumably food he'd picked up in Burnley. He shut the car and dragged them in and didn't come out again.

She could leave now. Slip down the stairs, get in the car, headlights off, and go. Abandon Mount Skillion and keep running. Drive as fast as she dared back down, eyes on the rear-view, ensuring John wasn't following. If he did ... well, she would cross that bridge if she came to it. But if she had enough of a head start, she could be far away before midnight.

She looked at the ceiling.

Far away *where*? Any other ski resort meant people. People meant phones and phones meant news. The same problem if she tried to get some work on a farm, as if she'd have the first clue how to convincingly pull that off. She was confident she could learn, but not fast enough to not arouse suspicion. And she didn't have enough money to go on without work. She'd bought her sedan months back, second hand, figuring she could sleep in it if need be – and had, many times – but it had also cleared out much of the cash she'd fled Melbourne with.

Maybe she could head to Western Australia. She doubted the coverage would have been as intense over there. She could get a job in a mine or something. She imagined Uncle Mac's reaction to that. She imagined ...

No. She did not think about him anymore.

She leaned back. Closed her eyes and breathed. Cleared her mind.

What, exactly, was she so worried about?

It was nothing specific, she had to concede. She didn't see danger, looking at that jovial, beaming man. But even someone as seemingly harmless as John might look at her too closely, conjure up a moment of buried recognition, and start making phone calls. Even if he never figured out anything, he'd still be there. Which was dangerous for her. What if she ignored approaching footsteps or sounds in the night because she assumed it was him?

But none of that changed how deeply tiring the idea of running again was.

Around nine, the lights in White Republic went off. She was still sitting at the window, occasionally checking the shadows either side for hints of movement. Nothing.

She opened a search engine and typed in *Australian writers.* A bunch of semi-familiar faces – Leo Grey's all too familiar – but none were John. She checked Liam's email again for a surname, but she'd been right in thinking there was none. She searched *Australian writers John.* Still plenty of names and faces. None resembling the man in the lodge across from her.

A lack of online presence wasn't indicative of anything. John was a common name, as common as it got. She could likely spend plenty of time searching and still miss him completely. Besides which, maybe he wrote under a pseudonym and was too modest to tell her what it was. Maybe he published under 'J.F. Smith' or something. Maybe he was a first-time author, or a ghost writer, or a journalist.

She imagined what it would be like for that to be your life. Fingers on keys and no bigger worry than grappling with a plot hole or publisher's demands. She felt a jealous ache. It was all too easy to veer down the many 'what-if' roads, to re-examine every path not taken. An exercise in pointlessness.

John, as it turned out, was true to his word about not bothering her. In fact, she didn't speak to him at all for the next few days. She still kept an eye on White Republic in the mornings, saw him set out smiling and with a spring in his step. He'd then vanish inside until the evening, when he would sit out on the balcony with a glass of wine and watch the sunset. Charlotte was careful not to let herself be seen, often watching him from between the blinds, but it was curious to her that John never read a book or checked his phone. He'd just sit and watch until it turned dark, then head inside. He wouldn't come out again until morning.

Unbidden, Dominic's face was there in her mind. She flinched. What would he think, seeing her now? Ducking and hiding and watching and fretting while an oblivious middle-aged man waddled about the place.

She didn't have an answer. His face remained, but wordless. Faded a little, maybe.

Would he laugh at where she had ended up? Would he be proud of what she had learned? He'd so hated a lack of caution. Or would he just be sad, seeing this ghost he'd once loved?

She closed her eyes. *He'd once loved.* God, wasn't that ever naïve. She didn't know if Dominic had loved her. Even in those golden early days, part of her had wondered what he was doing with her, how somebody like him could look at awkward, insecure, gawky Charlotte Laurent and believe they were right for each other.

Well, now she knew.

On the second day after John's arrival, Charlotte chanced her usual walk, all the way to the bone forest. She was still carrying the knife in her pocket, and half expected cracking twigs and heavy breathing from behind as John rushed her, but it never happened. He stayed in his lodge, working on his book, she supposed. Again, that queasy jealousy.

She wondered what he was writing. How he'd got his start. She wondered if he'd ever met Leo Grey.

She didn't want to think about Leo Grey.

Later, she was coming back from a routine check of the lodges when she found John sitting cross-legged on the boulder outside White Republic, fiddling with, of all things, a Rubik's Cube. She slowed. Passing him she'd have to say something. But then, maybe it was the chance she needed to get a better sense of who he was.

He smiled as she approached. 'Hard at work?' he asked.

'Sure. You?'

'Trying! Might risk a new walking route soon, but worried I'll get stuck if the path turns narrow.' He patted his stomach with a chuckle. 'Hey, I have to say: the sunsets up here are spectacular. You ever watch them? Oh shoot, look at me go, advising you like *I'm* the local. You must think I'm a big duffer.'

'No, they're good. The sunsets.'

'Better than, I reckon. I'll tell you what, how good is the phone reception up here?'

Charlotte frowned. 'You get reception?'

John laughed. 'Not at all, that's the point! No distractions. It's just me and the work. It's so, I don't know, cleansing. Sharpens the mind, don't you think?'

Maybe, although Charlotte was inclined to see the poor reception in a very different light.

John went back to his Rubik's Cube.

Charlotte still hovered. 'You should ... I mean, if you haven't, you should get up early and try the sunrise. They're even more beautiful.'

John looked at her, eyebrow raised. 'Is that so?'

'Yeah. Something about the way the light crawls down the hills. It's like ... like gold washing over the landscape. It always makes me ... I dunno. Feel alright.'

John looked at her, considering.

She shrugged.

John nodded. 'Alright. I'll take a look tomorrow.'

That third night, she left the office early and slept undisturbed. If John had planned to overpower her and return her to Melbourne, he'd had plenty of opportunity. The next morning, she got up early. From the office window, she saw John's silhouette heading up to the slopes as the sky lightened. She half considered going out and watching with him. But she didn't.

On the fourth night Charlotte bustled around the kitchen, playing an old CD she'd found here and quite liked – Nancy Griffiths – as she made a cup of tea and considered cooking up one of her frozen steaks. Her cooking was grim at the best of times but she was sick of eating out of cans.

It was as she opened the freezer that she heard the knock at the door.

She moved fast for the office. Keeping the light off, she peered through the window, struggling to get the angle right to see below.

John standing there, alone.

With a spike of irritation she remembered what he had said about not bothering her. But then there were plenty of valid reasons he could be knocking. The boiler might have broken or a light blown.

There were also other reasons.

He knocked again. She straightened up, forced two deep, steady breaths. She patted the knife in her pocket and went downstairs.

CHAPTER SIX

Then

Charlotte took a moment before opening the door. She resisted the urge to touch her hair; it had looked perfect in the mirror before, she didn't want to risk ruining it. Although, by that stage, he had seen her looking far more dishevelled. The thought made her blush. She turned the handle.

They'd been dating a few weeks (she said 'a few weeks' when people asked, but knew it had been exactly six) and every time she saw Dominic she still felt the initial fumbling need to try to act cool and normal. To modulate her voice, to not grin like an idiot, to walk with the kind of grace and poise that would be expected of whoever was on his arm.

He stepped into the hall and kissed her. He was in a suit, but without a tie, the top two shirt buttons undone – it made him look roguish yet sophisticated. Charlotte gestured around, although to what she was directing his attention, she had no idea. Her dad's house – her house, still – was boring. The hall lined with a few photos of the two of them. All the photos with Uncle Mac were long gone. Charlotte wished, briefly, that he was here. She was kind of dreading Dominic meeting her father. Uncle Mac, with his booming laugh and cheeky winks, would have offset that a lot.

'So this is El Casa De Laurent.' Dominic took his time down the hall, smiling at some of the photos. 'Is this you?'

'I know, I was fat.'

'You were cute! I mean, you could have cleaned the peanut butter off your face but—'

Charlotte shoved him. Still laughing, Dominic followed her into the dining room.

Charlotte's father straightened up from the table as they entered. He wasn't smiling. Not that Guy Laurent ever did, really. She remembered his grins when she was a kid. Now, his face was perpetually set to scowl. He was a short man, getting a little dumpy, balding and greying. Still, Charlotte had imagined him towering over Dominic.

He didn't. Dominic stepped up to him and took his hand in both of his own.

'Mr Laurent, it's fantastic to finally meet you. I'm Dominic.'

If Dominic thought that would prompt a smile, he was mistaken. 'So you are. Hungry?'

Charlotte had expected dinner to be a muted, awkward affair, but it seemed that Dominic could talk to anyone. Even when her father was gruff and monotone, Dominic had a way of keeping the conversation going, taking every grunted word and spinning a whole new topic out of it. Her dad didn't say much through dinner. Dominic talked about the nightclub business, the challenges of working for multiple venues that had to appeal to vastly different clientele. He asked her father about his own career and did a great job of seeming interested as he heard all about import tariffs and shipping permits. Charlotte picked at her food and watched them as though it was a down-to-the-wire tennis match.

Dominic helped her father wash up when they were done, insisting Charlotte stayed put. She sat at the table and sipped her wine and tried to make out what she could of the low voices from the kitchen.

Then it was coffee and dessert and Charlotte watched them both closely, wondering what had been said, but Dominic was just as charming and her father just as surly. A surge of irritation. *He couldn't just try?*

Dominic said his goodbyes, shaking her father's hand again and kissing her on the cheek. As she walked him out she whispered 'I'm sorry' but Dominic waved that off.

Charlotte didn't return to the dining room straight away. She lingered in the hall, trying to work out what to say. What she felt.

When Charlotte entered the room, her father was sitting at the stripped table, sipping a whisky, eyes on a fishing trip photo on the mantlepiece. One of the only ones that didn't have Uncle Mac in it. He'd been behind the camera.

'Very smooth operator,' her father said.

'What's that supposed to mean?'

He shrugged.

'Did you … like him?' The question seemed so childish, so stupid. Her father still wasn't looking at her.

'Pretty young to run that many nightclubs,' he said finally.

'He's really smart, Dad. A super-hard worker, a great business mind. It's a shame Uncle Mac couldn't be here, they'd …'

Her father tensed. Charlotte wished she'd kept her mouth shut.

He left without finishing his drink.

She caught up with Dominic for brunch the next day. He was strangely distracted. Still smiling, still charming, but it was clear that something was off.

After five minutes of moving food around her plate, Charlotte finally, quietly, asked him what he thought of her Dad.

A pained edge to his smile. 'I don't think what I thought of him matters. I think it's more what he thought of me.'

'He's like that with everyone,' she said quickly. 'He's just, I dunno, grumpy. I mean he basically drove Mum away, back to Paris.'

She knew that wasn't true. Her mother was flighty and irresponsible and impossible to pin down. Charlotte missed her sometimes, but she also felt relieved that she'd spent most of Charlotte's childhood a long way away.

'That's kind of you,' Dominic said. 'But trust me, I can tell when someone doesn't like me.'

'It's not your fault,' Charlotte said. 'I promise.'

'I don't think it is.' Dominic rested his chin on his fist, looking out the window. 'It's ... no, it doesn't matter.'

'What?'

'Nothing. Really. Eat up.'

'Dominic.' She put down her cutlery. 'Tell me.'

He sighed. 'Okay, look. I get that fathers can be protective of their daughters and everything. But there's protective and then there's controlling. Wanting everyone else to do things your way.'

Suddenly clear in her thoughts: yelling from behind the locked door of her father's office. Charlotte, fourteen, ducking around the corner into the kitchen. The door shoved open, the frame cracking off the wall.

'I swear to God,' her father's voice raised and trembling, 'you manipulative prick, I swear to God if you ever bring this up again—'

'Tone it down, Guy.' Uncle Mac, trying to stay calm, only managing cold.

'Get out of my house.'

'It's business, mate. That's all.'

'Out.'

Heavy footsteps and the front door slammed.

Charlotte, shaking, walked into the hall. Her father leaned against the wall, breathing heavily. She didn't speak. She didn't know what to say.

'We're done with him.' Her father didn't look at her. 'Understand? Done.'

Now, with Dominic, she remembered the simmer of resentment at that. As if his business disputes had anything to do with her or made her feel differently about Uncle Mac.

Dominic was watching her. She shrugged.

Being Dominic Ford's girlfriend was, Charlotte imagined, what being on drugs must feel like. Minus all the side effects. It was as though every moment was some beautiful shining gift that was hers for the taking.

Early on she had waited for the catch. But days passed, then weeks. The dates kept coming, always somewhere fancy and expensive, always paid for by Dominic. The nights after, each as spectacular as the first. And Dominic himself; attentive, interested, making her feel ... well, she wasn't entirely sure what the right word was. Special? Sexy? Wanted? They all seemed so cheesy and so right at the same time.

When Dominic looked at her, it was like standing in the one sunny spot on a cloudy day.

Still, at times the differences between them seemed enormous, like a chasm that was almost impossible to cross. Dominic was only a few years older than Charlotte, but everything from his knowing what wines to order, to his luxurious inner-city apartment, to the suits he wore and the way he carried himself seemed to belong to someone much older, someone on a whole other level. Charlotte still thought of herself as a girl, not much beyond the awkward, insecure kid she'd been in high school. Forking out for a pub meal rather than fast food felt like fine dining to her. Spending ten dollars as opposed to five on a bottle of wine was luxury. Then there was the fact that she still lived at home, that she still felt like she had to sneak in early after staying at Dominic's, even though she was an adult and her father had never once asked where she was. Sometimes, it made her feel like they were star-crossed lovers irresistibly coming together despite being so far apart, a thought that made her feel as warm as it did ridiculous and childish.

She worried, at times, that thinking it was all too good to be true would curse her, somehow. As if any kind of internal acknowledgement of the thought would make it reality, as if she would discover at that point that there was some terrible secret, some punchline just waiting to be sprung on her.

Maybe that was why she had felt so mixed about Dominic meeting her father, and Mel. Part of her wanted to see their reactions, their shock and disbelief that Charlotte was dating someone like this. But then, that shock and disbelief would only confirm what she most worried about – that Dominic was too good for her, that she didn't deserve him, that there was, somewhere, going to be a catch.

In lonely moments with nothing to distract her, she stood naked in front of the mirror and tried to work out what he saw in her. She guessed she was attractive-ish, but she was too tall, too skinny, had always thought she looked bug-eyed and buck-toothed. She knew, of course, that everyone was hard on their own appearance, that she probably looked fine, but 'fine' was not what Dominic Ford should be seen with. He looked like he should be arm in arm with supermodels, plural – not with her.

So what was it? What did he get out of the relationship? She wasn't particularly funny or brilliant. She thought, maybe, she could be a good writer, but knew she wasn't there yet. Sometimes she wanted to confront Dominic, to demand the truth. But that was what a crazy person would do and she didn't want him to think she was crazy. And even asking him seemed a risk, because maybe upon hearing the question some sort of spell would be broken and Dominic would ask himself the same thing.

There must have been something about her he recognised and she didn't. She just wished she knew what that something was. Or that she believed it existed.

As much as she loved the attention Dominic lavished on her, the fancy restaurants and classy nights out, in a way she couldn't quite define they made Charlotte feel just a little smaller each time. In their first week of dating, she'd told Dominic about the kind of stuff she wanted to write. He'd asked who her favourite author was and when, unthinking, she'd mentioned Leo Grey he'd raised an eyebrow. She knew he meant nothing by it, knew that liking Leo Grey *was* a little embarrassing, but still. It was just another harsh light shone on their differences, differences Charlotte was determined to make up for by being more cultured, more mature, more *worldly.*

And in the grand scheme of things, those issues were so tiny, and honestly her fault far more than his. In fact, even thinking about them seemed churlish. She was lucky to have him.

Charlotte had been so caught up with the top to bottom change in her life that she didn't realise the end of uni was approaching until it was almost upon her.

Her future was bearing down on her fast and she had no idea what to make of it. She was no closer to getting a book – getting *anything* – finished than she had been at the start of the year. She could go on to do a master's degree but the closest option she had for Creative Writing was Screenwriting, which didn't much interest her.

Then there was the job and house side of things. She knew she was at the end of her tether living with her father, and she hated the idea of working in cafés or bars any longer. On her nights alone, she would stare at the ceiling and imagine next year as a stalled, directionless meander through the same cycles she'd been trying to shed for so long now. Yes, Dominic made things better, but he didn't bring her any closer to her goals.

When she asked him over lunch if she should investigate more study, he laughed her off.

'Why?' he said. 'You can't stand uni as it is.'

'A master's might be different.'

'In Screenwriting? That would just be a different type of pretentious. Feels like more of a sideways step than a forward one.'

'How do I take a forward one?'

He leaned back with that confident smile. 'Charlotte, has it occurred to you that you need to live a little to have things to write about?'

He sounded almost like that awful tutor.

'I don't mean that to come off as patronising.' He took her hand. 'But really, if you're still living with your dad, still working in that café, still hanging out with Mel—'

'I *want* to change those things—'

'So do it.'

'How?'

'Move in with me.'

He said it so simply, so directly, that it had to be a joke. Charlotte blinked at him. But he was still smiling, still holding her hand.

'Move in with ... move ... What?'

'With me.'

'But we've ... we've only been seeing each other a couple of months and ...'

'And so?' He shrugged. 'I'm sure. Aren't you?'

The ease with which he said it made her heart swell and her eyes prickle. She was nearly breathless.

'Move in and I'll get you a job at one of the clubs. A good

one. I can look after you until you make better money, which you will almost immediately. You'll have time to write and we'll see each other more. What do you think?'

She should have reservations. She had to think this through. It was a massive decision. Probably irresponsible.

Dominic was still watching her, expectant.

Charlotte hiccupped a laugh. 'Yes. Oh my God, yes.'

She practically skipped home. Dominic told her she could make the move as soon as she wanted. He could send some of his guys around to move her stuff. She didn't have to worry about bond or a month's rent in advance or furniture or any of those things her friends had had to scrimp for. It was free and easy and she would *live with Dominic*. She said the words to herself over and over.

It was funny how your life always turned around right when you thought your path was set. At her lowest ebb, Dominic had come along and changed everything, changed how she thought of herself and her relationships. If she hadn't had that conversation with Leo Grey and felt the need to celebrate ... well, she didn't believe in fate, but it had made a pretty compelling case for its own existence.

Her excitement slipped away as she got home. It hit her, as she stood in the hallway breathing in the familiar, that this was maybe the biggest turning point of her life so far. Not only moving out, but moving out with her *boyfriend*. Fear flared, but as she looked at the old photos, so many of her as a kid, so few of her now, certainty returned. It was time to grow up. Time to leave old things behind. Leave the old *her* behind.

Her father's office door was closed, so she knew he was home. She hovered outside it for a while, trying to think through the words, trying to make them sound serious and adult and impossible to argue with. *I'm moving out. It's time. I'm going to live with Dominic.*

She knocked.

She stumbled through telling him while he watched her from behind his desk, expressionless.

Silence as Charlotte finished. Her father removed his glasses. It occurred to her then that she had absolutely no idea how he was going to react and wondered where along the way they'd stopped knowing each other.

'Charlotte.' His voice was a little gentler than usual. 'Are you sure about this?'

She nodded.

'You've known him five minutes.'

'I love him, Dad.'

'Does he feel the same way?'

'Why else would he have asked me to move in?'

'I don't know. But Charlotte ...' He grimaced. 'People like that, charming people, the ones who seem too good to be true ... they usually are.'

Defensiveness flared like a wildfire facing wind. 'What do you mean *too good to be true*?'

'I mean people like him; wealthy and charismatic and handsome and—'

'No.' Charlotte's voice was tight, coiled. 'You don't mean too good to be true. You mean *too good for me*.'

'That's not what I said.' He still sounded level, calm. 'Or what I meant. I just think you shouldn't rush into anything until you know for sure that he's everything he seems to be.'

But Charlotte didn't want to hear this. Not anymore. 'Just because Mum turned out to not give a shit about you, doesn't mean the same thing will happen to me.'

She'd wanted to hurt him, but if she'd succeeded, he gave nothing away. 'I'm not just thinking about your mother.'

'No,' Charlotte said, 'you're thinking about yourself and how much you'd hate it if I didn't turn out as miserable as you. Well fuck that. Dominic loves me and I love him. This is happening.'

She went to leave.

'Charlotte.'

She stopped.

He was standing now, eyes on his hands. He looked up.

'You're an adult now. I can't stop you. And I hope you're right. All I'm saying is that people like that don't shower others with attention unless there's something they want. And charm can blind us to someone's real agenda. So just, if you're going to do this ...'

Charlotte had heard enough. She left.

He called after her. 'Be careful.'

CHAPTER SEVEN

Now

'Hey there!' John smiled as Charlotte opened the door. 'I'm really sorry to interrupt you – feel free to tell me to get lost! But I was fixing a big old batch of bolognaise and I've gone and made way too much, even for the next few days. I don't really want to freeze it; you know how it is, it's never the same; besides the mince was frozen to begin with and I'm not too sure if freezing twice is the best idea – what can I say, I'm no chef!' He laughed. 'Anyway, I was wondering if you'd like some? No offense if you're vegetarian or you don't like bolognaise, although I'd prefer vegetarian to crazy, obviously. Can't speak for the quality but let's be real – it's pretty hard to screw up bolognaise. It's the time-honoured favourite of kitchen incompetents for a reason.'

Whatever she'd expected, it hadn't been a lengthy monologue about the limited merits of freezing bolognaise.

'Ah shoot, I'm babbling,' he said. 'Tell you what, how about I bring you a Tupperware container and if you decide to bin it just lie, alright? I'll choose to believe it was the best thing you've ever tasted and you never asked for more for fear of addiction.'

Smiling, John went to leave.

'I'd … I'd actually love that,' Charlotte said, before she could think it through. The idea of a home-cooked meal had been instantly, shockingly enticing. 'You're sure it's no trouble?'

'None at all!' he said. 'I'll dish up and drop it over then …' John hesitated. Glanced back at her, one eye squinting a little. 'Heck, I might as well ask. I'll completely respect it if you'd rather be left alone. But rattling around that lodge by myself – I'm getting a little loopy, especially with the lack of internet and no TV and all. Please do tell me if I'm overstepping, but would you be at all interested in joining me for dinner? Of course I'm sure you have a lot to do, but if you weren't opposed to a bit of a chinwag, well, the door's open. And the Tupperware is still on the table if not.'

Charlotte took him in. This friendly, pudgy, middle-aged man and his faltering, babbling offer. Faced with the prospect of actual conversation, of an evening not spent alone, she was finding it very hard to say no.

But she couldn't listen to that urge. Emotions betrayed you. If there was even a one per cent chance that John wasn't who he appeared to be, then she had to play it safe.

John must have seen thc indecision on her face. 'No stress, message received!' he said when the silence had dragged on too long. 'I'll drop the food around – you have a fantastic night.'

He turned to leave again.

'Wait,' Charlotte said. 'I'd love to come. Just gotta finish something up then I'll join you.'

'Brilliant!' John clapped. 'Oh, sorry, that wasn't very cool of me. Not too great at isolation – which probably doesn't sound very writerly of me! Anyway – wonderful stuff. I'll see you over there.'

Charlotte shut the door. She hovered, thinking over the exchange. She patted her pocket. The knife was still there.

In the space of a few days the interior of White Republic had been transformed, or at least it felt like it had. A fire roared and crackled, casting the room in flickering, cosy light. The smell of tomato and onion was thick in the air. John had arranged armchairs around the fireplace and thrown a cloth over the dining table. The Bee Gees warbled from the old speakers – 'Massachusetts'. John welcomed Charlotte in with a bad French accent and an insistence on taking a coat she didn't have, which he seemed to find hilarious.

'*Bonsoir, mademoiselle.* Come on through!'

Charlotte watched as John dished up the food. She kept watching until he'd placed her bowl down in front of her and even then waited for him to start.

The food was fantastic. John offered her a glass of red, which she turned down. As they ate, John idly spoke about things he'd seen on his walks, his excitement on encountering snow, a bird he thought was rare. There was something almost childlike about him, something Charlotte found oddly charming.

Upon finishing, John leaned back in his chair, hands on his belly and expression satisfied.

'I don't know what the spot is,' he said, 'but that sure hit it.'

Charlotte felt, if not at ease, then more unwound than she had in months. The music, the fire, the food – it was collectively pulling her towards something not far off relaxation.

'Thank you for this,' Charlotte said. 'It's very kind.'

John waved a hand. 'Please, you're doing me a favour. Sometimes I feel like all this time spent alone with the book is a little less than healthy.'

'What's it about?' Charlotte asked.

John sipped his wine. He considered her. 'Someone who needs help.'

'What kind of help?'

'Not sure yet. Still working that part out.'

'I used to write,' Charlotte said, surprising herself.

John's eyebrows went up. 'You did?'

She nodded. 'Loved it, actually. Anyway, I wasn't on your level but—'

'Oh, stop that,' John said. 'What does "on your level" even mean?'

'You know.' Charlotte drank her water and didn't look away from John. 'You have a publisher, right? You mentioned a deadline. Who are you with?'

John smiled. 'Not sure I can talk about that yet.'

'How many books have you written?'

'Would you believe this is the first? I mean, I've tried before. I came *this close*.' He held his thumb and forefinger together. 'But it didn't land the way I wanted it to. Something got in the way. Someone, maybe. But now I have this feeling that I can pull it off. If I can just figure out what this character needs.'

Still watching him carefully, she asked, 'How does your family feel about your work?'

'Not everyone gets it, unfortunately,' he said. 'What about you? Did your family support your writing?'

Charlotte shrugged. 'They didn't disapprove or anything. They just didn't ...'

'Believe in it?'

She nodded. It wasn't that her father had ever been against her writing, not as such, but apathy was its own kind of deterrent. In some ways, Charlotte felt, a worse one. Actively trying to stop her would have given her something to rebel against. Barely paying attention, giving the rare pieces she tried to show him only the most cursory glance, that stung more. And while he had never once urged her not to write, the occasional suggestions that she look at a teaching course or something practical instead were enough.

'Typical,' John said. 'Everyone thinking they know how you should live your life. What rules you should be following. What's good for you.'

'Isn't that what you're doing for your character?'

A strange, playful glint in John's eye. 'Ah. See? *That's* writer talk, if I ever heard it. You can't force characters into anything, you let them decide according to their natures. I think Thomas Harris said that. You know, *The Silence of the Lambs* guy? But you can give them a push. Create circumstances you hope they respond to. Beyond that, they'll make their own decisions.'

'You talk like a parent.'

'So, why don't you write anymore?' John asked.

She almost said something about Dominic. Nothing specific, just enough to speak to the truth of why she stopped.

But she caught herself. Concessions like that were how your guard started to drop. 'Life got in the way, I guess.'

'Does life get in the way up here?' he asked. 'I mean I don't want to assume anything, but I can't imagine looking over these lodges fills every hour you have.'

'Excuse me,' Charlotte said. 'This is very involving work.'

John laughed.

Charlotte hadn't smiled, really smiled, in months. The feeling overwhelmed her.

'All I'm saying is,' John, still chuckling, went on, 'maybe it's less a matter of not having time and more a matter of not having anything you *want* to write about. But if you ask me? The stuff you *don't* want to write about is the best stuff *to* write about.'

Charlotte didn't speak.

'Ah don't mind me,' John said. 'I'm being a Nosy Nellie! I think writers are like alcoholics – they want everyone else to be one too, so they don't feel so alone.'

'Do you feel alone?' Charlotte asked.

'Why do you think I invited you over?'

Charlotte searched for the appropriate wording. 'I guess I meant, in general. Do you have a wife, kids ...'

'I had a family,' John said. 'I don't anymore.'

'I'm sorry.'

'No need to be sorry,' John said. 'Sometimes the traditional paths aren't the right ones. It took me most of my life to realise that. When I did, it was like all the clouds suddenly cleared. I'd say I came back to myself, except I was never really with myself to begin with. But eventually I think the truth always comes to the surface. It's just up to us to decide what we do with it. Even if there's only one real option.'

'Which is?'

'Embrace it. There's no point in being anything other than who you are.'

Charlotte sipped her water and watched the easy smile on John's face.

'I'm glad you joined me tonight,' he said. 'You're a very interesting person.'

'You too,' Charlotte said, because she wasn't sure what else to.

She got ready slowly the next morning.

She'd dreamed of Dominic. She couldn't remember much of it. Just that it had hurt. Touches of the pain lingered and with it came something she hadn't felt in a long time, or had at least become very good at denying. She remembered the feeling of his arms around her, the taste of his lips, the way he had smiled. Thinking about Dominic was not, she had long since conceded to herself, something she could avoid. But she tried, in a feeble kind of compromise, to avoid remembering the best times.

Glimmers of the dream, vague and unformed and hard to identify, drifted through her mind with the queasy edge of something poisonous. She didn't believe dreams were important or meaningful, not really, but that didn't mean they couldn't weigh on you. She glanced at her notebook, sitting on the living-room table. She still hadn't written a word in it. Maybe now was the time, maybe if she tried to articulate the dream, maybe ...

She left it where it was. She didn't think about Dominic much. Or at least, she tried hard not to. Without Dominic she wouldn't be here, and from that perspective she supposed he was always present, his impact evident in everything that made up her life now. Maybe that was why each time she managed to banish his smile or his voice from her thoughts, she counted it as a victory.

Sometimes, though, that wasn't possible. Sometimes she swore she could feel him right there with her. And sometimes – in the worst times – she was glad of it.

Across the few relationships she'd had, Charlotte had developed a theory. People grew in all kinds of ways during their lives, like vines stretching out. In a relationship, parts of both of you grew together and, as that happened, the vines became tangled – too tangled, too wrapped up in each other to know anymore which was which. The longer the relationship, the stronger and more tangled the vines got. For some, that was a good thing.

But the end of a relationship, whatever form that took, meant the vines being pulled apart. And whether it was a careful cut or a sudden wrench, what was pulled away took parts of you with it and left traces of the other person, traces that could never be removed. In time, parts of you would grow back. Others wouldn't. Whatever the case, you would never be the same person again.

She almost laughed at that thought. The same person again. She hadn't known who she was before Dominic. She had certainly not known while she was with him. And now …

Well, there was one big difference now. Because now Charlotte understood that there was no luxury more complete than being able to worry about who you were. The most self-involved question on the planet, something you only ever thought about, probably, because those around you were too busy asking the same functionally pointless question of themselves.

She stepped out into the chilly morning. John was seated on the front steps of White Republic. He lifted his coffee cup in a salute.

'Morning, Katie!'

'Morning, John.' She wondered if this was how it would be every day from now on: him sitting outside early waiting to greet her. She wondered if that would be a problem.

'I love cold mornings, don't you?' John said. 'I mean, too many, no thanks, but every now and then? Gets you started fresh and clear-headed. Especially with a coffee. Want one? Brewed up a batch and I reckon it's alright. Best beans this side of ... well look, they're probably not the best, I'm no coffee snob, but they're pretty good.'

'Sure,' Charlotte said, because it seemed rude not to. Promising he'd be 'back in a jiff', John left his own mug at a slight angle on a tilting rock and ran back upstairs. Charlotte shoved her hands deep in her jacket pockets and looked towards the slope and the trees beyond. A haze of mist hung over it all, the grass still touched with frost, the sky a murky white. A bird called out and kept going, warbling somewhere deep in the trees.

John's coffee didn't taste much different to her own instant, but she smiled anyway and told him how good it was.

'The art of the plunge,' John said. 'I daresay I've mastered it.'

'Well, if the writing doesn't work out, at least you've got options.'

John rolled back on his heels and looked towards the mist. 'You know I was planning a walk but this weather's putting me off. How's your day looking?'

'Lots of checking that no windows have been broken by non-existent hooligans.'

'I wish I could offer some hooliganism for you,' John said. 'Make things a bit more exciting. Unfortunately, all I can offer is coffee. Tell you what, I think I will take a chance on that walk after all. Feel like showing me the sights?'

She led John down her normal route, the trail winding and rough between mossy rocks and grey-dappled trunks. She would have preferred he was in front, but given he didn't know the way that wouldn't make much sense. Occasionally she patted her pocket to make sure the knife was still there.

Neither spoke as they headed deeper into the bush, their breath misting ahead of them. Every now and then John would let out an excited squawk at a deposit of dirty snow deep in the trees. The closing-in trunks and branches muffled any sound but for their own footsteps. If there were animals out there, they weren't making themselves known. Behind her, John hiked with confidence, never slipping or tripping, knowing exactly where to put his feet to avoid losing balance. It had taken Charlotte a long time to master that.

They arrived at the little clearing. John suggested stopping to catch their breath, despite not appearing to have lost it. Charlotte nodded but said nothing. Now they were here, she wasn't sure she was entirely at ease with John having seen this place. For so long now it had been private and personal to her. Inviting someone else in felt like a violation.

She watched John pace the trees, occasionally leaning in to look more closely at a pattern in the bark. She went quickly through what she had learned about him from the night before. That he had had a family. But there was a lot that could mean, and no ring on his finger.

'So you were married,' she said.

She hadn't meant to be so abrupt. She'd planned to work up to the question through casual small talk. But now it was out and she braced for the evasion.

John gave her a considering, slightly wry look. 'I was. What about you?'

Charlotte nodded.

John blinked. 'You are married or you were?'

'I was.'

An alarm bell, somewhere distant. *Careful, Charlotte.*

John laughed. 'Well then. I'm sorry. You seem far too young. But I guess that's me being presumptuous about your generation. I thought thirty-five was the earliest you'd even consider it.'

Charlotte shrugged.

John leaned against a tree and looked at the sky. 'I think my marriage ending made everything a lot clearer. My whole life I had been controlled. I don't want to say she told me what to do or anything that straightforward. But expectations can be just as bad. Ticking those boxes, hitting those marks. All the things you're supposed to do.' He looked at her then, expression curious. 'Do you know what the term actualised means?'

Charlotte shook her head.

'It means nothing more or less than for something to become actual. Real. *Itself.* Which sounds so simple! But I have this theory that most people are perfectly happy to contort themselves into what is best for the herd. It's evolution, right? The colony falls apart if the worker bees defect. But if free will is what sets us apart from every other species on the planet, then that's as much a curse as a blessing because we have to decide to *exercise* that free will in order to become actualised.'

Somewhere distant and unseen a bird cried out again.

'Do you miss him?' John asked. 'Your husband.'

'I wish I didn't.'

'Because of the pain?'

She nodded.

'Then think of the pain as a fire burning away the old so that the new can grow.'

Charlotte didn't reply. John looked away through the trees, grinning as though what he could see was beyond beautiful. 'This place. How lucky, right? To get to spend so much time somewhere like this. It's so damn unique! Even those flowers – what are they?'

He took a step towards a slightly wider gap in the trees, through which a bush dotted in bluish flowers sprawled.

A rush of queasy fear. Charlotte knew that gap and those flowers. When she'd first arrived there'd been a sharp, steep ditch between them. Charlotte had spent days finding large sticks to sharpen and drive into the bottom, before covering it all in leaves and easily broken twigs. From here, it just looked like undergrowth. In the midst of her lonely paranoia in the first days here, she'd gone a little overboard, placing several traps out in the trees, just in case someone followed her on a walk and she had to lure them into one. She knew there wasn't much point in it. But it made her feel at least a little more in control.

'I wouldn't.' Charlotte tried to keep her voice easy, a little cautious rather than anything more. 'Lot of stinging nettle around there. I don't know how the stuff gets in your socks but it does.'

Charlotte didn't know if that was what stinging nettle did. She hoped John didn't either.

John, about to step through the gap, hesitated. Turned back with a wink. 'Maybe when I have better shoes, eh?'

It was strange how, after weeks of solitude, this new routine formed. Whoever was up first would wait for the other with a coffee. They'd chat in the icy morning air before Charlotte headed off to do the checks and John went back inside his lodge to write. In the afternoon they'd take a walk, different paths every time. Charlotte had removed the trap near the clearing, but there were others she had to be careful to keep him from. Sometimes they'd talk. Sometimes they'd walk in silence. Either, to Charlotte, was fine.

Most nights they'd have dinner together. Or rather, John would make dinner and Charlotte would promise to try one of these days. She'd warned John she was a dreadful cook, which he had laughed off while insisting that he was happy to handle the food given Charlotte's free tour guide work. To her that assessment was a bit generous, but she didn't complain.

She'd known on some level that she was lonely, in the same way she knew that the weather up here was cold. There wasn't a lot she could do about it, so she hadn't put much thought towards doing anything. But John's presence had upended that. He had reminded her of what good company could be like. There was something almost intoxicating about how *easy* it was to be in his company. He never pressed anything, always pulled back if he got the sense that his questions were too pointed. Without words he'd identified that there were things Charlotte did not want to speak about, and while others might have taken that as a challenge and tried to get the answers out of her, he never did.

Charlotte had to wonder if there was an implicit quid-pro-quo in that. For all their conversations, she still didn't know very much about him. He was good at saying a lot, at sharing reflections and experiences, without ever quite getting specific. She still didn't know the name of his ex-wife. She didn't know if he had children. She didn't know what his book was really about or what his job had been before he took up writing. And while she supposed it would be fair enough to ask, there seemed to be an unspoken understanding that if he wasn't going to delve too deeply into her past, she could return the favour.

But that led to a deeper concern. Because one practical consideration of placing herself up here had been that if she *was* found, the fallout would not affect anyone but her.

She knew that enjoying John's company was a form of selfishness. If she was truly being as cautious as she could, she would have long since removed herself from the mountain – not just for her own sake, but for John's. On her daily rounds she found herself pausing for longer and longer intervals, watching the carpark and the mouth of the mountain road beyond, tense as she listened for tyres on gravel, looked for a flash of headlights. Wondering what exactly she would do if those fears ever came true. Telling herself to leave before they did.

'Why do you think you write?' Charlotte asked John one morning, as they traipsed through the peeling trees and scratchy undergrowth. It was a frosty, brisk morning but the walk was doing a little to hold the chilliness at bay.

'Ah, the billion-dollar question.' John, slightly ahead, looked back. 'I've come to believe that the only way to find anything close to happiness is to do what makes you happy.'

Charlotte, hands in pockets as she stepped over a fallen log, said nothing.

'What about you?' he asked.

'I wish I could agree. Except I haven't written in ages, so ...'

'So what, you'll never write again?'

Charlotte shrugged.

'Oh, come on,' John said. 'Will you get anywhere with *that* attitude? Come on Katie, rage against the dying of the light!'

'That quote's about death, not writing.'

'Ah,' John replied. 'But not doing what you were born to do might as well be death, right? Here's a question for you. What are you afraid of?'

She was reminded of that first conversation with Leo Grey, a world away, a life ago.

Charlotte stopped. John kept walking. A pull of tension in her gut. Her hand, unconsciously, went for her pocket.

What if he knows? What if he's lured me out here? What if—

Stop. *Stop.*

'I'm afraid I'm no good,' she said, walking again.

John looked back at her, eyebrow slightly raised. 'Is that true?'

'Yeah.'

'Why wasn't it true back when you *did* write?'

'Because I was stupid. Because I was young.'

'You're still young. The difference now is that you're limiting yourself. Overthinking. Being scared and paranoid. Seriously. This afternoon, grab a notebook, sit down, don't think, and see what happens.'

'I never liked writing by hand,' Charlotte said. 'Generational thing I guess.'

John laughed. 'That's not generational; it's just sanity. I'm the same, hand gets too cramped. Computers for me, thanks. Which, by the way, you have. In your office.'

'You caught me,' Charlotte said, but in the back of her mind she was trying to work out if the office set-up was visible from the street outside.

The next morning dawned sunny and almost warm. It came as a pleasant surprise, a hint that maybe the cold was starting to creep away. She watched the blue sky as she poured a coffee out the front of Snowhaven, enjoying the touch of heat on her face until John joined her.

'Great day for it!' he exclaimed, pouring his own.

'For what?'

'Sitting inside and writing.' He winked. 'But no, I think I'll take a decent walk first, try to soak up some Vitamin D. Want to come?'

'I wish,' Charlotte said. She'd found more mould in one of the Bushmill bathrooms that she'd have to deal with before it was too far gone. 'Gotta spray and scrub. Work on your tan for me, would you?'

John saluted. 'Roger that!'

Charlotte returned the mugs and pot inside then headed next door to Bushmill, a bucket of cleaning supplies in hand. She could see John sauntering off into the trees, looking for all the world like he was headed somewhere enormously exciting.

Bushmill was chilly and stale-smelling. It had been recently renovated, with exposed wooden beams and stone benchtops giving it some refined, classical charm, but to Charlotte its mere two exits (one at the front, one through the drying room) compared to Snowhaven's four made it less than ideal. She cracked a few windows to air the place out then got to work in the bathroom. The mould was stubborn, but after about an hour she'd managed to remove most of it. She piled everything back into her bucket and washed her hands, then returned to the windows. The smell didn't seem much alleviated.

She stood for a moment outside in the sun. She whistled to herself walking back to Snowhaven, some Bee Gees song John had insisted on playing several times.

Stepping back inside Snowhaven, she left the bucket by the front door and headed upstairs, flicking the kettle on.

She might spend an hour in the sun with a cup of tea and her book – she'd ditched the romance and had started on *Great Expectations* – then head through the other lodges to open the windows.

She crossed into the living area, to where she'd left her book on one of the armchairs near the window.

'Keep still, please.'

Charlotte jerked upright, a bolt of ice rammed through her chest.

Anders in the chair by the fireplace. All in black. One ankle resting on the opposite knee. Held steady above it, a silenced pistol in a gloved hand.

CHAPTER EIGHT

Then

Everything had changed, and Charlotte was struggling to keep up. The club was big; a multi-storey venue with several different bars co-existing on different floors. There was the quieter, classier cigar bar on the top level, a more traditional pulsating dance club in the middle and a rowdy, sweaty live-music venue in the basement. As manager, Charlotte had to oversee all of them, and her first few nights there were spent running around trying to seem like she knew the slightest bit about what she was doing, all the while staving off the strong desire to hug herself in the toilet.

Freddie didn't help; a scowling, brusque man in his thirties who had worked behind the bar since before Dominic bought a stake in the place. Freddie had immediately made it clear that he didn't think much of Charlotte's qualifications – or the idea that she even had any. Which Charlotte found hard to counter given he was essentially right.

'You want me to shift stock downstairs,' he said to her one night, 'despite the fact that this level is where we make all our money?'

'The gig is going off, Freddie. We need—'

'Charlotte.' He adopted an ingratiating, infuriating smile. 'What you're doing is super impressive, really. But I've been here a while, okay? You think you can just let me do my job?'

Charlotte didn't have much of a comeback to that and later had to bite her tongue when the downstairs staff complained about running out of beer mid-show.

On another occasion when the upstairs bar was short-staffed, she asked if Freddie could help tidy the tables before the next wave of customers.

'You want me to abandon this during service?' He gestured out to the blue-lit floor of writhing dancers. 'You know you're capable of cleaning too, right?'

'Of course, but I've gotta make sure downstairs—'

'You don't think there's someone else you could ask? Like, anyone?'

'I'm asking you.'

'And I'm saying no. Unless you want to explain to your boyfriend – sorry, *boss* – why everything went to shit on a hectic night?'

Later, back at Dominic's apartment – their apartment – Charlotte paced the floorboards and vented while Dominic reclined on the couch with a whisky.

'I can't stand him,' she seethed. 'It's like nothing I say is worth listening to, even when I'm proved right. I *know* I'm good at this, Dominic. I know I'm across it. But he just ... I dunno if it's my age or me being a girl or, or *you*, but he just thinks I'm this idiot and then everything falls apart because he won't take me seriously.'

Dominic finished his drink, stood and crossed to the towering, varnished liquor cabinet. He chose a fresh glass and a new whisky, poured, then turned his attention to one of the paintings lining the wall.

'The way I see it, there are two ways to handle this,' he said. 'One is that I speak to him, but that will do more harm than good if you want him to take you seriously.'

'What's the other?'

'That you draw a line. Show him who's boss.'

Charlotte collapsed into the couch as Dominic poured her a wine. 'That's the thing,' she said. 'I don't *feel* like his boss.'

'But you are. That's an indisputable fact.'

'He's disputing it.'

'He's in no position to. He's an employee. You have the power here.'

Charlotte laughed. 'Power. Sure. As far as he's concerned, I'm an unearned title.'

Dominic swirled his whisky, thinking. 'Alright, let me throw you a thought experiment. Where does power come from?'

'Money, status, age.'

'Illusions,' Dominic said. 'Power is in the eye of the beholder.'

'Well, this beholder's eye doesn't see it. And I can't blame him.'

'Then create the illusion. Change the way he sees things.'

'I dunno,' Charlotte said. 'You start a fight with someone bigger and stronger, seems to me they have the power.'

'So pull a gun,' Dominic said. 'Find a way to shift the scales. Every revolution in history has proved just how flimsy the perception of power really is.'

All of which sounded wonderful but didn't really give her a concrete way to deal with the prick.

A few nights later the club was, again, inundated with customers, the staff run off their feet. When Charlotte heard that the bar team downstairs were struggling, she took a deep breath, reminded herself of what Dominic had said, and found Freddie on his phone out the back.

He didn't even look up. 'I don't work downstairs.'

'Tonight you do.'

'Tonight isn't any different to any other night. I'm needed here.'

'You're needed there. So hurry the fuck up and go.'

Freddie glanced up, amused. 'Or what? Gonna send your boyfriend to give me a smack?'

'Or you're fired.' Charlotte had to concentrate on keeping her voice steady.

Freddie's laugh stoked a glowing ember inside her into a blaze.

'Sure thing, sweetheart,' he said.

The unsteadiness was gone in an instant. 'Alright. Go home then.'

Freddie raised an eyebrow.

'I mean it,' Charlotte said. 'You're done. Get your stuff and go.'

Freddie rolled his eyes. 'Whatever, fine. I'll head down.'

'You'll head home.'

Freddie snorted. 'The place will collapse without me.'

'Actually,' Charlotte said, 'I reckon we'll be fine. You're fired. So get the hell out.'

Freddie gaped at her.

She pointed at the door.

Charlotte thought, briefly, he might hit her. But instead he spat at her feet, muttered 'bitch' and stalked off, leaving her trembling with fury but feeling, in the best way possible, like an electric current had gone through her. Like she could do anything.

Charlotte didn't know if word had spread or if she just *felt* different, but everything changed after that. She no longer entered the club believing she was an imposter. She no longer hesitated before giving staff members instructions, and they no longer hesitated before following them. Maybe they never had to begin with, maybe she'd been imagining it. But she wasn't anymore.

Dominic had laughed when she told him what happened. 'Jesus, you *fired* him? Well, good riddance. It's on you to find a replacement now.'

Which once might have daunted her, but Charlotte got the interviews organised quickly and soon was speaking to a range of qualified candidates, finally hiring a woman of about her age named Claire, whose straightforward, no-nonsense competence made Charlotte as proud as if it had been her own.

Then one night she arrived at work, humming and excited for the challenge of a full-on Friday, only for Claire to pull her aside and whisper, 'He's back.'

Charlotte didn't need to ask who she meant. Over one too many post-work drinks she'd told Claire the whole story of Freddie, only leaving out Dominic's part in it. Charlotte had known this might happen – some of the other staff members had reported that he'd been talking a big game about turning up and being disruptive. And while the prospect of dealing with that made her a little queasy, Charlotte figured she had kicked him out once; she could do it again.

She found Freddie slumped in one of the corner couches up in the cigar bar, a pint in hand and eyes unfocused. She stood over him, hands on hips, reminding herself all the while that other staff members were nearby in case this went bad. He looked up. A slack grin spread across his face as he took her in.

'Sweetheart!'

'What are you doing here?'

'Grab a seat, would you?'

'I'm working.'

'That'd be a first.'

'If you're going to be a dickhead, I'm calling security.'

He raised what she guessed was supposed to be a placating hand. 'No need, no need. I come in peace.'

'Why come at all?'

'Because I wanted to talk.' He raised a veering finger and pointed. 'To you.'

'About what?'

His eyes narrowed. 'You think you're pretty smart, don't you? Think you're across all the shit that goes down here?'

Charlotte didn't give him the satisfaction of a reply.

Freddie snorted. 'Yeah, course you do. 'Cos you got big bad boss boyfriend backing you up. 'Cept you don't know as much as you think you do.'

'That all?'

There was a mischievous edge to Freddie's smile now. 'Maybe you *do* know. But I doubt it. You'd be running scared if you did. Not everyone can handle that shit.'

'What shit?'

Freddie laughed. 'See unlike you, I been here long enough to know what really goes on. And lemme tell you: darling Dominic, he ain't who he says he is.'

A twinge in her stomach. 'So who is he?'

Freddie stood, swayed and belched. 'If you're too stupid to figure it out, it's not on me to tell you. Ask him yourself.'

He knocked his beer to the floor before leaving.

She wanted to brush off what Freddie had said. He was an idiot and he'd been drunk. He was bitter about what had happened. He was trying to stir shit up and was resorting to cheap, pathetic ways to do it.

But.

Lying next to Dominic that night, she found sleep hard. She'd glance sideways at him and wonder. The next morning over breakfast, she tried to bring it up with him. But she couldn't form the question. Maybe because she knew she wouldn't believe the answer.

What really ate at her was that one thing she hadn't felt while listening to Freddie was doubt. It had taken her time to admit that to herself. But hadn't she, from the start, wondered if Dominic was too good to be true? She couldn't chase away that feeling because from the moment Dominic had approached her, she had been waiting for the catch. Time had helped her convince herself that maybe there wasn't one, maybe things had finally fallen into place for her.

But.

She tried to suppress the snowballing worry. She knew Dominic. She loved him. He had changed her life. He adored her.

But Dominic, in his late twenties, didn't quite add up. How *did* someone his age own shares in several nightclubs? Where did that kind of self-assurance come from, that ability to wear suits and act suave and not feel like a total idiot doing it? The more she fretted over those things, the more she realised how little she knew about him. She knew he had grown up in Sydney. She knew his parents were lawyers. But beyond that, he'd told her next to nothing about them; not their names, what they were like. Shit, she didn't even know if he had siblings. Whenever she'd asked about how he got into this line of work, he made some joke and moved on. And Charlotte, always too enamoured to push the issue, left it.

And now, whatever confidence her firing of Freddie had given her began leaking away. She kept screwing up at work, kept forgetting obvious things or making beginner's mistakes. She knew the staff were starting to notice, to talk. Claire quietly asked if she was okay. And around Dominic, despite all her best efforts to act normal, she was getting twitchier; short-tempered and fidgety.

She needed to know.

It was almost embarrassing how fast her insistence to herself that she respect his privacy evaporated. She couldn't ask him outright – she knew he'd laugh it off, tell her that Freddie was just trying to get under her skin and she was silly for letting it work. She'd believe it too, or tell herself she did. Until the next thing that looked out of place, the next discrepancy that would bring that wondering right back.

Mid-service on a night she knew Dominic was tied up at one of the other clubs, she excused herself. She headed into the 'staff only' area and down a carpeted hall to where the big offices were. Outside Dominic's she paused, looking both ways, briefly eyeing the security camera. But Dominic wouldn't check that and anyone who did would know she was his girlfriend. It wasn't locked. She went inside.

Dominic's office was plush and expansive, with a leather chair behind a vast oak desk. It looked more like it belonged to an academic than a nightclub owner. She pulled the door closed behind her and listened, but there were no footsteps, no yells or pounding fists.

She approached the desk. She hesitated, hand resting on it, knowing that the moment she looked a trust would be broken. But if Freddie was right, it already had been. She rounded the desk and sat. She tried one of the drawers. Locked. Then the next. Also locked. A brief rush of relief mingled with sticky self-loathing. She pulled the handle one more time and as she did the door opened.

Charlotte shot upright, so fast the chair fell backwards.

Dominic, looking mildly surprised, stood in the doorway.

Words vanished.

'What are you doing?' he asked.

She should have thought this through. She should have come up with a cover story. But anything remotely convincing was out of her reach.

Dominic stepped into the room and closed the door behind him. He didn't look angry. Just concerned. 'Charlotte?'

She swallowed. 'Freddie ... um, Freddie was here the other

night. And he told me ... well, he didn't tell me much. But he said you were ...'

Dominic's expression didn't change.

'He said that you aren't who you say you are. That you ... I don't know but I couldn't get it out of my head and I was scared to ask you and ... but it's stupid, right? It's all just Freddie being an arsehole and I'm overreacting. I'm sorry. I'm really sorry. I know you're not ...'

She wanted him to be angry, offended, hurt, to erupt over the betrayal of trust. She wanted all of that because whether it was true or not, she would believe it. She would believe it because she had to, because all she needed was his rebuttal so she could preserve the perfect fantasy her life had become.

'He was talking shit, right?' Charlotte said.

Dominic looked away. Frowned. Faced her again.

She didn't want to hear it. She didn't want to know.

He told her anyway.

CHAPTER NINE

Now

Anders inclined his head but did not take his eyes from Charlotte. 'Keep still,' he repeated.

Pins and needles all through her body. She hadn't checked the thread in the hallway.

How did he get in?

'The other man,' Anders said. 'He is out on a walk, yes?'

How long has he been watching us?

'Yes?' Anders repeated.

Charlotte nodded.

'When will he return?'

'I don't ... I don't know.'

'Based on past experience?'

'Sometimes he, sometimes he takes an hour, sometimes two. He's probably back already.'

'He is not back,' Anders said simply. 'But he likely will be soon. Is there another exit from this lodge?'

Charlotte nodded.

'Good,' Anders said. 'In that case we will wait until we are sure he is back inside, then we will go. Until then you will keep quiet or I will shoot you and then I will shoot him.'

'Do you ... are you sure you have the right person? I don't—'

'Your name is Charlotte Laurent,' he said. 'You have been on the run for months now.'

There was something wrenching in hearing it aloud.

'I didn't kill him,' she said.

'That does not matter to me,' he replied.

'It should matter to *them*,' Charlotte spat. 'I didn't kill Dominic, okay? I didn't.'

Anders just watched her.

Hopelessness closed in like a vice. She had tried. She had taken precaution after precaution. She had convinced herself that, with enough care, she could stay ahead of her past. But now here it was in front of her. There was almost a kind of relief in it.

If Anders shot her now, at least she'd die quickly. At least it would be over.

'Do not run,' Anders said, as if seeing into her thoughts. 'Bullets that do not kill can still cause pain. I would not like that and nor would you.'

There was something so unsettling about the way he spoke. He was so polite. Like this was nothing more than an errand for him. He had to know that bringing her back to Melbourne would only end in her death. But Charlotte had long since learned that there were some people for whom that sort of thing was no bother at all.

'I saw you in the supermarket,' she said. 'You waited until now?'

'I had to find you first.'

'You *had* found me.'

'My employer insisted on discretion. Had I taken you in the supermarket I would have had to kill the attendant and anybody else who saw you. That would not have been very discreet. That would have drawn police. There would have been witnesses and the whole thing would have been ... what is it you Australians are so fond of saying? A headache. My employer would have been irritated.' He shrugged. 'So I took my time. It would seem there was no rush. You did not run when you had the chance.'

She should have followed her instincts. She should have known.

'So.' With his spare hand Anders slapped his knee and stood, the gun barrel rising with him. 'We go together to the front office. You can see there if the man has returned from his walk and then we can discuss our next steps, yes? Remember: if you scream or try to warn him, he will die and that would be unfortunate.'

'But my death wouldn't be,' Charlotte said.

'Many deaths are unfortunate,' Anders said. 'Just as many are self-induced. Shall we?'

Self-induced. She wanted to roar back at him; she had been a kid, innocent and stupid and in love, too starry-eyed to realise the waters were rising around her neck, stormier and more dangerous by the second.

But Anders wouldn't care. Men like him never did.

She started to back away, towards the hall. Anders followed at an easy pace, the gun never wavering.

'Did you follow me here?' she asked.

'I did not have to. I asked the attendant at the supermarket what you did.'

Barry had lied to her. Probably out of guilt.

'He told me you were the caretaker up here,' Anders went on. 'After that I watched the mountain road for a while, to see if you would try and leave. I suspected not. Where else would you go? Besides, the longer I waited the lower your guard would get.'

He had predicted her perfectly. The thought would have made her furious if there weren't more pressing matters on her mind. She was passing the kitchen now, backing into the hall proper, under a brick archway. Passing it, she hesitated, placing a hand against the wall on the other side. She closed her eyes and took a deep breath. She could hear Anders' footsteps, soft on the floorboards. She looked at him again.

'Please,' she said.

'You are past please.'

'I'll do whatever you want. Please just don't ...'

'There is no point in begging.' Anders was passing under the archway now. 'You have made your choices. I have my job. Do not make this more—'

Charlotte grabbed the wire dangling down the wall and pulled hard.

For a dreadful second she thought it hadn't worked, that she had misjudged. A flicker of confusion on Anders' face, then the flash of movement behind his head – a loud, far too loud crack, and he lurched forward. Charlotte jumped back as he hit the ground on hands and knees. His gun clattered towards her. She snatched it up.

He squinted at her.

She brought the butt of the gun down on his head, then again. His face smacked the floorboards and he was still.

Charlotte staggered back, struggling to breathe. She didn't let go of the gun. Anders wasn't moving but he could be faking it, he could get up any second, he could—

Enough.

Losing it helped no-one. She had known that something like this might happen and so she had prepared. A loose brick above the archway – she had wrapped it carefully in wire that she had run through tiny brackets down the doorway and to the other side of the arch. Simple. Potentially dangerous if it went wrong. But it had worked, perfectly, and now she had an unconscious hired gun on her hands.

Fuck.

Anders still wasn't moving. She thought, briefly, about shooting him – just in the leg or something, to keep him incapacitated. But she doubted she could aim straight and even if she could, then what? She'd have to patch him up, stop him bleeding to death or going into shock.

Or I could just kill him.

Her hand steadied.

The past months, always looking over her shoulder, always looking out for men like him when all she wanted was to be left alone. And the way Anders had spoken to her; no doubt or questioning whatsoever, even implying she *deserved* this.

She was shaking again, but not with fear.

She gave herself another second to breathe. Then, moving fast, she backed into her room. She felt around under the bed until she found the backpack taped to the slats, the one with her fake IDs and cash hidden in the bottom. She tugged it loose and ran back into the hall, lifting the gun. But Anders remained where he was.

She found the handcuffs buried in the bag with everything else. They were cheap, homemade by a guy she'd met in a bar who did metalwork as a hobby and had probably imagined Charlotte had something else in mind when she asked to buy the cuffs off him. Once Anders' wrists were secured, she rolled him over. He groaned slightly but didn't wake. Checking that the safety was on, Charlotte stuck the gun down the back of her jeans then got her hands under Anders' arms. He was heavy, heavier than she would have guessed from his build. She half expected him to wake as she dragged him towards the stairs, but he didn't. Sweating now, struggling to keep him upright, she pulled him down step by step, his boots bouncing off each one.

The boiler room thrummed with warmth. She managed to get Anders over to the right side of the concrete floor, where a series of sturdy metal pipes ran along the wall. Getting the gun out again, she rolled him onto his side and undid one cuff. She stepped back, waiting for him to take his chance. He didn't. She cuffed his right hand to the pipe, then scanned the surrounding area, making sure there was nothing he could use to free himself or attack. Finally she patted him down, checking his pockets. Only some car keys, which she removed and put in her own pocket.

She crossed to the other side of the room and sat watching him, the gun hanging from her fingers. He still hadn't moved.

Run. Run now and don't look back.

But she needed to know how he had tracked her to Burnley. She needed to know exactly what his employer expected from her. Maybe there was a deal she could make, maybe ...

No. She knew better than that.

She exhaled. Then there was John. If she ran without warning him, then sooner or later he would come to the lodge looking for her. He would find Anders, believe whatever bullshit story the captive man cooked up, and let him go. Then ...

She could feel the tears welling up, the pressure in her chest. She left the room, locking the door behind her. She shook with quiet, angry, hopeless sobs. She went back upstairs, into the office. It was, absurdly, still sunny outside, still beautiful. There was no sign of movement inside White Republic. She stayed where she was until John reappeared bouncing along the road, clearly singing something, a big smile on his face. He glanced up, waved when he saw her watching from the window. She waved back, then retreated into the shadows of the unlit room before he could realise anything was wrong. She thought of him going about his business with no idea of what he had walked into – what she had pulled him into purely by being here. She thought about Anders, probably concussed, down in the basement, still a threat even if she'd overpowered him for now. She thought about the gun resting in her lap. She picked it up, feeling its all-too-familiar weight.

CHAPTER TEN

Then

Somebody was knocking. Charlotte shook herself out of the moment and called, 'Come in.'

Mel opened the door in that slow, careful way, like stepping in on somebody five minutes from death. It was annoying, but mostly it made her wonder if Mel was overreacting or if Charlotte really had been that bad.

'Hey just checking in,' Mel said, hushed and gentle.

'I'm fine,' Charlotte replied, even though the room was a mess and there was a half-empty bottle of cheap wine on the bedside table. But those things didn't seem all that important right then. What was important was the laptop she had open in front of her as she sat on the bed. She'd been halfway through writing something and she'd felt pretty good about it.

Mel, of course, took no notice. She sat on the bed beside Charlotte, casting a pointed eye over all the strewn-about clothes. Charlotte, hoping she'd take the hint, started typing again, even though she'd completely lost the buzz.

'How you feeling?' Mel asked.

Charlotte kept typing, just random words now. 'I'm fine.'

'Writing?'

She nodded.

'About?'

A shrug. More random words.

'About him?'

Charlotte closed the laptop. 'Got a better suggestion?'

Mel shook her head. 'No. Not at all. It's probably healthy.' A glance at the bottle.

'Right, well.' Charlotte cleared her throat. 'Anyway. I'm feeling better. So ...'

'Cool.' Mel still didn't move.

Charlotte opened the laptop.

'It's just ...'

The dithering was really starting to piss Charlotte off. She wished Dominic was here, and *that* thought almost had her reaching for the wine.

'Okay look,' Mel said, a little firmer. 'I've loved having you here, Charli. But it's been three weeks and Shae is asking how long you're gonna stay and honestly it's fine if you want to stick around, really. But you'll have to like, pay some rent?'

Charlotte blinked. That shouldn't have been a surprise. What struck her more was the fact that it had been three weeks. It felt, simultaneously, like more and less time had passed. Like she'd been falling through a void ever since Dominic stood in his office and told her—

'So, like ...' Mel shot Charlotte a pained look. 'I mean, what do you think?'

'No, of ... of course,' Charlotte said. 'I'm sorry, I've been so out of it.'

'Babe, you've just been through a breakup.'

The word set her teeth on edge.

'I mean if you stayed here, I'd love it, really! But I'm sure you could go back with your dad and ...'

Charlotte almost laughed out loud. She hadn't spoken to her father in over a month. He had no idea that she and Dominic had broken up or that she was staying with Mel and unemployed. If she could help it, he never would. The thought of all his patronising warnings still stung.

'You sure you're okay with me staying? If I pay, obviously?'

Mel nodded. 'Really, yeah. You just, you know, gotta pay.'

She smiled, squeezed Charlotte's ankle, and left.

Charlotte resumed typing. She'd been writing about her and Dominic's first night out together. It was big, flowery, over the top. But it didn't feel false. It was how that night had felt. The problem now was reliving it and trying to accept that that feeling could have been wrong.

She'd written more here than she had in a long time. It wasn't like she'd arrived on Mel's doorstep and immediately started smashing out words. But after the tears and the hours of staring blankly at a wall, she'd had to do *something*. And the crush of disappointment and anger and self-loathing and every other bitter, poisonous, wild thing she felt had become too much to just sit with. It had to go somewhere. So, with no structure or thought, she'd started writing about Dominic. About their relationship. About the good times. About her doubts.

What she had not touched on, what she didn't think she *could*, was the night it all fell apart. Because as much as the words he'd said popped unbidden into her head, as clear as they had been when he said them, she didn't think she could write them down. Writing them down would make them real.

* * *

'I'm a drug dealer.'

He had said it simply. Directly. Never looking away from her.

And Charlotte had laughed. It was wild, high-pitched, crazy sounding. She thought it was a joke. Something an actor would say in one of those terrible crime shows on television.

But Dominic wasn't smiling.

The laugh tapered off. She stared at him.

'A drug dealer,' she repeated.

He nodded.

'But you … how …'

She wanted him to say something, to step in, to explain. To tell her it *was*, in fact, a joke. He didn't.

'You can't be,' she said.

Still he didn't reply.

'But you don't …' She gestured at his suit, at the office around her. 'Drug dealers don't …'

He still said nothing.

Realisation was barrelling towards her. She could feel it; huge and overpowering and too big to fully take in.

She'd met drug dealers before. Not many, but a couple at school and uni. That time she and Mel, giggling, had bought a foil-wrapped nugget of weed from a spotty, lank-haired guy with a baggy shirt and the strong smell of someone who'd never heard of deodorant. She and Mel had run off exhilarated, caught up in how *bad* they were.

Until Charlotte's father caught them. The memory still made her sick.

But that guy, that miserable, grotty loser, *that* was what a drug dealer was supposed to be. Pathetic. Off-putting. More sad than anything else. But Dominic, Dominic was a *businessman*; he was impressive, he was smart and charming and ...

Realisation in her face now.

She swayed.

'How much ...' She didn't know the question to ask. How much did he make? How much did he sell? *What* did he sell?

Enough to make him wealthy before thirty. Enough to pay for all those fancy dinners and his huge apartment. Enough for the designer suits and the luxury car, enough that he needed ...

She swallowed. Her mouth was sandpaper.

He needed a nightclub, *several* nightclubs, to launder it. Charlotte didn't know much about the drug trade, but she knew that big operators needed big businesses to cover what they made.

Which meant Dominic made a lot.

'Take a seat,' he said. 'I'll answer any questions you have.'

Charlotte, even though she could barely stand, didn't.

'Listen,' he said. 'I can understand you being surprised, but it's really no different to any other job.'

Did he believe that? Did he *actually* believe that?

'I mean it, Charlotte,' he said. 'I'll tell you the truth. All of it. It doesn't change anything. Not to me. Not how I feel about you.'

Questions spiralled through her head but she didn't want to ask any of them. She *couldn't.* News stories, one after another. That kid who had been pulled out of the Yarra, throat slashed, after getting involved in the drug trade. Gangland shootings. Police stings ending with multiple casualties.

How many of them had Dominic been involved with?

'Charlotte,' he said. 'Listen.'

She ran. Past him, through the door, down the hall. She expected him to yell out. She expected security to grab her.

Down the service stairwell and out of the club and into the stinking alley. She turned, faced the door, backing away. She could hear the music throbbing from inside. She could hear the city beyond. She remembered their first night together, the way the reflected buildings had twinkled in the Yarra.

That boy, limp and waterlogged, the news footage of his screaming mother.

Her father's words.

People like that don't shower others with attention unless there's something they want.

Head down, she staggered into the city. Waited for her phone to ring. It never did.

* * *

Charlotte hadn't thought she would ever have to fill out a résumé again. She'd figured she would stay at the club, rising through the ranks while writing in her spare time until she sold a manuscript and published a book and then that would be her future, turning up to glamorous literary events looking beautiful in dresses she'd paid for herself. Dominic on her arm, her handsome, perfect, businessman partner.

She hadn't realised until now, trying to make all those dead-end café jobs sound more impressive, how entirely she'd believed that would be her future. How despite all her fears – that Dominic would get bored of her, that he was too good, that none of it was real – she really had thought her path forward was set.

God, was there anything as cruel as the backwards plunge? As being tricked into thinking everything had changed, new steps had been taken, you were on your way to a shining tomorrow, only for it to be pulled out from under you and leave you lying in the dirt where you'd started, the ladder gone and no way back up?

I'm a drug dealer.

Sometimes, late at night, kept awake by the sound of Mel fucking whomever she'd brought home, Charlotte would turn those words over in her head. She'd ask herself if, really, it mattered. Would she have felt differently if Dominic was an arms dealer, if he sold black-market cigarettes or unlicensed booze?

Maybe she would and maybe she shouldn't. Maybe the thin line of legality was all that dictated what Charlotte would be willing to tolerate. But she could not look away from the fact that Dominic, clearly, made a *lot* of money, and she found it very hard to believe he could do that and keep his hands clean.

It wasn't that Charlotte had a problem with drugs either. Not really. She'd smoked a bit of weed here and there, and taken a pill that made her feel sick once. Just because it wasn't really her thing didn't mean she had an issue with it. But there was a difference between selling some stuff to pay for a personal habit and the scale Dominic clearly operated on.

She just hated how often she had to remind herself of the fact as she filled out applications.

Life had become a weird, spiralling cycle. She rarely knew which day it was. She would lie on the bed, writing, sipping wine and slipping back into those happy days with Dominic, unencumbered by reality. She'd drink and she'd write and she'd read it over and feel almost like she had stepped back in time, then she'd wake up already late for a job interview.

Her hangovers, on those days, were always worse.

Then the interviews. One after another. Sitting across from harried-looking men and women in oppressively warm cafés, trying to act like she really wanted this menial job, wondering later how obvious her disinterest had been when the phone never rang. She'd go back to bed and write and drink.

Then the nights out with Mel, who had recently made a crew of new hairdresser friends. They were beautiful and friendly with booming laughs and a collective love of prosecco. In different circumstances, Charlotte probably would have liked them. But sitting in those bars as they gossiped and checked out guys and bought Charlotte drinks, her thoughts would return to Dominic. What he was doing. Whether he missed her. What he'd say if she called him now.

He'd probably found someone new. All he had to do was go to another club, sit at the bar, and wait for someone else to fall into his lap. While she drifted through this pointless new existence, was he walking with another woman past the twinkling reflected lights, buying her drinks, taking her home ...

She reached for her phone.

And then, like a klaxon in her head, the memory of her father's fury. Red-faced and screaming, ordering Mel to get the hell out, Charlotte thick-tongued with embarrassment – she'd never, *never* seen him like this before.

'It's just weed,' she'd managed to say as he slammed the door behind Mel. 'Everyone does it.'

He hadn't faced her. His hand against the door, pressed so hard she almost expected the wood to splinter.

'I don't give a fuck,' he'd snarled.

'But Dad—'

'No. *No.* A bit of weed is how it starts. A bit of weed is one innocent-looking corner of that business. The rest is a fucking sickness that infects everything it touches.'

'How do you even know that?' Charlotte had demanded, not because she thought there might be an answer, but because what the hell would her dad know about any of this?

He faced her then. She wished he hadn't.

'I won't have drugs in this house. Never again, Charlotte. Never again or I swear to God you'll be on the street.'

Logically she knew he didn't mean it. Of course he didn't mean it. He couldn't.

And through the heart-pumping, hot-faced fear and confusion, something occurred to her.

'Was Mum ... was she involved in this stuff?'

He said nothing.

'Is that why she left?'

Charlotte wondered then if this was the missing puzzle piece to her life. Her father's violent hatred of drugs. Her mother's distance, the occasional brief phone call from France and nothing else, so far away for so long that they might as well be strangers.

'It doesn't matter,' her father said. 'We'll say no more about it, Charlotte. But if it happens again ...'

Staggering home from the bar one night, just the two of them, Charlotte kept her mouth shut as Mel spoke.

'We can do this all the time – I promise Shae is really cool once you get to know her! We'll have movie nights. We can go out. We can find you someone better, I promise.'

Maybe Mel was right. Maybe this was okay. Living with Mel, nights out. She could write. She would find someone. Dominic and the club and her brush with a darker, more dangerous life would just be a story she drew on for inspiration. In time it wouldn't hurt anymore. In time, she would know she had made the right choice. At that moment things were flat and colourless, the future ahead a barren hinterland, unremarkable and empty. But that would change. The pain would fade. So would the yearning. Time would give her perspective. She would be okay.

'Do you think he was a bad guy?' she asked Mel.

Mel didn't have to ask who she meant. They walked down the empty street in silence for a while.

'I don't know, Charli,' she said. 'I really don't. I mean, I've known drug dealers. Ones who were nice, ones who were pricks. But I'd never met one like him. Which makes it hard to guess what kind of person he is.'

Charlotte said nothing. Their footsteps sounded, to her, too loud.

Mel slung an arm over her shoulder. 'Anyway. He's in the past now. Onwards and upwards, hey?'

And that was what she told herself, even though she didn't believe it, even as she lay in that uncomfortable bed and stared at that peeling ceiling and thought about the apartment she'd so briefly shared with Dominic. It had all been so good. A fairy tale. A dream. And now every aspect of it had been replaced by twisted parody. Two-dollar cleanskins instead of expensive vintages. Pubs at happy hour rather than the fancy restaurants. T-shirts and jeans replacing form-fitting dresses, making coffee for next to nothing instead of managing a club, listening to Mel have sex instead of those magical, overwhelming nights with Dominic.

Onwards and upwards.

She got ready Monday morning for her new job. She dressed neat. Checked herself in the mirror. Pushed away the tug of draining despondency. It would be okay. It would suck for a while, but she would adjust. She would get used to it. Dominic would only be a memory.

Onwards and upwards.

She walked into the chilly morning, bag over her shoulder. She whispered the words to herself again and again as she walked for the train and it was only as she was about to get on that she realised her phone was ringing.

Dominic.

She stood there, staring at his name on the screen. She felt nothing. No, less than nothing, like a total void of emotion.

She had made her choice. She was moving on. She was done with him.

People like that don't shower others with attention unless there's something they want.

She rejected the call. The train was leaving. Still she stood on the platform, watching her phone.

He called again.

Her thumb hovered over the reject button.

Onwards and upwards.

People like that don't shower others with attention unless …

Was there something Dominic wanted from her?

It didn't matter. They were done.

But then, how could she know for sure unless she answered? How could she move on?

The phone was still ringing.

She answered.

They met at the bar on Southbank they'd gone to that first night. Charlotte dressed determinedly plain, in a t-shirt and jeans. Dominic was waiting out the front. They hugged for a long time without a word. When he stepped back he looked apologetic.

'I hate to ask this,' he said. 'But I need to know you're not wearing a wire. May I?'

Not wearing a wire. The words were so jarring and strange and foreign she almost laughed. But she didn't as he put a hand on her waist and slid it up under her shirt, running it across her back, her stomach, up to her breasts without touching them. Charlotte was unsteady. Dominic gave her an embarrassed smile and gestured to the bar.

They sat in the same booth. Dominic ordered a bottle of wine without asking her what she wanted. She didn't mind. She felt like she'd need at least a couple of drinks. He poured them both a glass and sipped without offering a toast. She just watched him.

'I won't waste your time,' he said. 'I'll just explain. If you'll let me?'

She nodded.

'It started with my brother.' Dominic drank. 'Isaac. He was a lot older than me. My hero, as you can imagine. Until he got pulled into the scene.'

The scene. Said so casually, as if she should know what it meant.

'Things went bad,' Dominic said. 'He was dealing and he was using. Sometimes used what he was supposed to sell. My parents tried to help, but it wasn't enough.' A beat. A flicker of pain. 'He died. An overdose. Heroin. Problem was, his debts didn't die with him. His employer came looking for the money. By that point I was at uni and my parents were barely coping. They weren't working and they'd spent way too much trying to help Isaac. Rehab, court costs, all of it. And the man Isaac owed was not patient. So I had a choice. Find a way to make the money, or risk them coming after us.'

'You couldn't go to the police?' Charlotte asked.

Dominic's smile was sad. 'The police aren't interested in a dead junkie's debts. You know what they are interested in? The chance to get at a criminal defence lawyer. Which my parents were. One crack in their façade, one hint that they'd done anything illegal to help Isaac – given him money, covered something up ...'

'Did they?' Charlotte asked.

'Of course,' Dominic said. 'Wouldn't your dad do anything to help you?'

She remembered, sudden and sharp, his threat to kick her out.

'So no,' Dominic went on, 'the police weren't an option. I struck a deal with Isaac's employer: move enough product to erase the debt.'

'You became a drug dealer even though the business killed your brother.'

Dominic nodded. 'I didn't see a choice. At first.' He leaned forward. 'Time passed. Things happened. I got good at it. I made money. And do you know what I realised?'

Charlotte didn't reply.

'How many industries profit off what kills?' Dominic said. 'Tobacco, alcohol, guns. All legal, all above board, all advertised and celebrated, depending on where you live. And beyond that – you look at the drink-driving statistics, at people killed in boozy fights or just straight up drinking themselves to death. You take those statistics and the deaths from smoking and you put them side by side with how many people die because of my industry. You want to take a guess at how comparable they are? I'll give you a clue – they're not. So in the grand scheme of things, what makes my business so bad?'

She had asked herself the same question and found an answer.

'The violence,' Charlotte said. 'Gangland wars and—'

Dominic laughed. She hadn't expected that.

'Yeah the media love to toot that trumpet, don't they?' he said. '*Idiots* die, Charlotte. Idiots get wrapped up in stupid turf wars and make a show of it and go down because they can't help swinging their dicks around the place. That's not me. That's not Adrian – my boss.'

'But what happened with your brother—'

Dominic was nodding. 'Yeah. You can argue that drugs destroyed my brother. You can also argue that a smart guy like him, under no illusions about what that first needle might mean, destroyed himself. He made a choice. The difference between the drug trade and those others is that we do not push anything on anyone. We don't have product placement in films. We don't have billboards or glamorous TV ads. And whatever idea the media likes to insist on, we don't stand on street corners pushing gear to teenagers. If somebody wants what we sell, they must *really* want it to go to the lengths they do. And who am I to deny a consenting adult the thing they want? Who are any of us?'

He let the question hang. Charlotte didn't answer it.

'But beyond that,' Dominic said. 'Beyond the moral grappling, is this: working in an industry – and it *is* an industry – that is outside the law offers a staggering amount of freedom. The ability to make choices on your own terms. To live outside the parameters that everyone sets for you, as if they have any right whatsoever to tell you how to live your life. Now this, what I do; it won't be forever. It might not be for much longer. But if I can end up in a position where I have all the money I could need, then my life going forward is my own. I will never again have to make a choice because somebody forced me into it or because some vague notion of propriety told me I should.'

Charlotte was lightheaded.

'I won't lie to you,' Dominic pushed on. 'I can't. You're too smart for that. Too special. And that's why,' he took her hand, 'I want to offer you the choice to come on this journey with me. To be a part of it. I knew you wouldn't turn me in. I knew I could tell you the truth even if it took some time for you to digest it. Because I knew that you would understand. You're special, Charlotte. I mean that. And I know you'll see this for what it is. Not some terrible nightmare truth. But an opportunity. A chance for both of us to be something spectacular. Together.'

He smiled. Sipped his wine. Charlotte didn't trust herself to pick up her own.

'So,' he said. 'What do you think?'

CHAPTER ELEVEN

Now

A clench in her chest as Anders stirred. Charlotte, sitting against the boiler-room wall a safe distance from him, raised the pistol and rested it on her knee. She kept her expression carefully blank as he sat up, wincing. One eye closed, he looked around the room. Paused only briefly on Charlotte, as though she was no more interesting than anything else here. He rubbed the back of his head. His hand came away bloody.

'How long was I out for?' he asked.

'Ten minutes. Give or take.'

He leaned against the wall. Tugged at his handcuffed wrist, but only once, as if to make sure the cuffs were really there. He dropped his arm and took in the gun aimed at him.

'Are you going to shoot me?'

'Depends on what you tell me.'

'What did you hit me with?'

'Excuse me?'

'I was backing you into the hall and something hit me in the head. What was it?'

An opportunity.

'*Who* was it,' Charlotte said. 'It—'

'My head hurts too much for lies,' Anders said with a hint of impatience. 'I have been watching you long enough to know you are alone, besides which I searched the lodge before you arrived. Your friend over ...' He angled his head, flinched, and exhaled. 'Well, wherever he is relative to us, he had no way of knowing you were in trouble. It was not him. So, what did you get me with?'

'A trap,' Charlotte said.

Anders' eyebrow twitched. 'I should have checked for traps.'

'Well, you didn't,' Charlotte said. 'And now you're here. How did you find me?'

He squinted at her. 'You did some things very cleverly. Others not so much. I paid a visit to your old friend Mel.'

A swooping in her stomach. Her hand on the gun tight. 'You—'

'I did not harm her.' He spoke almost lazily. 'I told her your father had hired me to help find you. She could have checked but I suppose she is not too bright. She told me you had contacted her.'

The phone booth in Thredbo. Fuck. Fuck, fuck, fuck.

'She guessed where you might be,' Anders went on. 'I went to Thredbo. Followed the trail from there.'

'Who else knows where I am?'

Anders said nothing.

Charlotte stood. A tremor raced up her arm.

'Who else knows, Anders? Is someone on the way?'

Anders said nothing.

'Fine,' Charlotte hissed. 'You want to live, tell me what I want to know.'

Anders' almost bored expression did not change.

Charlotte's jaw tightened. Even now, reinforcements could be coming up that road, surrounding the resort. A wave of cold swept over her. She should have gone already. But ...

'In case there is any confusion,' Anders said, 'I should clarify your options for you. You can try to leave via the road, but there may be men waiting for you. You can try to leave via the trees, but I doubt your chances of survival in the wilderness on foot. You have no time to pack or prepare adequately. And even if you take any of the above risks and survive them, you will be leaving your friend here at the mercy of potential attackers. He could come looking for you. He might break a window to get in. I will lie to him and he will set me free and then I will kill him. If you tell him who I am and why I am here, you risk him calling the police and turning you in himself. I suppose he might leave with you, but civilians are so very stupid about their safety, are they not? He probably thinks this can all be worked out over a cup of tea.' Anders had recited all of that without discernible emotion, but now a glimmer of amusement crossed his face. 'Ultimately you have to decide whether or not I have told anyone where we are.'

Charlotte stared at him. No sign of fear. It was as though he genuinely didn't care about the outcome. As though he was no more than vaguely curious about which way Charlotte might go.

'I could torture you,' Charlotte said.

'How?'

'Shoot you in the kneecap—'

'I will scream.'

'Nobody will hear.'

'This old lodge is not soundproofed. What will you tell your friend when he comes knocking? He doesn't seem the type to have heard a gunshot before, true, but up here I'd imagine you couldn't mistake it for much else. And you certainly couldn't mistake the screams. That is not a risk you want to take.'

'I'll gag you and—'

'You would have to get close to me,' Anders said. 'I have a free hand. You could keep a gun to my head but I doubt you could gag me one-handed. Not without me finding an opportunity to attack.' Anders shrugged. 'But the choice is yours, along with the risk.'

Silence.

'But then,' he said, 'you do not plan on torturing me. Or killing me. You would have cuffed both hands around the pipe if you wanted me fully incapacitated. You plan on keeping me captive.'

'I plan on keeping my options open.'

'By closing off the most useful ones? You must teach me more about your approach to strategy.'

Charlotte knelt. Looked him in the eye. Hoped she wasn't giving away the pulsating terror threatening to send her trembling to the ground.

'You haven't called anyone,' she said.

'Such certainty. Where does it come from?'

'From the fact that if you *had* you would be doing everything in your power to convince me you hadn't. But instead you're toying with me. Trying to confuse me, leave me unsure of what to do.'

'You may interpret what I say however you wish. Just as you may choose whether to kill me or not. It's simply a matter of how fully you understand the consequences.'

Charlotte stood. Kept her eyes on this strange, calm, smiling man. He was almost impossible to read. Would he be this relaxed if he *didn't* have help on the way?

Back up in the living room, she stood for a moment, cradling the gun. The shaking hit her hands first. It ran up her arms, down her body. Her lungs seized. Her vision blurred.

They had found her. After everything, every side road, every fake name, every disguise and double back and lie and precaution, they had found her. Just one bounty hunter for now, but it would not stay that way. Maybe there were men coming this way from Burnley. Maybe they were on the way from Melbourne.

But they were coming.

She focused on her breathing. Doing so was hard, like wrestling an out-of-control horse. But she did it. Four beats in. Four beats hold. Four beats out. Four beats nothing. Repeat. And repeat until she felt, again, in charge of herself.

Still unsteady, she made for the office. She crouched low and looked out over the desk, through the window. Stillness. No approaching figures. She listened. No yells or gunshots or barked orders. No sound of approaching cars.

Then, faint, whistling.

Anders was right about one thing: her presence had put John in danger.

She looked again at the gun in her hand. The main advantage she had, not that it would mean much against a squad of trained hitmen.

She exhaled. Sat on the floor and leaned against the wall. She was cornered. There was no clear path forward, no move that didn't come with a major risk. A small, nasty voice in her head whispered that she should just wait here, let them come and accept what she deserved.

No.

She crushed that voice.

She didn't have time to waste. It was true that men might be waiting in the lodges or along the road, ready to ambush her. But taking the time to search upped the risk of them finding her. Better to drive straight out and not slow down until she was far away from here.

She knocked on John's door but heard nothing. There was no time to wait. The choice twisted her stomach, but she had to make it. Once clear she could call White Republic and warn him.

She threw her bag into the back seat of her car and got in the front. A last glance towards the lodge that had been her home.

She turned the key.

Nothing.

CHAPTER TWELVE

Then

Dominic had promised there would be no awkward questions about her return to the club. Still, Charlotte was nervous when she arrived for her first shift back, sure the other staff members were looking sideways at her.

But soon enough it became obvious that nobody thought anything was amiss. Dominic had concocted some story about her being sick, and it appeared to have been roundly accepted.

Claire gave her a big hug and told her how great it was to have her back. Everyone else just progressed the same as before. And Dominic, when Charlotte commented on the fact, just smiled and said, 'See? Told you.'

On the surface, everything was the same as before. She was back in the apartment. Back at work. They were going out for expensive dinners and to dimly lit cocktail bars. But something fundamental had changed.

One night, Dominic asked her to meet him at a restaurant he'd chosen. He arrived ten minutes late, his tie loose and his hair out of its usual shape.

'Everything okay?' Charlotte asked.

Dominic's smile was strained. 'Fine.'

'You sure?'

'Let's just order, yeah?'

They did. Dominic was on his phone, texting something fast. His expression tightened, with what could be anger. Or fear. Charlotte watched him. He pocketed the phone and placed both hands on the table.

'Sorry about that. Busy day.'

'Doing what?' she asked. Dominic hadn't been at the club. Charlotte had been overseeing stocktake all day.

'Just work stuff.'

'What work stuff?'

Dominic's brow furrowed very slightly. 'Do you really think this is the place?'

He said it without inflection. Charlotte's cheeks burned. How stupid could she be? She barely spoke for the rest of dinner and when they got home she didn't ask him again.

Dominic had laid it all out for her and given her the chance to walk away. And she hadn't. She couldn't return to her old life. But the cost was being okay with something she didn't know how to process.

When Dominic told her it was just a business, it made sense. When he argued for the morality of it, she understood. In her head, all of that was clear. But that didn't change this strange, displaced feeling that had her lurching awake at night, from dreams she couldn't remember but made her feel queasy and shaken.

The worst part was that she couldn't talk to anyone about it. She wasn't sure what the others at the club knew or didn't about his business. And beyond that, she was so busy with the hours there that she barely had time for anyone or anything outside of work or Dominic. During the time she'd lived with Mel, her writing had picked up. Now, it had slowed again, to almost non-existent.

On a rare night off, she called Mel. The phone rang out. Mel didn't call back.

Charlotte wasn't surprised. Mel had been furious when Charlotte explained that she wouldn't be moving in after all, that she was getting back with Dominic.

'In what world is that a good idea?' Mel had demanded as Charlotte packed up her room.

'The world where I love him and he loves me.'

'Charli, he's a—'

Charlotte spun, stared her down, unblinking.

Mel shut up. Charlotte went back to packing.

Now Charlotte wished she'd handled it better. It was all well and good to entertain this idea of an exciting new life with exciting new friends, but when you didn't have time to make them, the fantasy slipped away fast.

Often she'd come home late to see the light on under the door of Dominic's study. She'd wait in the living room with a glass of wine, but he wouldn't come out. Once, she went and listened. She heard him speaking low and harried. She went to bed. He never joined her. The next morning she came out to find the study door locked and no sign of him.

She had chosen to commit to him, despite what she knew. Now she had to be an adult and see it through. She had to show Dominic that he had made the right choice in asking her to come back, that she wasn't just a stupid, naïve girl.

Dominic always woke early, so one morning she joined him in the kitchen before dawn, as he made a smoothie. She took his hand and looked him in the eye and said, 'I'm here, you know? Whatever's going on, I'm here. Whatever I can do to help you, I will.'

Dominic said nothing, but a hint of the old smile flickered across his face. He kissed her and returned to the study, leaving Charlotte standing in the still-dark kitchen.

The next day, Dominic called her at work. She answered the phone immediately.

'What are you doing tonight?' he asked.

'I'm in the club till late. There are a couple of events and—'

'Okay, I'll tell Claire to handle it. I'm having dinner with Victor and Elizabeth. You should join us.'

'Elizabeth?'

Silence on the other end.

'You don't remember.' Dominic's voice was flat.

'No, I do, of course I—'

'Elizabeth Bates, Charlotte.'

She scoured her memory for the name.

A heavy sigh.

'I remember,' Charlotte said. 'Of course. It will be great to meet her.'

'Seven, then. The Rode Institute.'

He didn't offer to pick her up.

Charlotte arrived at the restaurant ten minutes early. She'd spent over an hour in front of the mirror trying to get her makeup right, pairing it with a new red dress. She wanted to look striking, beautiful, glamorous. She'd never met Victor

Caine, Dominic's associate, before and still had no idea who Elizabeth Bates was. But Dominic inviting her to the table with them was a big deal.

She walked into the restaurant then came to a halt. At a corner table, under a low-hanging light that cast the white tablecloth gold, Dominic was already deep in conversation with two others. Charlotte checked the time. She *was* early; he had said seven, right? On edge now, she approached them.

'Charlotte.' Dominic stood and kissed her on the cheek. 'Have a seat.'

She didn't know how to act in front of these people. Victor Caine looked too big for the table, for his straining suit. But more than that, he looked *wrong* among all this propriety, with his brutish features, hairy knuckles and close-cropped hair, more bouncer than businessman. He said nothing as Dominic introduced her. Just watched with a slightly open-mouthed smirk. She felt his eyes remain on her after she turned her attention to Elizabeth Bates.

The other woman was older, quite a bit older, maybe in her forties or fifties. But she was beautiful in a way Charlotte could only describe as classy. She was dressed in black, her magenta lipstick muted, her dark hair even and immaculate, hanging just over her shoulders. She smiled as she shook Charlotte's hand, but there was no warmth in it and her attention seemed almost clinical. Charlotte was suddenly self-conscious of her bright red dress, almost childish now. She was aware of Victor watching her. She was aware of how close to Dominic Elizabeth Bates sat.

'Tell us about yourself, Charlotte,' Bates said once they had ordered, with a smile like a patronising kindergarten teacher.

'Well, um ... I mean I'm working in the club. And outside of that, I guess I write.'

'You guess?' Bates looked faintly surprised. 'You don't know?'

Charlotte tried to laugh, but she could feel Dominic's steady gaze.

'Are you published?' Bates asked.

Victor Caine leaned in slightly.

'N-no, not yet but—'

'Not even in a literary journal or something?'

'I mean, it's hard with the club and the workload and—'

'Well, I'm sure Dominic could have a word to management, get them to drop your hours,' Bates said.

'No, I didn't ... no, I like the hours, I do, I just ... And I mean I'm a manager myself so ...'

Bates's smile had turned almost sharklike. Charlotte drank.

She was flailing and what was more, Bates seemed to know and relish it. Dominic said nothing. Victor Caine just watched.

Dinner arrived. Topics flew from politics to some opera Charlotte had never heard of to profit margins and projections and other things she couldn't keep up with. Every time Dominic made a joke, Elizabeth Bates would hold his arm as she threw her head back and laughed.

She gathered from the conversation that Elizabeth Bates was Dominic's and Victor's lawyer, but Charlotte had to wonder how involved she was in the business. Nothing else explained how cosy she seemed with Dominic.

Almost nothing.

Charlotte drank. She couldn't shake the heavy feeling that she'd been brought along for a test that she'd failed miserably. She just wished she knew what it was.

Dominic didn't speak the whole way home. Charlotte knew she'd somehow let him down. The thought sparked a flash of anger. She hadn't had any clue *how* she was supposed to behave, or what he had expected.

Victor had thrown her. Compared to Dominic, he was far closer to what she imagined a career criminal would look like. She'd never once felt in danger from Dominic but, looking at Victor, for the first time she had wondered what it might mean for her if they ever broke up again, this time with her knowing more about what Dominic did. She didn't like the way Victor had watched her. She didn't like that smirk. She didn't like that she couldn't tell what was going on behind those dark eyes.

And then there was Elizabeth Bates. It was possible Charlotte was imagining it, possible those touches were just collegial. Maybe. But seeing Bates, so sophisticated and confident and *adult* ...

She was older. Older than her and older than Dominic. But Dominic had always seemed beyond his years. Didn't it make sense that he would be drawn to someone who would match him in maturity? But then, she thought with a horrible twist of keening desperation, why the fuck had he gone for her in the first place?

Days passed. Every time Dominic didn't answer his phone or came home late, the images would fill Charlotte's head. She imagined Bates in an opulent mansion, waiting with a cocktail, dressed in something silky and easy to slip off and then Dominic arriving and ...

She was at the club almost every day. Getting there early to ensure all the stock was in place, to take calls for events, to check they had the staff they needed. Staying late, often into the morning, overseeing the cleaning. She would get home and collapse into bed and then it would all start again. Even on her rare days off she was so tired she could barely do anything else.

She once again considered asking Dominic to lessen her shifts, but then one night as Charlotte tried to stay awake during the movie they were watching he squeezed her shoulder and said, 'Hey, you know I really appreciate the time you're putting in at the club. I need someone there I can trust.'

Wide awake and speechless, suddenly.

Someone there I can trust.

Maybe she was wrong. Maybe she *was* important to him from a business sense. Maybe she had a place in his life after all and they were both just busy and maybe she was overthinking.

Maybe.

But.

There were nights at the club when Victor Caine would arrive. She was hurrying across the cigar-bar floor one evening when she felt someone's eyes on her. And there he was, alone in a corner booth, watching. Smirking. She'd raised a hand. He hadn't reciprocated. He'd just sipped his whisky and watched and smirked.

Once, she approached him. Not because she wanted or had much reason to, but because she didn't like the idea of him telling Dominic she was ignoring him.

'Hi there.' Her voice sounded unnaturally bright, forced.

He said nothing.

'Good to see you. Wondering if … if there's anything I can do to help?'

'Help with what?' His voice was low, rough with a hint of amusement.

'Just … anything.'

He laughed and drank and didn't say anything else.

She kept an eye out for him after that. Most nights he wasn't there. But when he was it was always alone. Always watching.

She couldn't work while so on edge. She couldn't keep walking to her car with her keys between her fingers. So, one night over dinner, she raised it with Dominic.

'I see a bit of Victor around the club.'

'Well, he is a stakeholder,' Dominic replied, focus on his steak.

'Yeah, of course. It's just … I dunno. Maybe I'm being paranoid. He's always watching me. I just … is there some reason he's interested in me?'

'Have you done something to interest him?' Dominic asked. There was a playful note to his voice but that didn't stop her feeling a nauseous shiver. She stared at him.

'No … I mean, what do you … What have I …'

'I wouldn't worry about it,' Dominic said. 'Really, it's just Victor being Victor. Unwinding after work. I'll have a word with him.'

The weird question about what she might have done to 'interest' Victor aside, Charlotte was happy enough to take that. He'd listen to Dominic. She could put it out of her mind.

A week later Victor was back. Same position. Same smirk. Watching.

She didn't mention it to Dominic again.

One night, she was alone in the cigar bar, cleaning as a handful of lingering customers finished up. Her phone buzzed. A message from Mel. The surprise of seeing her name came with a warm rush of something not far off relief.

It was a link to a news article. Above it, Mel had written, *Isn't this that guy you fired?*

Charlotte opened it.

The image of Freddie's smiling face took the breath out of her. She wondered, absurdly, how the media always knew which photos would instantly tell you somebody was dead.

She lowered her arm. A current through the hand around the phone. She looked up and her eyes immediately found Victor Caine's. In his usual spot. She looked away but did not want to see Freddie's face again. Did not want to read the article.

What would it prove? If somebody believed Dominic was involved, the police would already be after him. Freddie was a mouthy prick who could have pissed off any number of dangerous people. That didn't mean ...

A whisper of tremulous doubt. Freddie had exposed a drug lord to his girlfriend. Charlotte had told Dominic what he'd said after she'd fired him.

Breath coming short and sharp. Weakness in her legs.

If something had happened to Freddie because of her, because of *Dominic* ...

She thought of Victor Caine's smirk. She thought of her father's warnings.

She closed the article without reading it. She deleted Mel's message.

CHAPTER THIRTEEN

Now

Heavy understanding was settling even as she tried again and again and still the car didn't start. She could check the petrol, look under the hood, go over all the menial problems that might be stopping it. But she knew this wasn't menial. Anders had made sure she wasn't going anywhere fast. She punched the dashboard, too hard. Tears filled her eyes.

She was trying to do right. She was trying to stay out of trouble, to not hurt anyone. She could be no possible use to the police or to Dominic's old associates. And yet here she was, at their whims, with the only decisions left to her the most pointless ones. She remembered the intoxicating rush of power she had felt when she fired Freddie. It seemed, now, a bad joke. Worsened by the realisation that she'd never had power, not really. Just what small, token amount she'd been allowed.

She looked in the rear-view, towards the road. It had been just under an hour since Anders' appearance (how was that possible?) but she could not afford to waste any more time. She did not think the road was being watched – if Anders had other men at his disposal then he'd have brought them with him, not wasted them on surveillance. But she very much doubted he had not at least alerted his employers as to where he was, probably with an instruction to send backup if he did not call back within a short time. Well, time was slipping away, and with it Charlotte's theoretical escape window.

She got out of the car. Before anything else, based on her first instinct, she popped the bonnet. Checked the engine, the way Uncle Mac had shown her. Sure enough, the spark plug was gone.

She wanted to scream. Anders hadn't had the spark plug in his pockets, and it was obvious he wasn't going to tell her where it was without a fight. So what could she do?

John.

She stood upright. He had a car – he'd moved it into the garage behind White Republic just yesterday. Except ...

The flare of hope was gone, leaving behind only a bitter, burning guilt. It was almost certain Anders had done the same to John's car. If so, her only remaining option would be to hike down the mountain, a trip that would take far too long and leave her without a car at the bottom. A journey of three hours by car might take days on foot.

As clear as if she was there again, she saw Dominic at the end of their vast dinner table watching her with that empty, mocking smile.

You've made your choice, now you have to live with it.

'At least I'm alive, you prick,' she muttered at the memory, then felt immediately stupid.

If they were coming for her, she wouldn't make it easy for them. She would hike down if she had to, use the time to work out a plan. Better to take even a tiny chance than to just give up. She had, as Anders pointed out, made her choices. She had had the opportunity to step away from this world, once, and been too stupid and naïve. Too in love. But John had not chosen to be a part of it. And the least she owed him, after putting his life at risk, was a warning. If his car *did* work, they could leave together. But she had to be ready for the alternative.

From the crates in Snowhaven's storage room she dug out a portable camp stove, a tent, a sleeping bag and a pot. She could cook some of her canned foods on the way down. Try to find relatively dry places to sleep, in elevated spots or even up in trees. She didn't know how long the trip would be – given the terrain, probably longer than she wanted to hope. But those were not concerns for now.

She stuffed what she could into the backpack before finding rope to lash the rest together. It was awkward and cumbersome – even the most casual hiker would laugh at her – but that didn't matter. As long as she could get clear of here, into the bush, with what she needed to stay alive, she could manage. She had got through worse.

Lugging her supplies, she left the lodge, listening all the while. No cars or footsteps. In the gap between lodges she dropped her bundled bag, taking a moment to catch her breath. She leaned against the wall of Snowhaven.

What the hell was she supposed to tell John? *Hey, how'd you fancy a swift getaway? Life or death stakes – think of the material for your book*. She almost laughed.

He might be angry. Would have every right to be. He'd definitely be scared. The guilt again, like a punch to the gut. If she had only turned herself in, if she had ...

If, if, if. She couldn't agonise over ifs. That was a luxury survival would afford her, one day.

She would have to tell that kind, offbeat, gentle man that she had a bludgeoned bounty hunter captive in her boiler room. Tell him what she had done to bring him there, why she had done it and why he had to flee with her.

Leaving the heavy bag next to the door, she crossed to his lodge. Hovered on the doorstep. Glanced down towards the carpark and the road. Silence. She knocked. 'Please,' she whispered. This couldn't be drawn out. She had to get it over and done with before she lost her nerve. She knocked, again and again, louder. Nothing.

A slow, ice-cold fear was dawning. She hadn't checked the lodges. Including John's.

She drew the gun. Punched in the combination and unlocked the door. Stepped inside and raised the gun. Looked down the hall. Listened for breathing, for footsteps, for cocked weapons. She moved forward.

No-one in the living room. Embers in the fireplace, still warm. A lone coffee cup next to a crumb-covered plate on the table. She swept the room in a circle. Nothing. She didn't want to surprise John with a gun, but nor did she want to give anyone else in here a warning by calling out.

Something on the mantlepiece caught her eye. A dull sheen. She moved towards it, then stopped.

It was an axe, relatively new by the look of the varnished wooden handle. Except the head was gouged with furrows and scratches. Charlotte picked it up. Glanced at the fireplace. There was nothing suspicious about the axe being here. John used his fireplace. He needed to chop wood. Except it didn't look like it had been chopping wood. Nor did it look familiar. Had he brought it with him?

Back down the hall. She checked the drying room. One of the guest rooms. Then up the stairs, slow and quiet but for the pounding of her too-loud heart.

The rooms upstairs were empty too. There were only two, apart from the bathroom. John wasn't here. Nor was anyone else.

She sat on his perfectly made bed, letting out a shaky breath. He must have taken another walk. They hadn't come for him, then. She would have to wait for him to get back and ...

Something itched at her.

She dismissed it. It didn't matter, it was so minor, it ...

But she had not survived this long by ignoring the sense that something wasn't right.

She stood. Pulled open the drawers. Checked the closet, the few hung-up clothes. John's suitcase was in the corner, empty.

There was nothing in the next room. Nothing in the bathroom outside of standard toiletries. She returned downstairs, raising the gun. She went fast through everything. Checked under beds and couches. On shelves. Even the kitchen cabinets.

The fear remained but it had shifted, somehow. Sharpened. She stood in the living room, eyes on the door, gun tight in her hand. Every interaction she and John had shared, every conversation, all of it raced through her head at once.

He had said he was a writer, that he was working on a book. So why, in this whole lodge, were there no papers, notebooks, pens? No laptop? Some of those things he could take with him. But he never left with a bag. And he had said …

She swayed on the spot. Reached out a hand to steady herself.

He had said he didn't write by hand. And there was no laptop charger.

She hurried down the hall. Paused at the door. Opened it. Nobody outside.

She'd lingered too long. Her thoughts were unbalanced, her mind reeling. *Later*, she told herself. Later she could unpack all of this. Now she had to be gone. Away from Anders. Away from John. Away from whoever was coming. She crossed back to Snowhaven.

Her bag was gone.

CHAPTER FOURTEEN

Then

It was late, and Charlotte was still at work, stuck in the tiny office Dominic had given her, going over the night's takings. She'd already screwed it up once and had to start again. In the dim light, carefully sifting through notes and receipts on her too-small desk, she again wondered what the point was, given the numbers were going to be fudged anyway when Dominic's *real* business takings were added.

But this was her job and so she kept at it. She'd just written down where she was up to when there was a knock at the door.

Claire, looking dead on her feet, stepped in. 'You all good?'

Charlotte nodded, focusing on the cash.

'Just finished the floors. Was thinking about having a knock-off. You almost done?'

'Almost.'

'Join me?'

Once Charlotte had put the cash and receipts in the safe and replaced the tills, she headed to the cigar bar. During operation it had a veneer of class at odds with the rest of the venue – all deep mahoganies and gold-rimmed tables and plush leather couches in circular booths. Now, with all the lights up and glassware drying in racks over the sinks in the bar, it looked like a disassembled movie set.

Claire sat in a corner booth, glass of wine in hand, eyes empty and distant. Charlotte poured herself one and joined her.

'Why haven't you run off home?' Charlotte asked.

'Too tired.' Claire's laugh was rough. 'I'm dreading the trip down the stairs then waiting for a train or a cab or whatever. Sometimes I think I'd be better off just living here.'

'Don't say that. It hits way too close to home.'

'Honestly, I don't know how you do it.' Claire drank deeply. 'You're always here.'

'Not always,' Charlotte said with a hint of defensiveness she failed to bite back. 'I've got the day off tomorrow.'

'Jesus, you deserve more than one day off. How much time do you get for yourself? Shouldn't you get some perks, given you're sleeping with the boss?'

Charlotte didn't know what to say to that.

Claire drank again. 'He must trust you like crazy.'

'You reckon?'

'Letting you oversee the place, handle the money, all of that? Yeah, I'd say so. How old are you, like twenty-five?'

She was younger, but it felt weirdly boastful to say so.

'Anyway.' Claire finished her drink. 'It's impressive. But I just hope you have a little *you* time as well, is all.'

For a moment they sat in silence. Charlotte glanced at Claire, then at her empty glass.

'Want another?' she asked.

* * *

Charlotte poured the last of the bottle into her own glass as Claire laughed, drank, then said, 'Right? *Right*? It's like she thinks she's, I dunno, like the maître-d' at some fancy restaurant when she's all "Um, the customers have requested" and I have to tell her, "Susan, the customers are pissing on the toilet floor and doing lines off the seats."'

'You know I sent her to check the toilets the other night?' Charlotte asked.

'You fucking didn't.'

'I fucking did. She was in the middle of telling some cooked business bro up here about the distillery his gin had come from and he kept being like "Uh-huh, sure, so interesting" and his mates were all laughing and I thought I was doing her a favour.' Charlotte could barely hold back the giggles at the memory. 'So she stares at me, all horrified, but she does it—'

'Because you fired the last person who refused a direct order.'

'Yep, that's it, I'm scary as fuck.'

Claire snorted into her wine.

'And next thing ...' Charlotte had to put her wine down; she was struggling to hold back the laughter. 'There's this ... this literal *scream* from the toilets and honest to God I thought somebody was being murdered so I run there—'

'Looking to tackle the killer until the police arrive.'

'Oh of course, secure them with a toilet seat, bludgeon them with a plunger, yeah, that kind of thing. Anyway, I burst in there and the screaming has got worse and there's

Susan clutching at the sink and carrying on and there's some guy who thinks he's in the Backstreet Boys—'

'Did he have frosted tips?'

'He absolutely did, plus a neon pink singlet but no pants because there's also a girl there trying to pull up her undies and shrieking at Susan for interrupting them and the guy is just standing there staring blankly at it all and he's still pantsless and I say ...'

Claire was now hiccupping with laughter.

Charlotte did her best to seem composed. 'I say ... oh fuck, well, first I yell at everyone to calm down and they sort of do and then I say the first thing I think of, which is ...'

Claire, convulsing badly now, had her head in her hands.

'Which is, "Sir, could you please put your penis away?"'

Claire lost it. Charlotte could hardly breathe. She couldn't remember the last time she'd laughed like this. The last time she'd felt so relaxed.

It took minutes for them both to calm down. Charlotte, tears in her eyes, sank back into the seat and finished her wine.

'Oh man,' Claire said. 'Oh *man*. I had no idea.'

'I didn't think I should tell anyone. Seemed unprofessional.'

'Unprofessional? They were fucking in a club toilet.'

'I know, but ... you know.'

'This.' Claire gestured between them. 'We need this. The debrief. See, I feel way fucking better than I did before. You should come for drinks with everyone more.'

'It's just time,' Charlotte said. 'Or the lack thereof.'

'Do you ever cut loose?' Claire asked. 'Like, actually party?'

'Dominic and I go for cocktails sometimes but—'

'With anyone who *isn't* your boyfriend?'

Charlotte thought of Mel. She shook her head.

'You poor goddamn thing,' Claire said. 'That simply will not do.'

She looked around. Took a sip. Leaned in close.

'Are there cameras in your office?'

'No.'

'Okay, firstly, more drinks?'

It had to be close to four o'clock in the morning, but the idea of stopping and going home now was suddenly overwhelmingly oppressive.

'Yes.'

'Good. Secondly ... well, let's go to the office for the secondly.'

Charlotte wanted to ask more. Instead she grabbed another bottle of wine and followed Claire downstairs.

Charlotte stood back from the desk as Claire, hunched in front of it, poured out a pile of white powder from the tiny bag. Then, with a bank card, she started to chop it. Charlotte was oddly transfixed, watching how the little clumps broke up, how it spread before Claire scraped it together and started dividing it into clearer lines.

Charlotte had never done coke before. She'd always seen it as the territory of tearaway movie stars. But then, she reflected with a rush of something uncomfortable and cold, it was the family business now.

'Alright.' Claire was rolling up a fifty-dollar note. 'This ought to give you a little kick.'

Charlotte didn't move.

'Charlotte?'

'I've never, um ...'

'Oh man,' Claire said. 'It's worse than I thought. Okay, well, you've seen literally any gangster movie ever right?'

Charlotte nodded.

'Well, there's your education.'

With a wink, Claire placed the note to a line, leaned over and then it was gone. She tilted her head back, sniffed once, twice. Rubbed her nostril with her thumb. Closed her eyes. A smile spread across her face. 'There she is.'

Charlotte didn't approach. She was already more than a little drunk and was having trouble thinking this through. Dominic had told her several times that the key to staying on top of his business was never touching his own product and that had suited Charlotte fine. She'd never wanted to get caught up in it herself.

But then, she also didn't want to say no. Not when she was having such a good time. And Claire was right. She *deserved* to cut loose. Given what he did, Dominic could hardly have an issue with this.

She accepted the note from Claire, who was watching her with slightly widened eyes. Charlotte put the note to her nostril and leaned over.

It burned. She smelled and tasted something acrid, chemical. But, like Claire, she put her head back. Sniffed. Put her thumb to her nostril. Sniffed again.

Nothing. Just the buzz of the alcohol and then ...

And then, subtle at first, a sense of sharpening alertness, of a vibrating, humming excitement. It wasn't overwhelming. It wasn't magical or euphoric. It was just ... good.

After that the night was off at a gallop. They poured more wines but even though Charlotte could feel the effect of the booze, she never got slurry or fuzzy. The coke not only held it at bay, but tinged everything with a glow of energy.

Talk moved on to their futures as Claire chopped more lines.

'Rapid fire,' she said, 'no thought, what do you want to do with your life?'

'Write.'

'Like books and stuff?'

'Yeah.'

'Awesome!' Claire slammed the table. 'Awesome. Good. What would you write, tomorrow, if you had the time? Go.'

She started chopping more lines. Charlotte hesitated.

'Rapid fire, go!' Claire snapped.

'Right so, okay, there's this girl. And like, she's got cancer. It's early stages and nobody in her life knows about it and she doesn't want to tell anyone. See like, she's sort of the responsible one in the family. Her parents are remote as hell but still expect her to answer the phone and listen to their problems whenever they call. Her brother is in and out of trouble with the police, expecting her to bail him out. Her best friend is in this fucking miserable relationship. And so she feels like if she tells anyone, she might burden them ...'

Claire stopped cutting the lines. She sat back and listened. And as Charlotte spoke, any hesitation slipped away, any worry about sounding like an idiot. Somewhere in the back of her head she knew Claire's transfixed expression probably had more to do with the coke than the story, but she didn't care. She'd forgotten, holy shit, she had forgotten how good it felt to have somebody hanging on your every word, to hear the gasps and the tense silences at all the right moments. And beyond that, to feel yourself slipping into the role of storyteller – emphasising this, going quiet for that, and to watch Claire react almost like a puppet.

'And at that moment, she unloads the gun.' Charlotte was on her feet. Claire hadn't moved. 'And the prick goes down. She's done. She's saved her brother. But as the adrenalin wears off she realises ...'

'Oh fuck,' Claire breathed.

Charlotte patted her stomach. 'Yeah. She was hit. She goes for her phone but she collapses and starts to fade. And we cut to a week later. To the news coverage. To her family and friends all wondering what the hell came over her. None of them know what she overheard. None of them know about the cancer. They just shake their heads and are all "Where did we go wrong?" and distancing themselves from her in the news and ... that's it.'

Charlotte sat down, snatched up the note, and did a line.

'You have to fucking write that.' Claire sounded strangled.

'When I have a spare ... I dunno, life.'

'You don't need a spare life,' Claire said. 'You need to tell your boyfriend that you're gonna pull back at the club. You need to devote more time to *you*. And if he loves you, at all, he'll respect that. He knows you write, yeah?'

'Yeah, but—'

'Well, there you go.' Claire's voice was firm. 'You've devoted all this time to his stuff. Devote some to yours. It's only fair.'

'It's not that simple. He trusts me to—'

'He can find someone else to trust,' Claire said.

Elizabeth Bates' cold smile appeared unbidden in Charlotte's head.

'Hey,' Claire said. 'Don't back down on this. Promise me, yeah?'

Charlotte barely remembered getting home. She'd crawled into bed not knowing what time it was but knowing the sun was up outside. She slept heavily and woke up to a throbbing head and a dry mouth and a blocked nose.

She lay alone in the bed, thinking back over the night.

Holy shit, she had missed that. Talking and laughing and bonding. The booze and the drugs had helped, sure, although her body disagreed today. But the main thing had been feeling, for the first time in so long, like she had a friend. A friend who actually encouraged her.

She took her time getting ready. She stood under the shower for ages, hoping the hot water would scour away the hangover. It helped, but not enough. She dressed in tracksuit pants and one of Dominic's t-shirts then dragged herself out to the kitchen.

Dominic was sitting at the table, in trousers and a shirt with the top buttons undone. It was as casual as he got. Squinting, Charlotte made for the coffee machine.

'What time is it?' she asked.

Dominic said nothing.

Charlotte turned to him. He didn't look at her.

It was then that she saw the tiny, empty bag on the table in front of him.

Bile rose. She swallowed it back.

'I stopped by the club this morning,' he said. 'Not long after you stumbled in. I wondered where you'd been all night. Especially when I noticed how many of the lights were still on. So I went to your office. And in the bin' – he rested a finger on the bag – 'was this.'

Charlotte said nothing.

'Where did you get it?' He still wasn't looking at her.

'Dominic—'

He slammed the table. Charlotte flinched.

'Where?'

'C-Claire had it. We had some drinks, m-maybe a bit too much and ...'

Dominic lowered his head slightly.

'Dominic, I don't, I mean it's just—'

'It's just *nothing*, Charlotte. I have told you before why we don't touch this stuff, right?'

'Yeah but—'

'You *cannot* do this and be with me. Do you understand for even a *second* the consequences of one mistake? One slip of the tongue, one door left unlocked? Hell, if the police had decided to raid last night, which has happened before, you know what finding this would have meant? The reason we get to live this life that you benefit from is because I am *careful*. All I ask of you is the same. And instead ...'

He exhaled.

Charlotte was trying to hold back the tears, trying to find the determination she'd felt the night before. He wasn't being fair. She had needed to cut loose, she had needed a friend and—

He stood. Finally faced her. Charlotte couldn't speak. She was seeing Freddie's smiling face again, the image she'd managed to repress for weeks. And with it came the icy, biting fear, the whispering worry of what could happen if she, like Freddie, fucked up. She'd never asked Dominic about the article. She didn't want to know. She didn't want to believe he was capable of that. But looking at him now, at those unblinking eyes, flared nostrils and drawn lips, she didn't doubt he was capable of anything.

'Are you stupid?' Dominic asked, quiet, cold.

She shook her head.

He held up the bag. 'Never again, Charlotte.'

He pocketed it. Made for the door. Paused.

'Claire has to go.'

'What?'

He didn't turn.

'Dominic, no. No, I can tell her not to do it again. I can tell her—'

'You can tell her she isn't to come back,' Dominic said.

Her mouth opened and closed. Stupid. Pathetic.

He looked back at her.

'I can trust you, right?'

Charlotte went straight to her office upon arriving back at work. She sat behind the desk where she'd drank and done coke with Claire and tried not to be sick. She hadn't eaten since the argument with Dominic. Although argument might have been too generous a word.

She told herself he was right. There was no choice. They couldn't afford a liability. Claire shouldn't have had drugs at work.

She checked the time. Four. Claire would have arrived. She stood unsteadily. She hesitated at the door and rested her head against it. Her palms were sweaty.

She found Claire on the main level, pulling stools down from the bar.

'Claire?'

She jumped then chuckled. 'Oh, you scared me. Sorry. Hey, how did you pull up? Such a good ...'

She trailed off at the look on Charlotte's face.

'Can we ...' Charlotte swallowed. 'Can we, um, go to my office?'

Neither spoke as Charlotte closed the door behind them. She asked Claire to sit.

She didn't. Just watched.

'Um. Okay so, we're going to have to, to let you go.'

Claire didn't reply. Charlotte couldn't meet her eyes.

'It's just, we can't have ... We can't have drugs on the premises and ...'

'Drugs you had no problem taking.'

'But you brought them in and—'

'Charlotte.' Claire's voice was low, hard. 'Don't embarrass both of us by tying yourself in knots trying to justify this. Dominic told you to get rid of me, right?'

Charlotte said nothing.

'Did you tell him any of what we spoke about?'

Charlotte said nothing.

'Did you tell him that you did the drugs too?'

'Yes, I didn't lie about—'

'But you also didn't get fired. Even though you did the exact same thing.'

Charlotte's clothes were sticking to her. It was warm in the office, too warm. 'It's not the same. I didn't supply—'

'You know the rumours about him, right?'

Charlotte said nothing.

Claire laughed. 'Not rumours then. What a fucking hypocrite you are. Both of you.'

She yanked open the door. Hesitated, breathing heavily.

'What if I go to the police? I might get in trouble for a bag of coke, but if I give them a reason to dig a little ...'

Dominic then, looking back at her. *I can trust you, right?*

Victor Caine's deepening smirk.

Freddie smiling at the head of the unread article.

Dominic again. *I'm careful.*

Charlotte straightened up. This time when she spoke, her voice didn't waver.

'I wouldn't do that.'

Claire faced her. Went to speak. Didn't.

Charlotte stared her down and hoped she'd leave before the shaking started again.

'You're fucking spineless,' Claire spat.

Her voice cracked on the last word. She left.

Charlotte got home late. The conversation with Claire kept turning over in her head. Even once she'd finished her shift she sat alone in her office for a long time, trembling until she felt strong enough to return home.

Dominic was in the living room, reading a book with an open bottle of wine in front of him. He looked up as Charlotte entered. He said nothing but the question was there.

Charlotte nodded.

He patted the couch beside him. She walked over and sat. He put an arm around her, pouring her a glass with his other hand. She drank.

Dominic kissed her on the head. 'I'm proud of you,' he murmured.

He rested his head on hers. Charlotte drank.

'You're brave, Charlotte. I love that about you. I love that you can do what needs to be done.'

She drank again.

CHAPTER FIFTEEN

Now

Fast and silently, she keyed in the code for Bushmill and opened the door. That musty smell again, worsened now by a touch of something pungent and oddly sweet. She hadn't got all the mould, then. That could be the next caretaker's problem.

She shut the door behind her, dropped the cleaning bucket and drew the gun. The drying room was empty.

She hurried through the hall, gun up and heart galloping, kicking open door after door, sweeping the rooms and moving on. Nothing. No waiting killer. No sign of her bag. She circled back to the drying room, paused for a moment to listen, then left.

She repeated the process at each lodge. Her focus was dragged again and again to the road between the trees, to any hint of approaching cars. The seconds were stretching too long. But the lodges were all empty. A strange mingling of relief and desperation clawed at her. If the lodges were empty, then Anders almost certainly didn't have backup already here. But that left only one option as to who had found her bag.

She already knew it couldn't be in John's lodge, unless – and the thought chilled her – John had taken it and already returned inside. She pushed that away and circled behind White Republic, to the garage where he'd moved his car. She unlocked it and slipped inside. It was dark and dusty, the car sharing the space with some canisters of fuel and some wood piled up to keep it dry. No bag. Instinctively she checked the handle to John's car, but it was locked. Not that she'd know what to do if by some stretch of luck it wasn't. She had no clue how to hotwire a car.

In the dark she leaned against the vehicle. Pounding rose in her head. She needed that bag. Her fake IDs, her money – fuck, even her *phone* had been packed in there.

Priorities. Yes, she needed the bag, especially if she planned on trying to walk out. But if she could get her car working, then she'd have to forget it and deal with the money and ID issues down the line. Survival came first. Always.

Back in Snowhaven she ran up the hall, shoved the office door open and snatched up the phone. She hadn't tried to call Liam since John had first arrived, but now with her bag gone and John's lodge empty, she needed information. She put the phone to her ear, watching out the window, watching for any sign of John or …

Or anyone else.

It took her a moment to realise what she was hearing. No dial tone. Nothing.

She put the phone down. Shifted the mouse of the computer. The screen stayed dark.

She circled around the desk. No cords leading from the computer or phone to the power points. She leaned close to the back of the computer. The end of a cable stuck out about a centimetre. It had been cut.

She stared at the empty gap behind the desk, trying to put it all together in her head.

The spark plug gone.

Phone and internet, disabled.

Her bag removed – with her mobile inside it.

Anders could have done the first two, but there was no way he could have done the last.

It would have taken a lot for Charlotte to call the police. Only the most desperate circumstances would be worth the risk of Dominic's associates having the first clue where to find her, of jail and the inevitable attacks that would come behind bars. But now even that option was sealed off.

Unless ...

Down the stairs and out the door again. Still no hint of movement in the dark windows. No sign of John.

A high-pitched whistle of wind.

She started up the road. A writhing feeling across her skin, worse by the second until she was running, running and gasping for air all the way to the ticket booth. She unlocked it, stumbled into the musty interior and searched, searched for the radio, even though she knew exactly where it should be, even though she knew it would be gone. She searched and she slammed the table with her fist and she collapsed back into the chair, staring out through the grubby glass at the empty carpark and the trees and the turbulent sky beyond.

Absurdly, suddenly, she remembered that strange feeling she sometimes got while walking through the dead trees. That Mount Skillion was like its own strange netherworld, somewhere Charlotte Laurent lived like a ghost surrounded by faded memories and colour-drained wilderness. Ever since she'd left Melbourne, fear had been a constant companion, but on Skillion she felt as safe as she had in a long time. Loneliness was its own kind of protection.

Except she wasn't alone anymore. She'd let a stranger into her life. She'd embraced his company and let her guard down and now Mount Skillion was no longer safe. Despite all the traps she'd made to protect herself, she hadn't noticed the one she'd walked right into.

She closed her eyes. One deep breath of musty air. Then she stood.

She'd escaped from traps before. This one, she decided, would be no different.

Charlotte burst into the boiler room, gun raised in one hand. Anders, who appeared to be testing the strength of the handcuffs, looked up with mild interest.

'Where the fuck is it?' she demanded.

'Where the fuck is what?'

'The spark plug. You took it from my car, right?'

'Do I look like a mechanic?'

A second hand on the gun and through gritted teeth: '*Where the fuck is it?*'

'Do you think cursing makes you seem more threatening?'

'I think a bullet will make me seem pretty fucking threatening.'

'Kill me, you get no … what was it? Spark plug. If I even took it. So possibly you get none regardless.'

'Don't fuck with me,' Charlotte said. 'I know you took it. I *know* …'

But she didn't know that, did she? The skin on the back of her neck crawled. She flinched, turned. Nothing through the door. She stepped out, gun in hand, looking up and down the hall. Listening. Nothing.

She was struggling to keep her breathing steady, to stop herself from collapsing on the spot and just crying.

Charlotte could take no chances. There would be time for wondering and theorising and feeling betrayed later. Right now, she had to get the fuck out.

She lowered the gun.

'Your car,' she said.

'Excuse me?'

'Your car. Where is it?'

Anders raised an eyebrow.

'Don't give me that,' she spat. 'You didn't fucking hike up here. You have a car. You parked it somewhere and you approached on foot and—'

He struck fast. A white flash. A snapping line of fire on the back of her neck and she was jerked forward like a snared animal, the gun clattering off concrete. She landed on Anders, squirmed, twisted, tried to force herself up and then felt the sudden, brutal vanishing of air as her throat closed in and her vision went red and he was hissing into her ear 'give me the key' and her brain went foggy and her hands clawed at where something was cutting into her neck and God she needed to breathe but she couldn't and—

The knife.

Haze now, only haze in her head and her vision and her ears. She dropped her hand. Forgot why she was groping blindly in her pocket, why she wasn't stopping the terrible thing being done to her neck but she found something and pulled it out and the haze was thicker but the instinct remained and she dropped her other hand. She pulled the blade clear and then swung her arm back and around to where—

Resistance. Soft. The cord around her neck loosened, just enough. The room rearranged itself in front of her. She sucked at a tiny sliver of air.

Charlotte held the tip of the knife to Anders' neck. He didn't loosen any further. She pushed harder. The cord slackened.

'Let it go,' she rasped.

He did. She dived forward, hitting concrete, rolling then scurrying away from him, the world tilting and unsteady as she pulled the makeshift noose from around her neck. She saw the white wire on the floor. She grabbed it, pulled, gathered it to her, then the gun, then her back was to the wall and she was still seeing double but she rubbed at her throat and forced in air and lifted the gun.

Anders put his hand to the side of his neck. He was bleeding.

He looked at her then closed his eyes.

She could see, now, where he had torn the old telephone cable out from where it ran around the base of the wall. He had fashioned it into a sort of lasso then, with more strength and precision than she would have guessed, almost killed her with it.

His eyes were still closed.

She picked up the knife. Closed it, the blunt side against her thigh. She lowered the gun.

Anders opened his eyes. Tugged once at the cuffs.

For what felt like a long, long time, they looked at each other.

And then, sounding almost disappointed, he spoke. 'You should have killed me.'

She staggered out into the hall, dragging the cable. She dropped it, shut the door. Rubbing her neck, still gasping for air, she slid to the ground. The shakes had started, hard and terrible. She had almost died. One slip-up and she had almost died.

You should have killed me.

She looked towards the stairs. Her thoughts were clearing. It was barely hope, what she felt. But it was there. John's car, likely disabled and still in the garage, was a risk. She'd need to get the keys off him somehow. But Anders would not have disabled his own car. With one road up, there were only so many places he could have left it.

She stuck the gun down the back of her jeans. Struggled to stand.

A knock at the door upstairs.

Charlotte froze. Her hands returned to the gun. She waited. The knock again. Not loud, not aggressive.

John.

She walked slowly up the hall, hoping John – if it was him – would just give up and leave. But the knock came again, then again. Charlotte moved up the stairs, hands still on the gun. She arrived at the front door and checked the peephole, ready to draw and shoot if she had to.

John, smiling and looking around and bouncing on the balls of his feet. John, her strange friend. John, who had made her feel okay for the first time in so long. John whom she had come to like and trust.

Who had very likely taken her bag.

She didn't draw the gun. She kept her hand behind her back. She tugged her collar up and opened the door.

'Katie!' There was nothing off about how John was acting, nothing outside of the jovial ordinary. Nothing that would indicate he had done anything to throw or unsettle her.

'John,' she said, voice hoarse. 'Everything okay?'

He blinked at her covered neck, her bloodshot eyes. 'Think I should be asking you that.'

'Accident,' she managed. 'I'm all good.'

A beat. John watched her, curiously.

'Anyway.' She went to close the door.

'Just thought I'd ask if you felt like lunch,' he said.

Could Anders hear this exchange? Maybe he was getting something, some buzz of voices. Enough to take his chance and yell.

'Not today, sorry John. I'm really snowed under.'

'Even without any snow!' John exclaimed with a laugh.

Charlotte forced a smile. 'Anyway. Another time.'

'A break might do you good, you know?'

'I'm sorry, John. I'm just flat out right now.'

'Gotta stop and smell the mountain air sometimes though, Katie. You shouldn't work too hard.'

'Just … not today.'

'Maybe dinner later?'

She needed him gone. 'Sure, maybe.' She went to close the door.

'Actually, Katie.'

She stopped.

'Just a thought,' John said. 'Maybe a silly one. But with what you've got going on, all that work and whatnot, I figure I should let you know that I'm here.'

He must have clocked Charlotte's confusion.

'To help,' he clarified. 'If there's anything you need. Even if it's tough or unpleasant. I'm more than happy to help.'

Charlotte went to reply but caught whatever was about to come out. Instead she thanked him and closed the door. Even through the heavy wood she could hear him whistling.

CHAPTER SIXTEEN

Then

Dominic woke Charlotte with a kiss. Squinting against the light, she pulled herself up.

'Happy anniversary,' he said. 'I've made breakfast.'

She could smell bacon and eggs. Dominic almost never cooked.

He'd put out a massive spread in the kitchen. It took Charlotte a moment to be sure it was real. Dominic beamed as he pulled out her seat. Charlotte went over the dates in her head. She'd forgotten completely.

'Two years,' Dominic said, pushing her seat in. 'Would you have imagined that when we met in that club? Now look at us.'

Now look at them. Things had changed. Her life was unrecognisable. The big house they shared. The two clubs Charlotte worked across. The clothes, the events they went to together, the company they kept.

Dominic poured her a coffee. Charlotte watched him.

He hadn't been this engaged in a long time. Dominic, nowadays, was more likely to be harried and under pressure, short-tempered and distant. When he'd asked her to take on the second club, she'd tried to tell him it would be too much, that she wanted to devote more time to writing. Dominic had given her a long, weary look, then said, 'Well, I guess if you don't think you can do it, there's no point.'

She'd started the next day.

But this morning, not only had he remembered their anniversary – which Charlotte had forgotten – but was going out of his way to make a big deal of it. And in these moments, the moments where the Dominic she'd spent that first magical night with returned, it was like nothing had changed. Like every bit of fear and frustration was worth it. Like maybe, if they just pushed through the difficult times, they could find the good ones again.

She smiled back at him and dug in.

'Today's going to be full on,' he said with an apologetic look. 'And I can't get out of the fundraiser tonight, *but* ...' He winked. 'Well, let's just say that might not be a bad thing. I've got a surprise for you.'

'Oh?'

'I promise you'll love it.'

He finished his breakfast and left to get ready. Charlotte watched him go. She cleared the table, feeling lighter than she had in a while.

Two years. Standing in the shower, she examined the concept, trying to work out if she could entirely believe it. On the one hand, she often felt like they were still in the early stages of their relationship. But then, the night she and Dominic met could have belonged to another life, years distant. She didn't feel very much like the girl she'd been then, so excited over meeting her literary idol and the belief that if she kept going, she could be just like him.

You're doing everything right.

She couldn't imagine Leo Grey would say that if they met today.

There were other changes, of course. She hadn't spoken to Mel in over a year now. Her other old high school and uni friends were even more distant. Her life was the club, was Dominic.

She'd seen her father once in the past year. He'd reached out and suggested a dinner, just the two of them. Charlotte had looked forward to it with a jittery excitement that surprised her. But it was as they ate that Guy Laurent had shown his hand.

'So, um ... you're still seeing that bloke.'

Charlotte put her cutlery down and fixed him with a steady look.

'He's being good to you?'

'He is.'

'Right. And he still, he's still running his clubs?'

'More, now. He's expanded.'

'You ever question how he pays for it all?'

'He's a good businessman.'

Guy looked at her a long time.

'What?' Charlotte said, an edge creeping into her voice.

'Being a good businessman doesn't make him a good man.'

'How the fuck would you know?'

'Because there are only a handful of ways somebody that young can get that rich, and he's not a movie star, so ...'

'What are you trying to tell me?'

'I think you know what I'm trying to tell you.'

'No.'

He leaned forward. 'Charlotte, I'm worried about you. There's been some stuff on the news, gangland hits and—'

Charlotte left. She didn't answer any of his phone calls after that.

He'd been wrong to worry. Of course he had. Charlotte wasn't in danger. Dominic was busy and he was under pressure but he was managing, they both were, and he still had time to make her breakfast and prepare a surprise for their anniversary. And that was the key to a good relationship, right? Still being able to surprise and excite each other even after all this time.

He picked her up at seven thirty that night. They drove in silence, Dominic with a secretive smile the whole way. Occasionally he reached out and squeezed her knee. Charlotte rubbed the back of his hand. She was lucky. She was so, so lucky to have him.

The fundraiser was taking place in a large function centre, packed with well-dressed people. The lights were low and the music too loud. A well-lit stage filled the far end, soon to be populated by various speakers. Tables along the walls carried complimentary drinks and lots for a silent auction.

Charlotte moved among it all, drinking her wine, smiling and nodding to people she vaguely knew through Dominic. She saw Victor Caine lurking in a corner, dark eyes scanning the room. She went back the way she'd come, just as Dominic caught her by the arm.

'Over there.'

He pointed. She looked.

It took her a moment to recognise Leo Grey. He was deep in conversation with an older woman.

Dominic put an arm around her. 'We've met a few times through the charity. Become pretty friendly, actually. I wanted to surprise you. So there he is.'

Charlotte didn't know what to say.

'You okay?' Dominic asked.

She didn't know how she felt about this being sprung on her. If Leo asked about her writing ... she had this horrible, churning sense that she was about to let him down terribly, that whatever she was now would pale in comparison to the bright-eyed, excited, ambitious student he'd met two years ago. She suppressed a hiss of resentment. She was being ridiculous. Dominic was trying to do something nice.

He gave her a gentle push. 'Go on. Say hi.'

She approached. Leo was still talking to the woman. Charlotte stood to the side, waiting. She could feel Dominic's eyes on her. Leo patted the woman on the arm, then turned towards the bar.

'Hi,' Charlotte said.

Leo blinked at her. 'Hello.'

It struck her how much older he looked. His hair was shorter, his face thinner, his cheeks hollow.

They stared at each other for several long seconds.

'I'm, um, Charlotte.'

'Right. Hi Charlotte, I'm Leo. I was just—'

'We've met,' Charlotte blurted before she could catch herself.

He just looked blankly at her.

Something desperate and unexpected rose in her chest.

'Sorry, where?'

'My old uni,' she said. 'Um ... two years ago today, exactly.'

A raised eyebrow.

'No, it's not ... it's not that I memorised the date or anything, it's just that I met my partner that night and today's our anniversary and ...'

'Right.' Leo's focus was on the bar. He finished his drink.

'You don't remember?' Charlotte couldn't keep the strain from her voice. Right then she hated herself, hated how pathetic she was, hated the way Leo Grey's expression had turned pitying.

'Oh yeah,' he said. 'Yeah, Charlotte, right?'

'We spoke about ...'

His eyes had moved to the bar again. They were slightly bloodshot.

'It doesn't matter,' Charlotte said. 'Sorry.'

She drank and backed away. Leo was saying something else, but she didn't hear it. She turned towards where Dominic had been, but he was gone.

She shut herself in a toilet cubicle, the one furthest from the door. She sat on the closed seat, put her head in her hands, and willed herself not to cry.

She was being stupid. Beyond stupid – childish and absurd. What did it matter if he didn't remember her? Why did she care? Of course he didn't remember her – he must have met fans every day. Maybe Mel had been right about him all along, maybe he did just want to sleep with her. Well, she was past that now and anyway, he hadn't written a good book in ages and ...

God, *why* was she so upset? What the fuck was wrong with her?

With quiet certainty it hit her. She took a long, ragged breath.

That day at her uni, sitting across from Leo, she had felt for maybe the last time an overwhelming sense of her own potential. That all she had to do was stay the path and she would succeed.

You're doing everything right.

In the last two years, she had grappled with the growing worry that she was getting further from that path, that she was no longer doing everything right. But she could get back to it if she just made time for writing, just focused, just stood up for herself.

Only now she was beginning to suspect that wasn't the case. She'd never been special. She'd never been remarkable. She wasn't some Cinderella, just waiting for her chance. She'd thought Leo Grey recognised something great in her, but two years later he didn't even remember her. That last little thread of hope that she'd been clinging to, that last thing that was *hers*, had never even existed to begin with.

She needed air. She stepped out into the hallway, moved for the fire exit down the end. It was slightly ajar. She began to push through and stopped when she heard voices.

'This is a mistake, mate.' Victor Caine's low drawl. 'You know that. Your boss ought to know that.'

'No, *mate*. What this is, is Ford's last chance to take the offer. Otherwise shit's about to get a lot worse. For him. For you. For—'

A cracking sound. Charlotte leaned a little into the gap, looking out into the darkened lot behind the function centre.

Victor Caine stood over another man, just a shadow in the night, trying to stand. Victor hit him again. And again. It wasn't like in the movies. It wasn't something that could just be shrugged off. The blows were powerful. The man's head hit pavement. Victor hit him again.

Charlotte stayed where she was.

The man on the ground wasn't moving. Victor straightened. He threw his head back. Rubbed his knuckles and inhaled.

Suddenly, he turned.

His eyes caught Charlotte's as she slipped back inside. She returned fast to the bathroom. Victor did not follow.

Back in the cubicle, she sat and closed her eyes and tried to breathe. Tried to banish what she'd seen. Tried not to think about Freddie. Tried not to imagine herself, in the dark, facing Victor's fists, or worse.

She'd never seen anyone get punched before. She wondered if she should go check on the man, should—

No. *No.*

She would bury it. With Freddie and her father's warnings and the rest. She'd made her choice.

It took a few more minutes for her breathing to steady and the shakes to stop.

She cleaned her face. Touched up her makeup until she was sure nobody would notice anything amiss. Then she walked back out into the midst of the event. She found Dominic, off to the side, eyes on his phone.

She crossed and embraced him, hard, tight. Taken aback, he held her. She didn't let go. She never would, never *could.* Because with nothing else left, at least she had him.

CHAPTER SEVENTEEN

Now

'Okay.' Charlotte entered the boiler room again. 'Here's the deal. Tell me where your car is, I let you go.'

Anders was not smiling. There was something calculating in the way he watched her now. 'You let me go, I will stop you and take the car myself.'

'I have the gun.'

Anders raised both eyebrows.

'Besides,' Charlotte said, 'I wouldn't let you go straight away.'

'Then why would I tell you the truth?'

'Because ...' Charlotte almost wanted to laugh with sheer disbelief at how annoyance overrode life-or-death panic here. 'Because I'll check. Then I'll come back and let you go.'

'Then I would overpower you.'

'Then I would shoot you. And anyway, I'm not going to unlock you right there and then, I'll ... fuck, I don't know. I'll tie the key to a candle and stick it up there.' She pointed to a pipe running around the top of the room. 'Light it and when it melts the key will drop to you. Or … something, I don't know. But I'll let you go.'

Anders frowned. 'You are quite inventive, aren't you?'

'I don't know or care. I'm just trying to stay alive.'

'And in doing so you would put me in the same position you are currently in. No car, no way out of here.'

'Well if you *do* have men on the way, you're in a better position than me.'

Anders' smile was wan. 'Yes, men of that ilk are always very understanding when they get brought to a location to find their quarry has vanished.'

'Not my problem,' Charlotte said. 'You want somebody to be sympathetic, don't try to strangle them. Now. The car.'

'Why didn't you kill me when you had the chance?'

'The car, Anders.'

'Why are you not asking your friend to use his car?'

'I'm assuming you took his spark plug too.'

'Are you afraid of what he'll say? What you'll have to explain?'

Charlotte didn't reply.

'Ah,' Anders said. 'You are afraid of *him*.'

'Is he working with you?' she asked, quietly.

Anders went to reply. Stopped. Considered. Then: 'No. He is not. But then I doubt I am the only one looking for you.'

'Why?' Charlotte could hear the desperate strain in her voice. 'Why toy with me? What does he want?'

'That I cannot answer,' Anders said.

Charlotte turned away. Took a deep breath. Tightened her hand on the gun and faced Anders again.

'Where is the car?'

Cool and level, he stared her down. 'I will not tell you that.'

She lifted the gun. Anders didn't react.

'Where is the car?'

'Your options are dwindling.'

'Where the fuck is the car?'

'You can search for it, but every minute you don't find it is a minute wasted. You can call the police, but—'

'The car,' Charlotte almost begged.

'You can shoot me, but you will not do that.'

Silence. Tears in Charlotte's eyes. Pain in her chest and her neck. She could feel her pulse through her hand. In the finger tight on the trigger.

Anders didn't look away.

Charlotte lowered the gun. Closed her eyes for a moment, then stepped out into the hall. Found what she was looking for. She returned and threw the bucket at Anders' feet.

He looked at it, confused. 'What is—'

'You're going to be here a while,' Charlotte said. 'You might need that.'

Anders' eyes widened. 'You expect me—'

'Many circumstances are unfortunate,' Charlotte said. 'Just as many are self-induced.'

She slammed the door on his horrified expression.

She ran. Through the empty carpark and into the shadows of the trees over the main road. She kept running, down the road that in winter would be edged with snow and full of cars. The gums grew thick, sloping downwards on her left, upwards on her right. Nowhere to leave a car. She kept going.

Once she could no longer see the carpark behind her she slowed. She stopped briefly, listening. Wind in the leaves. A hint of rain on the air. She was out of breath. Her lungs and muscles burned. The gun was heavy in her hand. She looked back towards the resort, debating her next move.

In weeks past she'd liked the way the Skillion village seemed to defer to nature. So small and tucked away and unobtrusive. Even the road felt squeezed by the trees and the slopes and sheer drops that alternately fringed it. The six lodges with their mostly silly names – Snowhaven, Bushmill, White Republic, Andrew's Alpine Escape, Bluebird and Bloomberg, plus the pub, ski hire and servo – sat cramped and shy around the single road, hunched together as if trying to stay out of the way.

Now, her surrounds felt less like a sanctuary and more like a tiny, fearful station under siege. The vast sweep of the trees and hills and mountains and cliffs constricted her, mocking her with an endless array of places to run to that, unprepared, would almost certainly kill her. The shadows between the trees were looming threats, the cries of birds unnerving, the fog a force moving against her, obscuring the many dangers even further.

Was there a bitter joke in all of this? In her lowest moments she'd thought of Skillion as a kind of purgatory, wondering if maybe she was already dead. Now the case for that was stronger than ever. The trappings of idyllic, nature-bound mountain life she'd loved so much had turned deadly, keeping her from running, forcing her into the orbit of somebody – maybe several somebodies – who had every intention of doing her harm.

Sooner or later, especially if she didn't return, Anders would call out. John would eventually hear something – or come looking for her. After that, what happened was in their hands. Maybe John wasn't dangerous. Maybe he hadn't stolen her bag. But nothing else made sense. Even if it was a stupid prank or something, even if he was harmless but a liar, whatever happened next was his own fault. At least, she had to convince herself of that.

She walked fast. A rustle in the trees to her right. She snapped her focus to it, gun up. Waited. It came again. A branch caught in the breeze. She swore under her breath. Continued, faster.

She was hoping that there was something she'd missed, some obscured turn-off or shoulder. She kept going, looking always for the car, but there was nothing. An abundance of caution might have led Anders to park a long way away and walk the rest, but, in the cold, she doubted it.

She checked her watch. She'd been walking nearly half an hour, a couple of kilometres maybe. A heavier gust of wind. A sprinkle of water blown from an overhanging tree. The sky above was darkening grey. How far could she go before the weather forced her back? How far *would* she go? Past an hour she'd be nearing nightfall, closer to the theoretical arrival of Anders' backup. She'd have to either return to the lodge in the dark or hunker down in the bush and wait.

Hopeless fury like a geyser threatening to erupt. She veered from the road and leaned against a grey trunk. She wanted to scream something hoarse and wordless and hateful. But if somebody *was* out there ...

At what point had this become her life? Every decision second-guessed, every choice shaped by threats real and imagined? *Life* seemed the wrong word for it. This wasn't living. This was a cruel mockery of it.

She remembered, then, sitting on the bank of an alpine river with her father and Uncle Mac. Six or seven years old and she had felt the tug of her first fish, shrieked with glee, then the slack as it somehow got free. She had been so angry. Her father had rubbed her back and told her that sometimes things were fated. Sometimes you had to just go with the flow.

But Uncle Mac had chuckled. 'Worst advice in the world, I reckon. Fight the flow. Make your own luck.'

She faced the road again. She had been brought here by going with the flow. Or, she now understood, going along with what others wanted. Always trying to please, trying to do what was best for everyone else with no consideration of whether it was best for her.

She walked. There was still no sign of the car.

It was getting colder. If she didn't find anything soon, she would have to turn back or run the risk of hypothermia. The temperature at night dropped dangerously.

She was weighing up how much further she could risk going when she saw a dark shape in the middle of the road up ahead. She stopped. From here she couldn't make out what it was. A big piece of bark or something?

It was then she saw the guard rail, the barrier that stopped cars from plummeting down the steep drop through the trees. It was torn apart, broken steel ends swaying out over the slope. The gap was big enough for a car to go through. It had not been there the last time she drove up.

Charlotte drew the gun. Got closer.

The item in the middle of the road was a steering wheel. She picked it up. Wires dangled from the back. She approached the destroyed barrier. The edges of the metal were jagged, uneven.

The scratches on John's axe.

It had got darker. The cold was biting through her clothes. She got as close to the edge as she dared. Down below, shadows among the trees, but also something else. A glint of far-off metal.

Charlotte staggered back. There was something written on the steering wheel.

She held it up. A single word had been carved into the leather.

DON'T.

CHAPTER EIGHTEEN

Then

Usually Charlotte would be asleep by now. Dominic never came home until well past midnight on a Sunday so Charlotte didn't bother waiting up for him. But she'd decided to sample an impressive new Chianti and was finding the bottle quite moreish, so she'd sat on their vast plush couch watching a movie and topping up her glass occasionally, enjoying herself, and the clock had just gone past twelve when she heard the back door open.

Momentarily, she thought it was in the film. But then came the click of it shutting – so soft it was obvious somebody was trying to do it quietly. A chill over her skin. She picked up the remote but stopped short of switching off the TV. She moved from the couch to the kitchen, all the while telling herself it was nothing, just Dominic, but then he never snuck around the back, and now all those long-buried worries started to crawl back; the full scope of who her partner was, what he did, and what that might mean for her.

It took her a couple of attempts to open the drawer and even then she dropped the knife, jumping back as it clattered too-loud on the tiles. She froze, but she could hear nothing else. She picked it up. Crept for the hall. Moved down it. A light was on in the laundry. That seemed strange. She lowered the knife and stepped into the doorway.

Dominic was hunched over the sink. His jacket was on the floor. The sleeves of his white shirt were rolled up. He was covered in blood.

Charlotte gasped, loud and sharp. Dominic stopped what he was doing but didn't look at her. He lowered his head. Closed his eyes.

'Dominic …' Charlotte breathed.

'Go to bed, Charlotte.'

'Are you …' She moved forward but couldn't bring herself to touch him.

He resumed scrubbing his arms. 'I said go to bed. I'm not hurt.'

It took a moment for the implications of that to hit her. 'Then who—'

'Charlotte.' He faced her. His eyes had widened, gone unblinking. His face was a mask of contained fury, a mask splattered in somebody else's blood. It struck her how tall he was, how he filled the room.

'Go to bed.' His voice was low. Quiet. But it allowed no room for discussion. Charlotte backed out of the room. She returned to the kitchen, put the knife back in the drawer. She stood there, unsure of what to do. Going to bed seemed absurd, impossible. But that was what Dominic had told her to do.

She lay under the covers in the darkened room and stared at the ceiling. She heard the shower start. It went for a while.

She didn't move. The water was shut off. Silence. Then the bedroom door opened and Dominic stepped into the room. She closed her eyes. She could hear him moving around. The creak of the armchair in the corner.

'I know you're awake,' he said.

She sat up, just a little.

Dominic flicked on the lamp. He sat there, hair wet, in a dressing gown, cast in shadow by the dim light.

'I'm sorry if I scared you,' he said.

She didn't reply.

Dominic sighed. 'There are things you don't know. Things I keep from you. Not for any reason other than to protect you. But I've realised now that I can't keep it all separate anymore. It's gone too far.'

'What has?' Charlotte's voice sounded like a child's.

'I have enemies,' Dominic said. 'Our organisation isn't the only one making moves in the Melbourne scene. For a while we were the biggest, but now we have a competitor moving in. A Sydney player. Large. Dangerous. Powerful. And ruthless. Not everyone in this industry is like me, Charlotte. Some are very, very bad people. And they will do anything to get what they want.'

'Are they trying to kill you?' she asked.

Dominic nodded.

The air had gone out of Charlotte.

'I wish I could lie to you,' he said, 'but I can't. Until now there was an uneasy truce. That has changed. And I have to decide what to do about it.'

Charlotte waited.

'I think we need to end this,' Dominic said.

A wrench in her stomach.

'I don't want to,' Dominic said. 'You have to know that. I want you, Charlotte. You're all I want. I see …' His smile was pained and sad and so beautiful. 'I see the most amazing future. I want to marry you. Have kids. Get out of this business. That was my dream. And there was a time when I thought that was possible. A little more money, a smooth transition, turn the clubs legit and whatever we wanted could have been ours, with no need to ever worry again. But now …'

'You could stop,' Charlotte said. 'Stop now, get out. We can do something else. Make money another way. The clubs don't need to launder. We—'

But Dominic was shaking his head. 'It's not that simple. I know too much. They'll come for me whatever I do, wherever I go. And I can't abandon the others, Charlotte. I can't.' His voice hardened on the last word and Charlotte's heart broke for him.

He leaned forward. Head in his hands. 'I'm sorry. I'm so sorry. But I have to protect you.'

Charlotte was out from under the covers and crawling across the bed, sliding off to Dominic's feet. She took his hands, pulling them away from his face. Saw the tears in his eyes.

'I'm in this with you,' Charlotte said. 'I love you. So much. I'm here with you until the end.'

'Charlotte, I can't—'

'Please.' She knew she was begging but that didn't matter. 'There must be something we can do. Please.'

Dominic was shaking his head but Charlotte didn't let him speak.

'What can I do?' she said. 'What can I do to help you?'

Dominic looked away. Took a deep breath. Closed his eyes again. A twitch in his jaw. Charlotte did not let go of his hands.

'There might be something,' Dominic said. He looked at her again. A tiny flicker of hope, somewhere in the dark. 'Something you can do to help. But it's …' He shook his head. 'No. No, I can't ask that of you. I *can't*—'

Charlotte squeezed his hands. 'Whatever it is,' she said. 'Whatever it is, I'll do it. Tell me what you need me to do.'

A long, heavy silence. And then, finally, he did.

CHAPTER NINETEEN

Now

Charlotte checked the darkness behind her then slipped through the side door into Snowhaven. She moved quickly through the lodge. With the gun ahead of her and the broken steering wheel under her arm, she swept every room. When she was sure they were all clear, she locked them up and jammed a chair under the handle of the front door.

She headed to the boiler room. Held the gun at the ready as she kicked the door open.

Only Anders inside, still secured, looking vaguely entertained as he watched her enter.

'Do you fancy yourself an action hero?' he asked.

Charlotte shut the door and threw the steering wheel at his feet. She watched him closely as he picked it up. As amusement dropped from his face.

'You recognise that, I take it,' she said.

'Where did you get this?' he asked.

'On the road where I'm guessing you left your car,' Charlotte said. 'I'm guessing you didn't hack away the barrier and push it down the slope.'

Anders ran a finger over the word carved in the wheel.

'I'm also guessing,' Charlotte said, 'that no crony of yours did that.'

Anders didn't speak.

'Now would be a really good time to tell me if anyone else is coming,' Charlotte said.

'I do not see how this changes my situation,' Anders replied.

'No?' Charlotte's voice was getting higher, wilder. She didn't care. 'Try this on for size. Someone up on this mountain either saw you arrive or figured out you were here. That same someone got rid of your car and left this as – shit, I don't know – some kind of fucked-up message.'

'A message to you, it would seem,' Anders said. 'Just as it would seem the removal of my car eliminated a potential escape route.'

'Even if that's true, don't you think it's a pretty massive risk to assume he's going to let you walk away? If I die, either he finds you or you're stuck here. Which is worse?'

'You say "he" with familiarity,' Anders said. 'You believe this is your friend.'

Did she believe that? Truly? She tried to picture John cutting away the barrier with the axe. Pushing Anders' car through it.

Why? Why would he do any of that? But then, why claim to be a writer?

'It could be somebody else,' Anders said, but he no longer sounded so confident.

'I found an axe in his lodge,' Charlotte replied. 'A new one but scratched up. Like it had been used to cut metal. Seem like a coincidence to you?'

Anders said nothing.

'Do you think the syndicate hired somebody else?' Charlotte asked.

'It's possible,' Anders said. 'It's even likely, but you know as well as I that they would be paying to have you discreetly returned. Not for ...' He raised the steering wheel. 'Whatever this is.'

Which was what?

Charlotte closed her eyes, rubbing her temples.

'What are you going to do?' Anders asked.

She hated that question. But she still had to answer it.

'Firstly,' Charlotte said, 'I *need* to know if anyone else is coming. Tell me, and I'll find a way to let you free once I've gone.'

'You still need a means of escape,' Anders said. 'It will take you at least two days to walk down the mountain, more. In this weather, without supplies.'

'And if I have to, I will,' Charlotte said. 'But first I need to know if I'm going to run into a pack of hitmen on the way.'

'You friend has a car, presumably,' Anders said. 'And you have a gun.'

'Is anyone else coming?'

Anders looked at her for a long time. Finally, he seemed to come to a decision.

'No,' he said.

'Okay,' she said. 'Okay ...'

She looked at the gun in her hand. Pictured herself walking across to White Republic, holding up John, demanding his keys.

She'd done worse. She could do this.

'Are you going to shoot him?' Anders asked.

'I'm going to make him give me the keys.'

'Which leaves him alive. And a threat.'

'I don't *know* he's a threat!' Charlotte snapped.

'He's behaving like one.'

She shook her head. None of this helped her.

'Be wise about this,' Anders said. 'This man is clearly strong and willing to do the extreme and unexpected. You must assume that he knows who you are and that he knows about me. This is not an instance where half measures would be advisable. Your best recourse is to kill him. He is attempting to seal off your routes of escape.'

'But I don't …'

Maybe she just didn't want to believe it. Didn't want to believe that the only friend she'd made in years could be, in the end, just another man who meant her harm. The thought dragged at her like a sucking drain.

'Charlotte.'

She looked at Anders.

He leaned forward. 'I did not take the spark plug from your car. I didn't think I would *have* to.'

She held his gaze. She believed him. She looked at the gun.

'Kill him,' Anders said.

Something you can—

No. Not that. Never that.

'He goes for a walk every morning,' Charlotte said, pushing past the memory. 'I can get into the lodge while he's gone, find his keys.'

'That means waiting overnight,' Anders said. 'Right now, he likely does not think you are a threat. Do it now. Cross the road, knock on the door, raise the—'

'Not everyone,' Charlotte said, 'sees murder as the only solution.'

Anders was quiet for several long seconds. Charlotte didn't look at him.

'It is scarcely the only solution,' Anders said. 'But it is, all too often, the best one. Besides which, there is a difference between murder and self-defence.'

She stuck the gun down the back of her jeans and turned away.

'What I am having trouble understanding,' Anders went on, 'is how, after everything you have been through, you are so reluctant to take the steps that will allow you to protect yourself. Do you *want* to die?'

'Again,' Charlotte said. 'I'm not you.'

Anders leaned forward slightly. 'Then consider another option.'

'What option?'

'The only one left to you.' His smile grew. 'If you will not harm that man, perhaps it's worth letting me do it.'

She locked the door and went back up the stairs. She would not sleep tonight. She would keep herself awake, keep watch. She did not entirely believe that Anders did not have reinforcements on the way, but for now her main concern had to be John.

Anders was right. She could take no chances. She reached the kitchen, flicked on the light and headed for the kettle. Start strong on the coffee. Keep watch. Then in the morning—

'Hi Katie.'

She spun, jerking back into the kitchen bench.

John was standing in the living room, hands in pockets, smiling.

Charlotte's entire body was ice. She couldn't form words. Couldn't move.

The gun.

'I thought we had dinner plans,' John said.

'We … I …'

'I couldn't find you,' he went on. 'So, I came to check if you were alright. No lights inside. I got worried so I came in through a window.' He laughed. 'Imagine that! Chubby old me, crawling through a window. What a sight. Glad you didn't see it.'

He hadn't moved any closer. He removed a hand from his pocket. He was holding something. In the shadows of the unlit living room she couldn't make it out. But through his fingers she saw a glint.

The gun. The gun, now.

'Anyway,' John said. 'Are you?'

'Am I …'

'Alright?'

She swallowed. 'I'm fine.'

John slapped his thigh. Charlotte jumped.

'Well!' John exclaimed. 'All's well that ends well, eh?'

He didn't move. Charlotte reached behind her. Her eyes were on his hand. How fast could he reach her if she pulled the gun, if she fumbled for even a second?

John took a step forward. Charlotte's sweat-slick hand closed around the butt of the gun.

Sudden movement. Something shining in the air. John had flipped a coin. He caught it. Winked.

'Heads or tails?'

Charlotte said nothing.

'Go on,' John urged. 'Heads or tails.'

'H-heads.'

John opened his hand. Looked at the coin. Whistled through his teeth.

'What ... what was it?' Charlotte said.

'All in good time,' John said. 'You have yourself a great night, Katie.'

Humming, he went for the stairs. She heard descending footsteps, then a scrape as he moved aside the chair she'd placed under the door handle. The sound of wind as it opened, then the click of it shutting and silence as Charlotte fell to the floor, gasping desperately for air.

CHAPTER TWENTY

Then

She almost tripped carrying the glass back to her corner booth. She slipped in and closed her eyes, giving herself a moment for the sense of swaying like a storm-borne ship to fade. She drank. The wine didn't taste like anything. She drank again.

Dominic was at work. Or so he said. He was always somewhere else these days. He still smiled and held her and said all the right things when they saw each other. The least he could do, given that they were getting married in a couple of months. That thought, that thought that once might have sent Charlotte into a giddy spin, landed dull and empty. She drank.

She was trying to hide this from Dominic. The nights alone here in this tiny bar. She would get home before he did and scull water until she was almost ready to be sick. Then she would scrub her teeth and swill half a bottle of mouthwash. Did he suspect anything? Did it matter?

Maybe he really was working tonight. Maybe that didn't matter either. Even when he was around, she saw his phone ring. Saw Bates calling. She drank.

There it was again. Something at the edge of her thoughts. She willed it away. She had nothing new to add, no new way to look at it. The memories. *Something you can do.* What came after and now the black hole inside her, sucking away everything that was left of Charlotte Laurent and leaving in her place ...

She didn't know what was left in her place.

Something you can—

She drank.

She was good at pretending everything was fine. At work she smiled. She gave orders and oversaw events and all the rest. The distraction was welcome. At first the thought of doing anything that required her to function was enough to send her to the nearest sink, choking back vomit. It had surprised her, though, how well she managed to keep up appearances, at least enough for nobody to know anything was wrong.

Wrong.

She almost laughed. So small a word. Not nearly reflective of what was going on here. Wrong had an opposite. Wrong could be righted. Wrong implied that something could be fixed. No, this wasn't wrong; this just was her, now and forever stained.

She drank.

Voices at the bar, loud and laughing. Her head throbbed. She wished they'd fuck off, all of them. Maybe it would be better for her to do this at home, but at home, somehow, the memories found her more easily.

'Charli? Oh my God!'

It took a moment for the blurred shape in her vision to cohere. When it did, Charlotte briefly wondered whether she'd fallen asleep.

Mel was sitting opposite her wearing a bright pink dress and a tiara. She wasn't smiling. She didn't look concerned. Just vaguely surprised. Pink shapes in the distance behind her. Charlotte drank.

'How are you?' Mel asked.

'Fine.'

'You don't look it.'

Charlotte caught herself before she told Mel to get fucked. Instead, she asked what she was doing here.

Mel shifted in her seat. 'Pub crawl. It's, um ... well, it's my hen's night. Can you believe it? I'm getting married!'

You and me both, Charlotte thought but didn't say.

'Congratulations. You should get back to them.'

Mel didn't move.

Charlotte drank.

'Charli, listen ...' Mel bit her lip. 'I know it's been a while. I know we didn't leave stuff on the best terms. But that doesn't mean ... that doesn't mean I don't care about you.'

Charlotte almost laughed.

'And like ...' Mel was fumbling for the words but Charlotte wasn't going to help her. 'I mean, shit Charli, you don't look well.'

'Couple too many, Mel. That's all.'

'Right. Except what *led* to the couple too many?'

Charlotte didn't reply.

Mel leaned forward. 'Charlotte, if Dominic is—'

'Dominic's fine.'

'You sure about that?'

Charlotte just looked at her. Willed her to leave.

Mel took a deep breath. 'Charlotte, listen—'

'No, you listen.' Drunk as she was, her voice was clear. Hard. 'You never liked him. I get that. But let's be real for a second. That had nothing to do with Dominic and everything to do with you not being able to control me anymore. Because you always saw me as your little puppet and you couldn't fucking stand it when I wasn't. When you realised I had way more going for me than you did. Or maybe you always knew that but Dominic just proved it.'

She wanted Mel to yell at her. To storm off or throw a drink in her face.

Instead, she smiled sadly and said, 'Charlotte, I always knew that. Always. Here was you, this creative, thoughtful, ambitious person, and then there was me. Maybe I was insecure about it, but I never for a second saw you as a *puppet* or wanted you to change. Ever. I loved you and I was proud of you. But after you met Dominic ...' She grimaced. 'You weren't the same, Charlotte. You became so desperate to please him. You know how much trouble it caused for Shae and me, after we got everything ready for you to move in and go on the lease and stuff? You never apologised for that. I mean, I could get over it, sure. But with Dominic you stopped writing. You stopped calling me. You stopped being *you*. And look, I'll take responsibility for where I screwed up. But if you really hate me that much, then I might as well say that it seems like Dominic has been cutting you off from everyone who cares about you for a long, long time. And I worry about how long it will be before he asks you to do something dangerous. Something there's no coming back from.'

They looked at each other. Charlotte reached for her drink. Mel caught her hand.

The tears then. Rising unbidden and overwhelming. Charlotte closed her eyes against them.

'Charli,' Mel whispered. 'We can go somewhere else. We can talk, okay? About anything.'

But they couldn't. Because Mel would never understand. Charlotte was changed now, different down to her atoms. She would never again be that wide-eyed wannabe writer. Her situation wasn't something she could write her way out of. It was too late.

She stood. Staggered out of the booth. She wouldn't break down here. She couldn't risk what she might say.

Do you understand for even a second the consequences of one mistake? One slip of the tongue, one door left unlocked?

Victor Caine's twisting smirk. Dominic washing blood from his hands in the laundry.

Mel caught her arm. Turned her round, so they were face to face. 'I'm here, Charli,' she said. 'I promise.'

Charlotte tried to pull away.

'I want to know you're safe.' There was an edge to Mel's voice. 'Charli, please. Tell me you're safe.'

Charlotte left.

* * *

Had there been a moment, one clear moment, when she could have stopped? Seen the path she was on and pulled away before things went bad?

In the few times she could think clearly, the times that weren't a blur of planning and dinners and work and all the rest, she wondered if even now she could stop. Could leave

Dominic. But she knew she wouldn't. Part of her, feebly, wanted to believe that was because she loved him too much. But she knew that wasn't true anymore. It was because, as she'd known the moment he got down on one knee, two weeks after she'd knelt before him and he'd told her there was *something you can do*, there was nobody else who would want her now. How could she lie next to someone new, knowing always what she had done, wondering when they would discover the truth and turn away from her in horror and disgust?

Dominic knew, and accepted her, and he would protect her; so she would stay. This was her life now. This was where she had ended up. If there had ever been the chance to go back, there wasn't anymore.

Their wedding was big. In a huge stone church she stood in her flowing white dress, fiddling with the gold band that did not seem to fit right, and saying all the words expected of her. The kiss and the cheers and the smiles, all the fake smiles in the lights of flashing cameras as Dominic stood shining and perfect and Charlotte searched for the bar.

Her father found her there. She almost told him to fuck off. Now, of all times, she didn't need to be told where she had gone wrong.

But instead he gathered her into a hug and kissed her cheek and said, quietly, 'I know we might have had our disagreements, Charlotte. But I love you and I'm proud of you and I respect your choice.'

And God how she wished, for the first time, that he was lying or mocking her. Because the way he looked at her told her just how much he meant it, and the *cruelty* of it coming now, that was too much.

But it was her wedding day and she would not cause a scene, so she kissed him on the cheek and thanked him and finished her drink.

She drifted through the reception. Between strangers and half-remembered friends. They all wanted to congratulate her, to tell her how stunning she looked, what a beautiful couple she and Dominic were. And it was all so bright and perfect, all a fairy tale come true, and nothing had ever felt so wrong.

Later, as the music ramped up and people danced and drank, she tried to find Dominic. She'd had too much, she knew that, and what she had held down for so long was threatening to overwhelm her. If it did, she would drown. Dominic would help. He could at least tell her the words that would help her believe, if only for tonight, that everything was okay.

He wasn't on the dance floor. He wasn't out the front with the smokers. She stumbled around the halls of the mirrored venue until she saw an open door to a side room.

Voices, low, teasing.

'Did I look good?'

'You looked convincing. That's the main thing.'

She didn't approach the door. Didn't need to see them to know it was Dominic and Elizabeth Bates.

'Performance of my life,' Dominic said.

'It's paid off,' Bates said. 'We look clean. And she played her part perfectly. We're almost there and—'

Charlotte backed away. Closed her eyes for a moment, something throbbing in her head. Then turned and went back to the hall. Whatever else was being said, whatever she was about to learn, she didn't want to know. Not now. Not anymore.

She could hardly stand. Another drink and she found a corner table. She sipped. Somebody joined her. It took her a moment to recognise Leo Grey. She hadn't realised he was here.

'Congratulations,' he said, raising his own glass.

Charlotte didn't reply.

'Charlotte, listen,' Leo said. 'Back at that fundraiser, the last time we saw each other, I *did* remember you. It had just been a full-on night and I was a bit all over the place. I've asked Dominic a few times to say something but—'

'Why are you friends with him?' she asked.

Leo blinked. 'What?'

'Why? You're an author. He's …' She waved a hand. 'Why?'

'He's interesting,' Leo said. 'You're married to him. You must think the same.'

Interesting. The last thing she had written had been about Dominic. Now, the idea of writing about him or anything that had happened to her was enough to bring bile rising. She stood.

'Charlotte.' He reached for her. 'Do you want me to call Dominic? Do you—'

'Fuck off,' she muttered, stumbling away.

She hated him then. Hated him because maybe if he'd told her that he remembered her, maybe she wouldn't be here, maybe things would be different, maybe …

But all those maybes faded as she leaned against a mirror and looked at her still-perfect wedding dress, at her curled blonde hair and made-up face a beautiful mask, as she looked at the woman in the mirror and did not recognise herself.

She knew, then, that there *had* been a moment she could have turned away. Many of them, in fact. And she had ignored each and every one. The only person who had brought her here was herself.

She drank.

CHAPTER TWENTY-ONE

Now

Charlotte sat in the office and watched White Republic through the window. No movement. No nothing. She checked her watch. It was ten in the morning and John hadn't emerged yet.

Exhaustion weighed on her. She'd spent much of the night on the stairs watching the door, gun in hand. Just the empty silence and then the irrational, gnawing fear that he'd somehow crept back into the lodge.

Anders' words again, in her head: *Perhaps it's worth letting me do it.*

She had ignored him of course. As if she'd release the hired gun who'd tried to strangle her and just hope he'd somehow changed his mind about collecting his paycheque. Sure, he might kill John, but only as a stop on the way to delivering Charlotte.

But in truth, even in the parallel universe where she could trust Anders in the slightest, that wasn't the outcome she wanted. The thought of John dead, even if he *was* some twisted freak, brought her no pleasure or relief. The closest she would get to either was escape, and even then it would be a momentary calm before the same old fears came right back. She would be running, again. She knew, now, that would never change. Maybe for the rest of her life. But then, maybe that was what she deserved.

A swell of childish frustration at John. She almost wanted to plead with him, *Let me get your keys, let me run, let me forget any of this ever happened.* She didn't care who John was or why he was doing this. She'd long since learned that motives counted for nothing. Not when the outcome was more pain.

She thought of Anders. Could she leave him to John's mercy? Or John to Anders'? With surprising clarity, it hit her that yeah, she could. She didn't want to kill. But nor did she owe either of them a thing. The moment she had the keys she would be gone.

She wondered if there was a difference between killing somebody and leaving them to die. She wondered if the following uncertainty would make the choice easier or harder. Maybe what we did mattered less than how we chose to look at it.

Something you can do—

Movement. Charlotte ducked, watched. John was strolling out the door, lips pursed in a whistle Charlotte couldn't hear. He closed his eyes. Took a long, deep breath. Spun in a near pirouette.

He looked up towards her window.

Charlotte stopped herself from darting out of sight. John was far more likely to glimpse a sudden movement, however small, than he was to notice the top of her head peering over a desk under half-lowered blinds.

John wasn't moving. Still watching.

Can he see me?

He started to walk, heading towards the trees. He kept going until she could no longer see him from the window.

Charlotte hurried downstairs, removed the chair and opened the front door. She leaned out as far as she dared.

She could just make out a figure crossing the slope. She watched until he had vanished into the trees.

She knew John's car was in the garage behind White Republic, but trying to get it would be pointless without the keys.

So she had to change that.

Fast and low, she ran for the door to White Republic.

She fumbled with the keypad to unlock the door. She stepped into the lodge and, as quietly as she could, shut the door behind her.

She had to be far more meticulous than last time. She checked the hooks set in a carved wooden backboard on the kitchen wall. The mantlepiece over the fireplace. The drawers of the sideboard in the entry hall. No sign of the car keys anywhere – it was very likely he'd taken them with him, but she still had to search. At the front door she paused, listening. John could be back any moment, likely without the warning whistle.

She went for the stairs. Stopped at the base, hand on the banister. Another glance at the front door. She started upstairs, knowing she might be walking into a trap. She was carrying the gun down the back of her jeans, but it was little comfort. On the landing she paused again, listening. Then she crossed into his bedroom. There was something unsettling about his perfectly made bed, no sign of the slightest crease or wrinkle. As if nobody had ever slept in it. She made a point not to touch or disturb anything as she went to the bedside table. She opened the drawer, saw a gleam, snatched for them. Hard and jagged in her hands.

A cool rush of relief that almost sent her laughing to the floor. She had a way out. Thank God, she had a way out.

She heard the front door open. Her heart seized.

Creaking floorboards in the front hall. No effort to be silent. He hadn't heard her. She waited for another creak and timed it with sliding the drawer shut again, hand tight around the keys to stop them from jangling. The drawer made a tiny scraping sound.

The footsteps stopped.

Charlotte held her breath, frozen with one hand around the keys and the other resting on the gun. Silence still from downstairs. Surely he hadn't heard anything. Surely.

Footsteps on the stairs.

A whimper escaped her. She dropped to her stomach and slid under the bed. Pulled the gun and clasped it to her chest. More steps, louder now. One on the landing, then another. Silence. Charlotte closed her eyes. She was already drenched in sweat – would he smell it? She couldn't get enough air into her lungs but she had to focus, had to struggle against every instinct, had to—

He was coming into the bedroom.

Tears in her eyes as he stopped again, just inside the doorway. Charlotte tried to remember if she'd left anything amiss, if she'd somehow disturbed the bedding, hadn't closed the drawer entirely.

His boots, stationary in the doorway.

Seconds crept by. He didn't approach. Tremors up and down her body. She angled the gun but her sweaty hands were making it hard to hold steady.

He still wasn't moving.

A minute had passed – more than, surely. What the *fuck* was he doing? Did he have his own weapon, aimed at the bed?

One step forward then another. His boots, clean and unscuffed despite the bushwalks, got nearer to her face, all too near. They stopped again, right by the bed. Then turned, heels facing her. A wheeze of protest from the bed. The mattress right over Charlotte's face bulged towards her. He was sitting.

Charlotte barely choked back a sob. Any second now some sound would slip out, would have to and then ...

John started to whistle.

It was familiar, one of the Bee Gees songs he loved to play. 'You Win Again'. It kept going. What was he doing? What was he trying to ...

There was no shifting of his weight on the mattress, nothing that would indicate he was doing anything other than sitting and whistling and ...

Waiting.

She aimed the gun at his heel. The shakes were coming in waves now; the barrel would hold then suddenly shudder again and again like she had no control over it.

He was still whistling.

At this range she would hit something, surely. Whatever happened next he would be incapacitated, if not dead. She had his keys. She could get to the car and be gone, take whatever she needed, leave Anders in the boiler room for his men to find, and John …

He was still whistling.

She closed her eyes.

John, who had been so kind and decent to her. Who had reminded her what it was like to have a friend.

John, who had lied about being a writer, who had stolen her backpack and the spark plug from her car, who had broken into her lodge and left warning messages in destroyed steering wheels and pushed a car off the side of the mountain.

Her finger tightened on the trigger.

Did she know for sure?

He was still whistling.

There might be something you can do.

She gritted her teeth. Her body jerked with repressed sobs. If John, somehow, *was* innocent and she pulled that trigger, if some third party was fucking with her and blaming him …

He stopped whistling.

Her eyes flew open. Her shallow breath caught in her throat.

The shriek of mattress springs as he stood. He crossed the room. She heard his steady footsteps descend, then cross the hall back to the door.

A click and he was gone.

She stayed where she was a long time, listening. No movement in the lodge. He could be waiting for her outside. But if he was, then all she was doing by staying put was worsening her chances of being caught.

She could at least check his car – although what she would do if the spark plug was gone there too, she had no idea. But she had to take the risk, get out of the lodge and get to the garage.

She rolled from under the bed. Got to her feet. Pocketed the keys, lifted the gun and moved for the stairs. On the landing she stopped, took a breath. Then moved quickly down and hovered at the bottom before sweeping both ways with the gun. But there was no sign of anyone in either direction.

She didn't go for the front door. If she was the predator, she'd assume her prey would run for the door. Instead, she moved through the kitchen and living area where she and John had shared dinners a million years ago (two days, Jesus, had it only been *two days* since Anders?). She arrived at the back door. Waited a moment, then pulled it open and stepped out into the cool air. The sky above was bruised, angry. Silence but for a gentle gust of wind. She replaced the gun in her jeans. Crossed towards the garage, half hidden in the trees, a dirt road leading from the closed, half-rusted roller door around to the main street. Her heart thumped, fast and hard. If the car worked, if the spark plug had not been removed, then she was home free.

So close now, just metres away.

John stepped in front of her.

'Hello Katie,' he said. 'Feel up to a little chat?'

CHAPTER TWENTY-TWO

Then

She veered from the door, propping herself up on the kitchen bench. A long, deep breath, then another and another. She dreaded returning. She drank more, then finished the glass. Stood back. The bottle, mostly empty now, was doubling. She blinked, waited for her vision to stabilise then made for the door. She noticed that she'd spilled wine on her dress. Expensive dress, too. She hoped Dominic noticed.

One step after another down the hall, past the photos. So many now. So very convincing. The two of them smiling and beautiful on trip after trip, at so many events. Testaments to a year of wedded bliss. It felt like more. The years had bled and blurred together and the fog around her had grown. She paused by one of the photos. Took in her smile. She'd got good at that. But the woman in that photo, for all that she looked like she belonged on the arm of a man like Dominic, didn't look very much like herself. Whatever the fuck that meant.

She'd known the line that had been crossed. But her reasons had been sound, right? It was all for them. All for the future. *We can get out after this. Out clean.* He had promised.

But then.

Now isn't a good time.

There's a lot of pressure. Sharks circling.

It's too dangerous.

You would never want to give all this up.

So Charlotte stopped asking.

She pushed herself back from the wall. Swayed, wondered dully if she would fall. She didn't. She went back into the dining room. Faint music and low lights, a spread of half-finished food on an ornate tablecloth. All those faces around it, all eyes on him, nobody so much as looking at her as she returned to her spot beside her husband.

One acknowledgement. 'You find the bathroom alright?' Leo Grey asked from beside her.

Prick. She didn't bother replying. She wondered sometimes if there was an unspoken agreement between herself and Leo. If they recognised in each other the signs of a problem drinker. Granted, he was better at hiding it. Always had a glass in hand but never seemed drunk. Dominic knew she couldn't stand Leo. That was exactly why he was seated next to her. Dinner and a show.

'Of course,' Dominic said, 'the Thai club scene is very different to the Australian one.'

'I'll bet.' Victor Caine winked at Charlotte.

Dominic raised an unimpressed eyebrow. 'Racism aside, there's a lot to learn. A trip like that really is the definition of a perk.'

Victor just laughed. He was watching her.

She felt sick. All of them dancing to Dominic's tune, all of them clawing for a little of his light. She didn't even know who was part of the business and who wasn't anymore. Dominic kept his company mixed. Hence Leo Grey, one of Dominic's colourful collection of minor celebrities – well-known enough to create the look of legitimacy, not public enough to draw attention. Years of being a fixture on the fundraising scene, a prominent young nightclub owner and pillar of the community had brought Dominic into some very gilded circles. And these relationships were mutually beneficial. Leo was a has-been at thirty or however fucking old he was now, a skinny, stringy-haired author who'd written nothing of any note since the early bestsellers Charlotte had once obsessed over. For guys like Leo, the orbit of charismatic, powerful and wealthy figures like Dominic must have been addictive, a way to believe that they were still relevant, like the best was ahead.

'Imagine it, Leo,' Dominic was saying – although how he'd reached this new line of conversation Charlotte had no idea – 'the next book launch at one of my venues. Deck the whole place out. Themed decorations. Invite some major players.' He clicked at a fat fuck stuffing his face down the end of the table. 'Phil writes for the *Herald*. He can make a show out of it.'

Leo drank. Of course he did.

Dominic leaned back, raising his wine glass with a satisfied smile. 'You know they always say that the creative industries are all about who you know. Well, that goes beyond just the creative. I think it's true of every line of work.'

What about yours? Charlotte thought.

Had Dominic climbed the ranks of the narcotics business through a few convenient contacts? Most of whom were dead by now – whether due to Dominic or somebody else? It didn't fucking matter. He was the king and it had all worked out his way. She drank. It took her a moment to realise all eyes were on her and another to realise she had spoken.

She lowered the glass. She didn't look at Dominic. She could feel his steady gaze.

What the fuck had she said?

'What *about* my line of work, Charlotte?' he asked.

She said nothing.

Dominic laughed a little. 'Well, I can't speak for what my wife is on about, but the nightclub industry certainly—'

'I'm not talking about fucking nightclubs,' Charlotte said.

She looked at him. No anger on his face. But it was there. She knew.

'Everybody at this table knows what I'm talking about,' she said.

Easy, relaxed, Dominic asked, 'Do they?'

And oh how quickly the squawking sycophants fell in line; a wave of reassurances and expressed confusion. They all knew, or at least suspected. Of course they did. But none of them would ever say it out loud. Better to be blind than banished from the kingdom.

She went to speak over them, to cut through the bullshit with what they all knew. A voice in her head, wild and reckless, demanded that she do it. Another, louder but worn down by the booze, insisted she stop, apologise, placate him. Pull back now and smooth things over.

Victor Caine was watching her with narrowed eyes.

She drank.

'I think you've had enough, Charlotte.'

The expert pitch of Dominic's voice. Not condescending. Not dithering. Firm and kind and sad. 'You remember what Doctor Clemons said.'

There was no Doctor Clemons. It didn't matter when all anyone saw was the reasonable, caring husband struggling against the alcoholic housewife, trying to invoke the words of an external professional to head off another fight. And when, in a moment, he suggested she take herself to bed, how he would milk the sympathy. He would be a tough but fair man at the end of his tether. His wife had a drinking problem. She said stupid things that made no sense. And every single man around that table would know she had been telling the truth and every single one of them would pretend otherwise.

'Maybe you should get some rest,' Dominic said.

It could have sounded patronising. But he was too clever for that.

Charlotte looked sideways at Leo Grey. That face, more lined and worn than it should have been, frowning and focused on his drink. Nobody would tell that prick he should get some rest. Nor any of the other boozehounds sitting around that table. How very easy it was to toe the line. The privileges it netted you.

She finished her drink, stood shakily and left the room without saying goodnight or waiting to hear Dominic's apologies to his guests. She carefully closed the door behind her. She went to their bedroom. Undressed in her giant walk-in closet. Cleaned her teeth over their gold-plated sink. She'd be hungover tomorrow but at least she wouldn't have stale red wine on her breath. She climbed into bed and lay under the covers and waited.

Go to bed.

Dominic in the laundry, scrubbing another man's blood off his hands.

And Charlotte, a child chastened for seeing too much. But she knew now he had always meant her to see. Had *needed* her to see. Because it was the seeing that would ensure she followed the other orders to come. Which she had done. Which she still did, even as all the reasons she gave herself – her love for Dominic, the future they would build together, the validation he provided her – slipped away like the mirage they'd always been.

She didn't sleep, just lay there and waited. The low buzz of conversation and occasional laughter (how quickly he'd regained the mood) continued. Then slowly it slipped away. She heard doors open and close. Footsteps. The door to their room remained shut. She waited.

This was her punishment. Or part of it. He knew she was awake. She knew her outburst would not go unaddressed. She would lie here until Dominic decided it was time to deal with her and until then he would let her stew.

She got up. Their ensuite had a high window that looked out to the front yard. On tottering tiptoes, she looked through it. Two silhouettes in the driveway. One large, broad. The other slim. Victor Caine and Leo Grey? What the hell were they talking about?

Whatever it was, it was done. They both left. There was nobody else. Charlotte went back to bed.

The minutes dragged by. The door didn't open. Time crawled.

Charlotte hugged her pillow, close and hard. Through the night her heart pounded. She shook. She wanted to scream. But as the hours passed, all of that was eroded to just an awful tiredness. She was, in the end, no different from those men around the table. Worse even. The world champion at looking away from all the things she didn't want to see. The problem was, of course, that eventually those things grew so numerous that you couldn't look anywhere else.

Light through the window. She knew she should get up, but some tiny childhood instinct told her she was safe under the covers. Stupid. Under the covers was where the danger slept, right alongside her.

But he wasn't here. Dominic had never come to bed. Probably fucking that dried-up cunt of a lawyer. Yeah, that would be right. When was the last time that thought might have made her angry? Like most changes, the shift in her understanding of her marriage had been so gradual that she couldn't quite identify when one attitude had given way to a different one. Whatever the case, it didn't matter. Now she was grateful for Elizabeth Bates. If Dominic was in her bed, it kept him out of Charlotte's.

For days she didn't leave the house. Just waited for Dominic to return. She ordered food. Went through bottle after bottle. Stood out in the yard under the swivelling cameras, glass in hand, staring into the pond, watching the fish come right up to the edges then veer hard away again. It was all she *could* look at. The high fences blocked out everything except the grey sky above. She stood there until it darkened. It felt like she'd only been there five minutes. She guessed hours had passed. She drank and went back inside. She headed for the dining room, pushed open the door and froze.

Dominic was sitting at the head of the table, alone, eating a steak. He did not look up.

How long had he been back? A merry-go-round of options in her head: back out, go to bed, sit down? She did none of them. Just stood there as Dominic cut away at his meat. Finally he finished. Put his cutlery together and slid the plate away. Only then did he look at her.

She remembered the first time she'd ever seen him. That handsome, charming, impressive young man at the nightclub. So sophisticated, so magnetic. So *different*.

'You are an embarrassment,' he said.

She didn't reply.

'What exactly were you hoping to achieve?'

She shrugged, like a petulant teenager.

Dominic snorted. 'Of course. Of course you have no fucking idea.' He stood, went to the bar and poured himself a whisky. 'If you have a problem, Charlotte, you can bring it to me. But to throw a tantrum in front of my friends, like a toddler? It's repulsive.'

'Dominic …' Words caught in her throat. She closed her eyes. Took a shuddering breath. And tried again. 'Dominic, I can't do this.'

He sat again. Drank. 'Do what?'

'This.' She moved for the table. 'Us. The … the business. I can't. I can't be a part of it. I can't be always waiting for the police or worse to kick down our door. I just …'

No expression on his face.

Even though she knew it was futile, she tried to use his own words. 'Didn't you … I mean you always said you wanted to get out eventually, right? That you had to secure your position. It's secure, Dominic. You're at the top. All your enemies are dead.'

A tired grimace, as though he was dealing with a deeply frustrating conversation. 'Not all of my enemies are dead, Charlotte. They just haven't shown themselves yet. But they're out there. The small-time dealer with more than half a brain, who realises playing smart can change his life. The lieutenant waiting for his chance to stick a knife in my back. The remnants of *his* crew, still out there, out for revenge. And more. No, I'm a long way from safe. One moment of weakness, and they'll strike.'

She grabbed the chair at the other end, pulled it out, sat and leaned forward. 'Then isn't this the perfect time? Get out before they come for us. Take our money and leave. No more of this. No more fear. No more …'

She didn't know what she was going to say there. Because there was too much of it. Blood? Guilt? The ugly and ever-growing tension between them?

Dominic still hadn't spoken. He just watched her.

'Why?' she whispered. 'Why not stop?'

'Because I don't want to,' he said.

It might have been the first time Dominic Ford had ever been honest with her.

She leaned back. Pushed tears away with the heel of her hand. Looked at the ceiling and breathed in then out. Faced him again.

'Then I want a divorce,' she said.

'No.'

'No? You can't ...' She was spluttering, lost for words.

'No, *you* can't.' His eyes, suddenly, were alight, his voice a hiss. 'You knew what you were getting into, Charlotte. You knew what this was.'

She was crying now, the sobs spilling out of her, racking her body. 'I didn't. I didn't have a—'

'What, a choice?' Dominic laughed. 'You had so many choices, Charlotte. You didn't have to leave that club with me. You didn't have to come home with me or come back to me after you learned what I did. You could have said no to everything that came after. You never once did.'

'You told me it was safe. You said it was—'

'Then you really are stupid,' Dominic said. 'Yes, I have run my business better and safer and— *Stop fucking crying!*'

She hiccupped. Swallowed. Rocked back and forth. But she stopped crying.

'We can't divorce,' Dominic said.

'You can have it all,' Charlotte said. 'I don't care, you'd win in court anyway, you have Elizabeth and—'

'It can't happen,' Dominic said. 'You know why. You made your choice and now you have to live with it.'

'Then I'll run,' Charlotte gasped out. 'I'll just, I'll just leave and—'

'And I will find you.'

He said it simply and directly without looking away and Charlotte knew he meant it.

She was curling in on herself. Just a child. Just an idiot girl in over her head with no way out.

Except.

'I'll go to the police,' she breathed. 'I'll tell them everything.'

No reply.

She was ready for him to pick up the steak knife. To have his phone in hand. Or a gun. But he just sat there and, for the first time in that whole conversation, smiled. She'd never seen him smile like that. Never seen such a cruel, charmless, vicious look on his face.

Because he knew exactly why she couldn't go to the police.

He finished his drink, stood and left.

The sobs returned with the closed door, making her feel like she was going to throw up. By the time they were done she was on the floor, sitting against the wall. She didn't know how she'd got there. Dominic hadn't returned.

She stood. Leaned against the table. And with nothing other than a sense of grim inevitability, she knew what she had to do.

CHAPTER TWENTY-THREE

Now

She knew the gun was there, knew she should reach behind and grab it and make him get out of her way, let her into the garage, but her hand was not responding to her demands.

John, unmoving, just smiled. 'Ah dang, I think I've gone and scared you,' he said. 'Sorry. Jumping out like that, what was I thinking?'

It was then she saw he was holding the axe.

Charlotte couldn't reply. Absurdly she just shook her head, as if to say it was all fine, no worries. As if anything about this situation was normal.

'Well, I promise I'm not that scary,' John said. 'Jumping out aside. I was just thinking there are some things you and I should discuss. A couple of little matters I ought to come clean about before you go running off.' He nodded towards the garage, as if he knew what she'd been planning. 'I was going to suggest dinner again, but you know, I don't want to keep you in suspense. So how about a drink? Glass of wine?'

Charlotte went to speak but John slapped his head. 'Ah what a doofus I'm being! You never drink, do you?' A wink. 'Tea then. Indulge me?'

The gun. Grab the fucking gun.

'Well?' He was still smiling. Still entirely at ease. She pictured that smile turning to terror as she pulled the gun. Imagined the contorted pain and slow slackening as he staggered and fell when she fired. And the years ahead, always wondering if somehow, maybe, she had been wrong about him.

'Katie?'

'Maybe ... maybe not today, John.'

John winced. 'Ah look, I'm afraid today might be the only day for it. It won't take a minute. Come on.'

He took her elbow. She flinched but he gave no sign of noticing. The axe swung from his free hand. He guided her to the back door of White Republic. Then let her go and unlocked it as her hand went for the gun, covered by the tail of her shirt. Then the door was open and John was standing back, arm outstretched, inviting her in ahead of him.

The axe, in his other hand, was no longer swinging.

She stepped into the lodge. John closed the door behind them. Axe now over his shoulder, he headed for the kitchen. 'Brisk outside, isn't it?'

She could get to the door, be gone in seconds. He would follow but she had the gun. But if he threw the axe ...

'Then, I suppose at least it's not snowing.' The kettle was starting to boil. John dropped a pair of teabags in two mugs. The axe now on the bench, within easy reach. 'Although I hear sometimes it happens in the off-seasons! How magical would that be?'

The gun would be the tell, surely. An innocent man would react with fear and surprise. If John was dangerous, the gun would reveal it.

'Alright,' John said. 'I can tell you're anxious for some answers.'

He sipped his tea, then picked up the axe. He turned, leaning against the bench. Watching her. Her own tea sat there. He didn't bring it over.

'The truth is,' John said, 'that I haven't been entirely honest with you.'

'You're not a writer,' Charlotte said.

John waved a hand. 'Well, that's neither here nor there. What really defines a writer when it comes down to it? I *am* working on a book, but that's not what's important. And it's not really why I'm here.'

His smile grew. Charlotte didn't move.

'But then, I'm not the only one keeping secrets, am I? There's a lot you haven't told me. About your husband, for example. About what brought you here.'

Charlotte said nothing.

'So,' John went on. 'I think maybe I'll offer a little truth for some of the same in return. Your tea is there, by the way. If you want it.'

John didn't move. Neither did Charlotte.

'I was married,' he said. 'She left me.'

He paused as though expecting her to say something, but Charlotte didn't reply.

'Afterwards, I tried to work out why. She told me there was no-one else, but I followed her and found out she was spending time with a much younger bloke, a guy she worked with. Sounds a bit stalkery when I put it like that, doesn't it?' He shrugged. 'Anyway. The young bloke was all charming and energetic, the life of many parties. And I thought, gee, maybe that's what's wrong. Maybe I'm too boring. See, I'd always been a rule follower, Katie. Always did what I thought was expected of me. You ever feel that way, Katie? Like the terms of your life were dictated by someone else?'

Despite herself, Charlotte nodded.

'Now I was a duffer, I'll admit it,' John said. 'Spent a bit too much time trying to be like that young bloke, to see if that changed things for me. You know, dressing young, going to bars. Typical midlife crisis stuff! It didn't work, obviously. So I did something a bit silly. I confronted the young bloke.'

A simmering, terrified energy through her. The truth, right there.

John's smile grew. 'What do you think happened?'

'I don't know,' she said.

'Take a guess?'

She didn't want to say it. Didn't want the confirmation. But what she wanted, clearly, no longer mattered.

'You hurt him.'

'What do you take me for?' John laughed. 'What I did, Katie, was I stopped hurting myself. I became actualised. I finally let go of what was holding me back and I *lived*. I've been living ever since. The adventures I've had, the people I've met.' He approached the table, axe still in hand. 'I'm *alive*, Katie. I'm free. It's wonderful. And because it's so wonderful—' He pulled out the chair. Charlotte flinched. He sat. Placed the axe down in front of him. 'Because it's so wonderful, I always feel terrible for people still held back.

Still weighed down by whatever it is that hangs around their neck. And then I think, well dang, wasn't that me not so long ago? Don't I have a responsibility to help?'

Charlotte didn't answer.

'Now, I've asked if you need help,' John said. 'You say you don't. But I think you're lying.'

'I'm fine,' Charlotte breathed.

He shook his head. 'No, Katie. I don't think that's true at all. I don't think you'd be hiding away up here, avoiding any mention of your husband or your old life, if you were fine. I think something has been eating away at you for a long time.'

The prickle of tears in her eyes.

'I'm fine,' Charlotte repeated.

John ignored that. He looked at her now without a trace of a smile and said, 'I think I know what's weighing you down, Katie.'

He wasn't holding the axe. She could draw the gun. She could hold him at bay and get to the car and be gone. Her hand slipped behind her back.

'What's that?' she asked.

John tilted his head to the side and surveyed her with such sympathy it almost made her head spin. Nobody had ever looked at her like that before.

'Guilt,' he said.

Silence. She didn't grab the gun.

'Am I right?'

Charlotte said nothing.

He leaned further forward. 'Katie. Why don't you forgive yourself?'

The answer was out before she could catch it. 'Because not forgiving myself is what stops me ever doing it again.'

A considering look from John. 'But it's also what stops you living freely.'

Charlotte almost laughed at that. Many things stopped her living freely. A psychopath who thought he was a self-help guru was among them.

'Guilt is a choice,' John said. 'It's a form of self-punishment, and self-punishment is pointless. It achieves nothing. It shackles you. And damn, Katie, I think an unshackled you would be quite the sight. But you need to stop running. You need to stop hiding. And you need to let go of that guilt.'

A sudden, desperate yearning to ask him how. She stopped herself.

He smacked the table. Charlotte jumped. He stood, collecting the axe.

'But! It'll take time. Ingrained habits are hard to break. Anyway. I wanted you to know I'm on your side. We'll get there together. Now, head on back to Snowhaven, yeah? We can catch up later.'

He remained where he was, holding the axe, smiling and unblinking. Charlotte went to speak. Didn't. She backed towards the door.

'Oh,' John said. 'One more thing.'

Charlotte stopped.

He winked. 'Do head straight back, won't you? Would hate for you to get lost.'

* * *

She closed the door of Snowhaven behind her and leaned against it. Her breaths came thick and fast. She closed her eyes. Tried to get a hold of herself. Tried to think.

What exactly was John's game? That he was crazy, probably dangerous, was obvious. But was there some twisted part of him that thought he was *helping* her? Well, clearly that was the case, but how the fuck did stealing her bag and disabling the car and all the rest achieve that?

She didn't know what to feel anymore. Fear was there, along with confusion and anger. It all churned together but somewhere in there was a tiny snatch of something totally unexpected, something almost like hope.

She stamped it down. She was being absurd. John was very likely a murderer. Whatever he said, the story about his ex-wife's new lover sounded a *lot* like it ended in death. It didn't matter that he was dangling in front of her the very thing she had wanted so badly for so long. What mattered was the only thing that had mattered all along – that she get out of here.

She checked the time. She had to get to the car before John noticed the keys were gone. Instinct told her to run straight to the garage, but she knew he would likely be watching. She had to give it some time.

Also she should probably feed Anders.

She placed the bowl of noodles on the floor and slid it to him with her foot. He reached for it, caught the edge with his fingertips and dragged it over. He held up the teaspoon and raised an eyebrow.

'Ideal for noodles.'

'Ideal for not stabbing.'

Anders sighed and started to eat. He grimaced. 'Cold.'

'You want hot food, don't try to kidnap people.'

'Something about pots and kettles comes to mind.'

'So does something about self-defence.'

Anders shrugged and kept eating.

'I'm leaving,' Charlotte said.

Anders stopped, looking at her.

'I got the keys.'

'Is he dead?'

She shook her head.

'Then you are still in danger.'

'Nothing new there,' Charlotte said. 'Anyway. He almost caught me. We spoke and he let me go, so in a few minutes—'

'You spoke to him.' Anders' brow furrowed.

'Yes.'

'And you did not pull the gun.'

'No. He had an axe. He—'

'You have a *gun*,' Anders snarled.

Charlotte blinked. She'd never seen him express this much emotion. He was angry.

'Do you not understand the danger you are in?' Anders pushed on. 'And yet you refuse to make the choices that will keep you alive. If you wanted to die this badly, you should have allowed me to take you in the first place.'

'Not wanting to die and not wanting to kill aren't mutually exclusive,' Charlotte said.

'Right now? Yes, they are.'

'How?' Charlotte could hear her own rising fury. 'I'm still alive. I'm armed and I'm free. Last I checked, you're the one chained up in a fucking basement shitting into a bucket.'

Anders leaned back against the wall. His mouth curled into a bitter smile.

'In my experience,' he said, 'having a moral code means nothing when your opponents lack one. But I suppose the trophy wife of a drug lord would not know much about moral codes.'

Charlotte snorted. 'Says the assassin.'

'It astounds me sometimes how naïve people can be,' Anders said. 'Even in the wake of experiences that should leave them anything but.'

Charlotte didn't reply.

'I was a detective, you know,' Anders said. 'Back in Sweden. Years ago. Lives ago.'

Whether he meant his own lives or others, he did not say.

'I had a case. Several murders. Strange murders. Apparently unrelated. Which, predictably, were linked to organised crime, like most killings are in the end. But these ... they were violent. Extreme. Painful. And the victims? Innocents. Except each of them knew something incriminating about a major player. Just a puzzle piece, really, not enough to make any sense without context. But enough for the major player in question to see them as threats and to think the best way to throw police off the scent was to make the murders look, well ... anything but professional. Most police were distracted by the methods. But I found the link. The mutual ... contacts. I brought it to my superiors. And then ...' A low, bitter laugh. 'Nothing. I was wrong, they said. We had a serial killer. The mob were not involved. I pushed further. I was removed from the force. A false accusation. But I didn't let it go. And so they came for me.'

He pulled up his shirt. A long, knotted scar up his stomach.

'My old colleagues, for a not inconsiderable sum of money, had sold me out to the men I was trying to bring down.'

Charlotte stared at him. Anders looked into his now empty bowl. Turned it, grimaced.

'I fled. Came here. And when it turned out a fake name and no history makes it next to impossible to get a legal job that utilises your skillset, I went for an illegal one.'

The absurdity of Anders' choice seemed, to Charlotte, enormous. 'So you started working for exactly the kind of men who drove you out of Sweden.'

Anders nodded. 'I did. Because the bitter truth of it was that I assumed everyone played by the same rules. They did not. They won. And in the end I was left with no choice but to do the same.'

'What's your point?' Charlotte said. 'That you're a fucking hypocrite?'

He met her eyes now. His gaze was cold and pitiless but Charlotte refused to look away.

'My point,' Anders said, 'is what you are failing to grasp about those who threaten you. Not just them. Human beings do not value life. They claim they do. But if that was true in the slightest, nobody would ever drink or smoke, never drive too fast or pour toxic swill into oceans. It staggers me that we can all know the dangers and still perpetuate the causes. Animals do only what they must to survive, but we seem hell-bent on doing the exact opposite, and then complaining when it blows up in our faces. As if we have been dealt such a harsh injustice. Look at yourself.' He leaned forward. 'You married a drug lord. You knew what Dominic Ford was. You knew his business destroyed people's lives. You knew, eventually, that he murdered people himself. Many people. I know you knew that.'

The bloody clothes in the laundry. Freddie. Victor's attack behind the function centre.

Charlotte still did not look away.

'And yet you stayed with him. You worked for him. You *loved* him. And then it all went wrong and you fled. And when I found you, as you must have always known somebody would, you somehow had the tenacity to look me in the eye and beg me to spare your life. As though you had not done everything in your power to place yourself exactly where you were.'

'What about you, then?' Something was humming through Charlotte, a low defensive anger. 'You think you don't deserve what you get?'

'On the contrary,' Anders said. 'I deserve exactly what I get. But I'm no longer under any illusions that my fate will be due to anything other than luck. For example – the luck of being kidnapped by somebody who refuses to kill.'

'There you are,' Charlotte said. 'The obvious that you're missing.'

Anders raised an eyebrow.

'If everyone's stupid choices damn them, then you don't really leave any room for them to learn to make better ones.'

Anders snorted. 'Because in your experience people do that so often.'

Charlotte looked at Anders for a long time. 'I think they do, actually. I also think it's up to them whether they change for the better or the worse.'

Charlotte left. As she went through the door, Anders called out.

'Charlotte.'

She looked back.

He was watching her, mouth partly open, like he wanted to say something. His jaw clenched. He looked away.

'What?' she asked.

He didn't look at her again. 'Nothing of real value. Only that ... only that I do not think you did it.'

Charlotte closed the door behind her.

CHAPTER TWENTY-FOUR

Then

Not all of my enemies are dead.

Well, it stood to reason, then, that one of those enemies might soon strike. Charlotte's task, now, would be to make it look right. The front-door lock could be broken with a hammer and a screwdriver. Muddy male footprints in the hall – she could stick the boots in the wood heater and light them up when she was done. Shatter the security cameras outside, destroy the hard-drive footage.

Which left the difficult part.

She had buried the gun, along with a silencer, several rolls of cash and a stack of fake IDs, in a nearby park. It hadn't been long after their wedding that she'd collected those things. Dominic never suspected that she'd paid attention, that she'd overheard things. That she'd know the places to go. Guns with the serial numbers filed off. Fake IDs fabricated in a matter of hours, no questions asked. None of it came cheap. Discretion never did. But she had the money.

The plan was to shoot Dominic, then leave the house as though on an errand. Dispose of the gun and return after a few hours to find her husband dead. Call his men in a hysterical panic, scream and cry and break down and drink. Do all the things they would expect of her, all the things that would fit the image Dominic had painted of her.

Maybe some of his closest associates would be suspicious of her. But she would ensure it was far more credible that the attack had come from an external enemy. Let Victor and his other lieutenants go to war and take each other out. Charlotte had swallowed enough pride over the years, she could swallow a little more to play dumb and then – when the smoke subsided – take her dead husband's money and get far away from all of it.

Now she sat at their kitchen table, a half-empty bottle of wine next to a half-full glass. In reality, Charlotte had not drunk a thing since making her decision. The wine had gone down the sink. The gun rested in her lap.

She pictured the scene in her head. She would sit here and stare blankly into space. Dominic would enter, spare her a single contemptuous glance, then head to the cabinet to pour himself a whisky, the same as he did every day before retreating to his study. As soon as his back was turned, Charlotte would shoot him.

She didn't want to see his face.

Which, of course, begged the question of whether she could do this at all. Whether she had it in her. But the worst part about that doubt was how quickly it was offset by the grim truth. Yes, she could. She could shoot her husband dead.

She glanced at the clock. Almost midday, on a Saturday. Dominic stayed 'in the city' on Friday nights, which almost certainly meant with Elizabeth Bates, but being an early riser, he was usually back before now. It could, she realised, be only seconds until Dominic was dead and she'd have to deal with the aftermath, whatever that was.

She closed her eyes and made herself think back to the start, to that night with Mel in the club. The way Dominic had made her feel so special. She played out the memory in her head and all the while tried to determine whether it sparked anything, some long-buried glimmer of that singular feeling he, and only he, had given her. Maybe she was hoping to change her mind, that something undeniable would gallop from her subconscious and show her how wrong she'd been to even consider this.

It never came. There was nothing left of what she'd felt that night, no recognition of the girl she'd been. Young and stupid and insecure, worried about failing friendships and fumbled dreams that she so easily could have picked up again had she just found her own confidence rather than relying on somebody else for it. She wondered, absurdly, how Mel's marriage was doing. What she would think if she knew where Charlotte was now. What she was about to do.

A knock at the door. Charlotte's eyes flew open. She sat up straight. She almost dropped the gun. He was here.

Except.

Dominic wouldn't knock.

Her thoughts spun. A visitor meant she had to call off the plan. It meant a witness. She would have to rework, take a step back and hold off and—

The knocking, again.

Charlotte put the gun down the back of her jeans and stepped into the hall. Through the frosted window in the door she could see a silhouette. She approached, slowly. A swell of cold fear in her gut. Unexpected visitors were rare, especially when Dominic wasn't home. She remembered again their last conversation.

Not all of my enemies are dead, Charlotte. They just haven't shown themselves yet.

She reached for the handle. Looked through the peephole. Blinked – confused – then opened the door and stepped back.

Leo Grey stood on the threshold, hand halfway raised to knock again. He dropped it with an embarrassed smile.

'Hi,' he said.

Of all the people she might have expected to see on the other side, he was not one of them. In fact, now that he was looking at her all stupid and uncertain and apologising if it was a bad time, fear was replaced with irritation. What the fuck could *Leo Grey* want that was so important?

'Can I come in?' he asked.

'Dominic isn't home.' She went to shut the door.

He caught it. 'Actually, it's you I was hoping to talk to.'

'Why?'

Leo gestured past her, into the hall. 'You mind?'

Charlotte stepped aside. Leo entered the hall. She closed the door. He walked down to the dining area. She followed. He didn't sit. He paced the room, looking through glass cabinets and over the probably expensive paintings Dominic had covered the walls with.

'He's got good taste, doesn't he?' Leo said.

Charlotte shrugged. The fear was back – low and crawling and uncomfortable. Nothing about this was normal.

'Why are you here?' she asked him.

Leo, moving along the wall with his back to her, stopped. He turned, looking her over. Then he took a seat at the table. He gestured for Charlotte to do the same. She did, down the other end. Leo looked at his hands.

'I've been given a message,' he said. 'To pass on to you.'

Charlotte stared at him, totally lost now. 'A message? From who?'

'I was told not to tell you,' Leo said. 'That it didn't matter.'

'What's the message then?'

Leo met her eyes. 'Run.'

All air went out of her. She couldn't speak. She couldn't do anything other than stare. Leo Grey, this vapid idiot who her husband kept around to look legitimate, the man she had once idolised, had just blown everything apart.

Run.

Somebody knew. Somebody knew she was planning to kill Dominic. And that meant ...

'Who?' The word came out choked, weak.

'All that matters is that they were adamant,' Leo said. 'I don't know the context. I don't know what's going on. All I know is that they were firm on that. Run.'

'But ... but why? How do they ... What else did they say?'

Leo was shaking his head. 'Nothing. Just that I get that message to you as soon as possible.'

Charlotte was frozen. She remembered seeing Leo and Victor talking in the front yard. But no, that was before she'd decided on this.

Run.

'Charlotte?' Leo said.

Run.

Tears in her eyes. A hollow terror in her stomach. The image of Dominic, covered in someone else's blood, seared into her mind. He had killed before, and would do it again.

'Charlotte?'

She still couldn't move.

Run.

'Charlotte.' He was calm. Direct.

Charlotte looked at him.

She remembered, then, the first time they had spoken. That perfect day after the lecture, she'd been so nervous and awed by the impressive young author, so disbelieving that he'd ever take the time to speak to her. Only three years ago. Jesus. Back then he had shone in the sun. Now he was in her life in a way that would have, to her younger self, been more than a dream come true. But her younger self hadn't known him, known how weak and pathetic and stupid he really was.

Looking at him now, drawn and tired but watching her with intense focus, she wondered if she was wrong even about that. If, maybe, there was more to Leo Grey than she'd guessed.

'What are you going to do?' he asked.

It was almost funny. That first meeting had set her on this path, sent her uncharacteristically into the night looking to celebrate. In the darker times it had been easy to blame him. As if any of it had been his fault.

But then, maybe there was something else at play here. Charlotte didn't believe in God or destiny or any of that. But if she allowed herself the belief that Leo Grey had started all of this, then maybe she could believe that this visit was, on some cosmic level, him ending it.

'Charlotte,' he repeated. 'What are you going to do?'

CHAPTER TWENTY-FIVE

Now

I do not think you did it.

It meant nothing, what Anders thought. In all likelihood he was just saying it to get her guard down, to invite another chance for him to strike. Still, somehow it hit home in a whirlwind of dizzying emotion. It took her a couple of minutes, there on the stairs, to realise that the prevailing one was anger.

She doubted this was a new realisation for Anders. In fact, she thought it likely that the people who had hired him thought the same. They were more concerned about the removal of a potentially dangerous loose end than anything else. That was all she was to them. A pawn that had to be taken off the board.

Unbidden, John's face appeared in her thoughts and with it a rush of searing hatred. Nothing gave him the right to fuck with her, to smugly make choices for her based on some vague bullshit about what would *help*. She could almost imagine him waddling along and seeing her bag, deciding to hide it because of some idiotic belief that the challenge would be *good for her.* What mattered to John, what had mattered to Dominic and Victor and Elizabeth and all of them, was what *they* wanted. Not that she was alive and autonomous and wanted to stay that way. His strange little speech back in the lodge echoed through her head. What patronising, pointless bullshit.

She walked up the stairs, tightening her fists. No more fucking around.

She opened the front door and drew the gun. She left the door open, not wanting to risk any sound that might give her away. She crossed the street at an angle. Stopped at the corner of White Republic, looking around to the dark mass of trees where the garage was. Waited and listened.

Leaves crackled under her feet as she moved. She reached the side door to the garage. Put her back against the metal. Searched for the handle. Gave herself another moment then opened the door and stepped in.

There it was. She'd been sure until that second that John would be a step ahead of her, that somehow he would have managed to move his car. But no, there it was, in the shadows. Something between a laugh and a sob, out before she could stop it. She pulled the keys from her pocket. It was over. She was going. In a moment she'd be in the car, driving away from the mountain, away from John, Anders, all of this. She was …

Something wasn't right.

Slowly, she looked down at the keys in her hand. Lifted them into the feeble light from the open door.

Whatever weak hope had been building slipped away. Charlotte leaned against the car. Closed her eyes. She hadn't thought to check them. But she should have known. Should have guessed it could never be this easy.

The keys were her own.

Morning. From the office window, the lodges were obscured by a heavy fog that had settled in the night. She could barely even see the street below.

She leaned against the wall, arms crossed, eyes on the window despite knowing it was likely pointless. She didn't look at the phone or computer. She was still holding her car keys.

When had he stolen them? Had he put them there knowing what she would do? Whatever the case, she was going to have to assume that almost anything she did from here on, John would have prepared for.

Some of the fog dissipated. She could see the door of White Republic now. It opened. John, rugged up warm in a coat, stepped into the cold and rubbed his hands. Charlotte leaned back. Waited a beat, then checked again. He was walking towards the trees.

There was no other choice. She'd set the traps out there for a reason. It was time to go after him and get what she needed.

You're brave, Charlotte.

How many times had Dominic said that to her? Always when there was something he needed, or when he was trying to convince her she'd done the right thing. Once, hearing that from him had been enough, a crutch that took the weight off asking herself any difficult questions. But a time had come when it wasn't enough anymore. And once, drunk, she had asked Dominic what he'd meant by that statement. What bravery, to him, was.

'That's easy,' he'd said, looking at her like she was an idiot. 'It's being willing to do what has to be done. No matter what.'

What has to be done. How noble that made it all sound. How difficult and tortured and justified. But now she understood, all Dominic meant by 'what has to be done' was harming somebody else. To him, that was courage.

Charlotte knew, as surely as she'd ever known anything, that that was not true. Courage was being willing to harm yourself *for* someone else.

She had harmed herself for Dominic plenty. Harmed others too – the two things were not mutually exclusive. But here was what ate at her: whatever courage she had demonstrated, what was it actually for? Was courage a virtue when the result was only destructive? How many soldiers had demonstrated the most remarkable courage in pointless wars, when cowardice would have served themselves and others so much better?

To do something awful and call it courage was, Charlotte felt, a very effective way to live with yourself. Would it be brave to kill Anders, or John? Maybe. But that didn't mean it was her best course of action.

Charlotte went to the kitchen. She found a calico bag and filled it with cans of food, along with an opener. She filled two water bottles and put them in as well.

Anders jerked awake as she entered the boiler room. She slid the heavy bag across the floor. Still bleary-eyed, he looked inside.

'I could use these as weapons,' he said.

'You could,' she replied. 'But there's not much point. You won't see me again.'

'I've heard that before.'

Charlotte ignored that.

Anders watched her. 'I do hope you plan on being a little more forceful if you want an outcome this time.'

'And I hope it won't come to that.'

Something that might have been sympathy crossed Anders' face.

'Either way, I'm gone,' Charlotte said. 'The moment I'm far enough away I'll call the cops and tell them where you are. If I ... if something else happens, well, you've got the food.'

'You might as well just kill me,' Anders said.

'You'll be fine,' Charlotte replied. 'Tell the police you're an innocent tourist. You recognised me and I knocked you out and ran. By the time they crosscheck you can find a way out.'

'That's if *he* doesn't find me first.'

Charlotte nodded to the bag. 'You can use those as weapons.'

Anders laughed. Charlotte smiled a little.

'You know, you never gave me a proper answer,' Anders said. 'About why you wouldn't kill me. It would be self-defence, essentially.'

'Not with you handcuffed there.'

Anders considered her a long moment. 'Are you hoping that he does attack you? That you can justify shooting him that way?'

'I'm hoping he gives me his keys and lets me go,' Charlotte said. 'If he doesn't, I don't know. Good luck, Anders.'

'Wait.'

She stopped in the doorway.

'That's not an explanation,' he said. 'You might as well tell me. Everybody thinks you're a killer anyway.'

Charlotte closed the door.

CHAPTER TWENTY-SIX

Then

She paid cash for the bus before taking a seat up the back. She pulled her hood down lower and hunched her shoulders, placing a hand on the backpack beside her. It was all she had brought. A couple of changes of clothes, the cash she had hidden and more from Dominic's safe, her fake IDs and the gun.

She looked out the window into the dark bus terminal, heart vibrating, fingers periodically tightening on the fabric of the bag. She only relaxed when the bus finally moved. There weren't many other people on it. All had been on before her. Still, she half expected a car to come careening out of nowhere, or else a volley of gunfire to shatter the windows.

Nothing happened. Not as the lights of Melbourne slipped away behind her. Not as the landscape outside turned flat and rural. Not as, around two am, she finally fell asleep.

Early in the morning, the sky somewhere between heavy grey and deep blue, she changed buses at a country-town terminal. Clutching a styrofoam cup of instant coffee, she watched out the window. Felt the ground below her steepen, saw trees thicken, undergrowth become denser, rougher. Finally, the sun now high and only a couple of clouds drifting around the mountain peaks that fringed it, she stepped out into Thredbo. She stood there in the gentle warmth, looking at the rolling green park and the stone façades of the lodges; at the steep brown and green slope that led up the side of the valley towards Mt Kosciusko, Australia's highest peak; at the chairlift running partway up it even now in autumn for the mountain bikers and hikers. She sat down on a bench. There were tears in her eyes. She smiled. Then she laughed, although it felt more like an attack of violent hiccups.

She was free. She had run and nobody had caught her and she was here in the most beautiful part of the world she had ever known.

Maybe Dominic would try to find her. But she knew well enough how to stay ahead of him. Once his fury died down, maybe he would decide to just leave it, to give up and count her departure as a blessing.

There was no reason to think he would look for her in Thredbo. She'd never told him about the trips up here as a child, how Uncle Mac swore that it was better away from winter, that all those skiers just ruined it. Maybe it was because those golden pockets of time were among the few purely happy memories she had had left. From before adulthood crept in and poisoned everything, when she could still believe that her father and Uncle Mac were nothing more or less than the people who loved her most.

As she sat in that mountainous valley under a high sky, breathing the freshest air she had breathed in years, the idea of murdering her husband took on an air of unreality.

She had not pulled the trigger. She had fled. And nobody knew where she was. In the bus station she'd worn the backpack on her stomach under her hoodie, kept her face covered, and adjusted her walk. If Dominic did somehow get his hands on CCTV footage, if he even thought to, he would not see his wife.

She sat there for a long time, eyes closed, enjoying the warmth on her face.

She had money and while she knew she should be careful with it, she was too overcome with a new and unfamiliar lightness to care. So she went straight to the lodge that she used to stay in with her dad and Uncle Mac. It would be melancholic. But that was okay. This time, this new day, could not be all perfect. And luck was on her side – the woman in the office hadn't let the lodge out yet. Charlotte babbled some explanation about why she was paying cash, but the woman didn't seem to care. She took the key card with a probably too-effusive thanks, then went inside.

It hadn't changed. Stiff couches under generic photos, windows all the way around looking out over the sprawl of the town and the slopes. Charlotte stepped out onto the balcony and watched kids playing in the street, barbecues and easy talk between neighbours, most of whom were probably tourists like herself. It wasn't summer but it was a warm day regardless.

She returned inside and fell into a deep, dreamless sleep better than she'd had in a very long time.

She woke up early the next morning, making a coffee and sipping it on the balcony as she watched the town come to life.

The chairlift was already going. Charlotte remembered how scared of it she'd been as a kid, feeling it jerk up beneath her, huddling into Uncle Mac who would laugh and tell stories about collapsing chairlifts and broken wires while her father told him to shut up despite barely being able to contain his own chuckles.

Today she rode the chairlift alone. It wasn't as warm as yesterday and fewer people were braving the walk up to the peak. Charlotte was buffeted by the wind, her hand on the backpack beside her. She hadn't been sure she should bring it, but doing so was better than risking somebody coming to clean the lodge and finding the gun.

At the top of the chairlift was a dark building that jutted from the mountain plateau like a gargoyle. There was a café inside, overlooking the town below. Charlotte got a hot chocolate and sat in the window, remembering doing the same as a child. Maybe it was the altitude, but she felt strangely breathless.

Things could never go back to the way they were. Too broken, too far gone. But she thought she understood now why she had come back here, and found herself strangely grateful for whatever impulse had prevented her from telling Dominic about Thredbo. Because now, despite everything, the high country still felt untainted, a last safe haven for the girl she had been. The perfect place for her to come while deciding who she would be now.

On gravel paths and the metal-grate walkways that carried hikers over rocks and streams and blueish mountain grass, she headed higher. Around her were gigantic boulders dappled with lichen, and the distant shapes of other peaks. She had never made it to the top as a kid. Too far, too steep. Her father would always take her back as Uncle Mac forged on.

But she remembered one thing. The right turn, onto another path that led to a giant valley, at the bottom of which was a sapphire mountain lake, the deepest, purest blue she'd ever seen. She'd been fascinated by it as a child, never having seen anything so brilliant in its colour. Now, she took what she thought to be the safe path, walking alone along a high ridge, striking off from the mass of hikers making for the peak. There was less wind up here. The sun was weak, the warmth barely there, but Charlotte didn't mind. She walked until she came to the lake. No different from how it had looked when she was a kid. Somehow she'd thought that time might dull it, or else she'd just discover she'd remembered it wrong. But no. It was still there. Still so strange and distinct and *other* it left her almost winded.

She left the path and walked down towards the water.

Down by the edge, it was vast. So strange to think that all these would-be adventurers passed it by in favour of a view not much better than what you got from the café. She sat on a large rock and watched the water. No ripples, no sign of the wind disturbing it. Still. Peaceful.

A glint in the sun drew her gaze. Her wedding ring. She considered it. Once she'd stared at it in disbelief. Later it had become something she absently toyed with, and finally something she tried to pretend wasn't there at all. She pulled it from her finger. Weighed it in her palm.

She threw it into the lake.

The ripples were gone in a second. It was as though the ring had never been there at all.

She looked over her shoulder, up the slope. She couldn't see anyone else.

She wasn't sure what she was doing until she took the gun from her bag. Felt the weight of it. More tears, then. Tears for who she'd been and who she'd never be again.

She threw the gun into the water. That time she saw the ripples.

Maybe everything she'd been through had served to poison even the good times. Because up here, among her favourite childhood memories, other ones, things she'd buried, were emerging. Uncle Mac sneering at her father when he tripped during a mountain walk. Guy watching his best friend with narrowed eyes as he channel-surfed in the lodge and dismissed everything as stupid, fake, brain-rotting.

She'd never fully understood their friendship. Guy, grumpy and stoic, was not an especially charismatic or impressive man. Uncle Mac was the opposite: with his big laugh and winks and robust opinions on everything, he had a kind of magnetism that she would have thought her father would be wary of, especially given all his warnings about Dominic. Or maybe that very thing had informed his warnings about Dominic.

She wished she could call him. And with that came a different kind of wish, another last vestige of the child she'd been. A wish that she could wait here, safe and warm, for her dad to come and collect her and take her somewhere else.

She hoped he was okay. She hoped he hadn't worried too much when he'd heard she was missing. One day, down the line, she could tell him she was okay. Maybe. But to do so now would send him on a panicked search that would likely bring him into Dominic's orbit.

She realised then, with a cold, sad certainty, that this was adulthood. Her dad could no longer protect her. It was her job to protect him.

But maybe there was something she could do. Something to ease his pain. After all, that was a kind of protection in and of itself, right?

Down in the village, she found a payphone. It was late afternoon, the courtyards and wide, undulating walkways starting to fill with families heading for restaurants, tourists to bars. She stood in the booth and closed her eyes and weighed it up and then she dialled Mel's number.

'Hello?'

'It's me. Charlotte.'

Silence.

'Charli? Are you okay?'

'I am. I just wanted you to know that.'

'You just ... what, where are you?'

'I'm away. Somewhere safe. Somewhere I was always happy.'

'What happened? Oh my God, Charlotte, the news, did you ... Let me call the police, I can—'

'Mel. I'm fine. I promise. Just ... do me a favour, yeah? In a few weeks, call Dad. Let him know I'm alright.'

'Charli—'

'I miss you, Mel. I hope you're really happy. I hope ...'

Her voice caught. She saw it then. The alternate life she could have had. Normal disappointments. Normal regrets. Another path.

But it was gone now, and she had to make do with what she had.

Tears in her eyes. 'Bye, Mel.'

She hung up. Stood there, breathing deeply, tears on her cheeks. Then, hands in her pockets, she walked into the cooling air.

She'd switched on the TV upon arriving back at the lodge but hadn't really planned on watching anything. She took a long, hot shower, scrubbing every inch of herself. Mel used to tell her that every time she broke up with somebody she would do that, a kind of symbolic cleanse. Well, it would take more than even the most thorough wash to remove all traces of Dominic. But this felt like a start.

He would know by now, that she was gone. He had probably taken steps to find her already. But then maybe he was trying to keep it quiet, trying to hide the humiliation. She wondered if he felt anything other than angry or embarrassed. If he would miss her. If he had any regrets.

She dried herself off, got dressed and made a cup of tea in the living room. The six o'clock news was starting on the TV. Maybe she'd head into town, get herself a nice dinner. Tomorrow she would have to start planning her next steps. Where she went from here, what Katie McCauley was going to do with the rest of her life. She carried her tea to the window and as she did she heard her husband's name.

'*Dominic Ford, a prominent nightclub owner and suspected gangland figure, has been found dead in suspicious circumstances.*'

Scalding water and broken ceramic at her feet. The teacup

forgotten. Dominic was on the TV, the worst photo they could find of him.

'Police are investigating the apparent assassination and are pursuing several lines of inquiry ...'

And then her own face. One of their wedding photos.

'Charlotte Ford has not been seen since the day of her husband's death. Police are urging anyone with information to come forward.'

A strangled, animal sound escaped her throat.

Dominic was dead.

There he was, in that club, smiling.

Dead.

Their wedding day, at the end of the aisle, perfect in his suit.

Dead.

The day he'd shown her the house they would share together.

Dead.

And then his face, troubled and tortured, as he said the words that would change everything.

There might be something. Something you can do to help.

Her mouth was dry. Her eyes burned. Her stomach heaved, like she was about to throw up. She tried to breathe.

Dominic was gone. The idea was too big, too impossible. She knew, logically, it was true. But all of that had to take a backseat, had to be filed away to sort out later.

Her face had been on the TV. The police were looking for her. What had the newsreader said? Nothing specific, just that she had vanished, that anyone with any information ...

She stood. Supported herself against the couch.

Why were they trying to find her? Was she feared dead too? Or was she ...

Run.

A suspect.

Her sluggish thoughts began to spiral. Each beat of her heart threatened to escape her chest. She faced the door as the pieces started to fall into place. The questions she should have asked, *would* have asked if she hadn't been so blinded by her desire to get the hell out.

Why Leo Grey?

Why send the author? Why not somebody intimidating, somebody connected, somebody who would ensure she did what she was told?

Because they weren't trying to protect her.

It had been a trap. One of his invisible enemies had moved against him. And whoever it was ...

Victor Caine and Leo Grey in the driveway, talking.

Dominic at the dining table, cutting into a bloody steak.

Not all of my enemies are dead, Charlotte. They just haven't shown themselves yet.

Victor Caine, always watching from the sidelines.

The lieutenant, waiting to stick the knife in.

Whoever it was had known that they needed a scapegoat. The unhappy wife everyone had seen try and fail to speak up against him. Who had fled the day of his death. As far as the police or Dominic's associates were concerned, it was far too convenient to be coincidence.

Whoever was behind this had enlisted someone outside the business to warn her. If she *was* caught, she wouldn't be able to identify exactly who the order came from. And when Leo Grey denied knowing what she was talking about, it would be far more likely the cops would believe him than her. Except ...

Pounding on the door. For a moment Charlotte was rooted to the spot, staring.

She ran. Grabbed her bag. More pounding. She went for the balcony. The sliding door was already open. Cold, night. She vaulted over the railing. Landed with too much weight on her left leg. Limped out of the yard. No police cars. She could still hear the pounding from upstairs, faint snatches of a female voice. The woman from reception.

Charlotte loped down the road. She tugged the hoodie from her bag, pulling it on and covering her face.

Maybe Dominic's killer was someone from his inner circle. Maybe not. But if Charlotte was the number-one person of interest for the police, she would be for the syndicate too.

Which meant ...

If the police brought her back to Melbourne, Dominic's men would find a way to get at her before she could prove she hadn't killed him. Before she could point the finger of blame at someone else.

Victor Caine's smirk.

She reached the central part of Thredbo. Saw a couple of cops leaning against their car, talking. Charlotte crossed the road. Kept her head down. Reached the bus terminal and sat. It didn't matter where she went as long as she was gone from here.

Dominic was dead and she would be too if she was found. All that mattered now was to get as far away as she could. To hide. To make sure she disappeared.

The bus was pulling in. She paid cash, got on and took a seat up the back. She waited, tense, until it pulled out and Thredbo disappeared into the night.

She had been wrong. There was no uncorrupted pocket of the world where she could again feel like the person she'd once been. There was no part of her left untainted. There was no blank-slate future.

There was only running. Only surviving.

CHAPTER TWENTY-SEVEN

Now

The winds had got higher. The fog had dissipated a little. She stood outside Snowhaven for a moment, hand on the pistol in the back of her jeans.

The keys. Get the keys, and get out.

She wondered again if any of this was even real. If she was a ghost, then what did that make John? Some otherworldly tormentor, a dangerous spirit she could never get ahead of. Every move she made, he pre-empted. Even the places she'd thought she was safe, he could access. She saw then, with dreadful clarity, her body lying among the bone forest, sightless eyes staring at a mocking blue sky, birds and foxes descending to pick at what was left of her, reduce her to a skeleton before the snow came and buried her. By the time it melted, by the time anyone wandered out that way again, would her corpse be distinguishable from the fallen white branches around it? And meanwhile the police and Victor Caine would keep hunting for Charlotte Laurent, never guessing that she had been claimed by her own safe haven, unable to imagine that what had finally done her in was not an assassin's bullet or an improvised prison knife, but a monster who would disappear the moment he'd finished her off.

She inhaled. The cold air, once so refreshing, now seared. She could taste, somehow, the bite of snow. It should have been months away. But it was coming.

Maybe her lonely, fearful fantasies were right. But succumbing to that belief would not help her. And if Charlotte had long since been disabused of the pleasant fantasies of her childhood and adolescence, then she had to banish the darker ones as well.

John was not a fairy-tale monster. He was a man, however twisted and clever he might be. And while, yes, he had walked the knotted mountain paths and familiarised himself with the lodges and the trees and the slopes, he still would not, could not, be as familiar with them as Charlotte was.

She started to walk.

She didn't look back at the lodge. She crossed the grassy slope. The trees loomed ahead. She didn't take her hand from the gun. She reached the path and slowed as she navigated the familiar peaks and troughs, the rocks and the fallen branches and trunks too thick to easily step over. She knew it all without having to look. She walked deeper into the bush. Between the more distant trunks all she could see was an eerie white, sometimes bleeding into the grey of the ghost gums. Between the clawing trees and the creeping white and the rough and tangled scrub, it was like she was walking through a dream. Or something worse. She did not linger on that thought.

It occurred to her that John could be waiting somewhere in the trees. But why? He didn't know she was coming.

Still, her eyes darted and she listened for any rustle or heavy breathing. For any sign that John, somehow, had anticipated this.

She found him in the clearing where she used to come to read. He was standing with his hands clasped behind his back, his gaze on the leafy canopy above. He'd been so out of place when he first arrived. Now he seemed part of the bush around him, some extension of the danger that lurked in the deep, dark places.

Charlotte stopped. She didn't pull the gun.

'It's even prettier like this, isn't it?' He still hadn't looked at her. 'The mist makes it ... ghostly, somehow. Like a projection from another world. All strange and mysterious. Which the bush should seem, I think. Don't you?'

Charlotte didn't reply. The icy wind bit through her clothes. Something cold that could have been rain, could have been snow, on her face.

Still smiling serenely, John looked at her.

'I need your car keys,' she said.

'But you have your own car.'

'It doesn't work.' Every word out of her mouth sounded bitten off, like she was getting them out before they could betray her. 'Someone stole the spark plug.'

Wide-eyed, exaggerated innocence. 'Well, that's a nuisance! Do you need a lift somewhere?'

What the fuck is his game?

'I know it was you.'

'Now why would I do something like that?'

'For fuck's sake,' Charlotte snarled. 'Enough of this. Give me your fucking keys.'

No reaction. Just the same unchanging smile.

'Or give me back the spark plug. Either way I'm leaving.'

'Leaving!' John exclaimed, mock-horrified. 'You can't leave! We're only just getting to know each other.'

Charlotte shook her head. 'I'm done getting to know you. Whoever you are, whatever you've done ... I don't need to know. I don't need answers. I just need to go.'

'Tell me,' John said, 'is this how you want to live? Always running away when things get challenging? Letting somebody else call the shots? Is that the future you want?'

Charlotte drew the gun and pointed it directly at his face.

John applauded, so loud and echoing in the forest silence that Charlotte instinctively stepped back. Somewhere in the trees a flock of birds escaped into the sky.

'Good!' John cried. 'Better than good, *brilliant*! This is what I'm talking about. You're taking action. You're making calls. You're stepping into your power.'

Tears in her eyes now. 'John, stop. Whatever you're trying to do, just stop, alright? I need to go. Please don't make me hurt you.'

'But I'm not making you,' John said.

'Yes!' Charlotte cried. 'Yes, you are! You've been messing with my head, forcing me into a corner. I just need to leave. People are looking for me, bad people. Can't you understand that? I need to get out of here or I will be killed.'

'So kill back,' John said.

'Why the *fuck* does everyone think that's the only solution?' Charlotte said. 'If you weren't so fucking caught up in whatever bullshit you're trying to pull, then this could just end. If you didn't ...'

She stopped herself. There was no point.

'The keys,' she said. 'Give them to me.'

'First, ask me why.'

'Why what?'

'Why did I take your bag? The spark plug? Why did I cut those cords?'

A distant echo of relief. It had been him. There wasn't some other enemy up here.

'Why?'

John took a step towards her. 'Because I was helping you.'

'I don't want your help.'

Another step. 'You don't want to be better? Braver? Stronger?'

Another step.

'*Stop*,' Charlotte spat. 'Not another step, you patronising fuck. Stay right there.'

John kept smiling. 'Or what?'

'Or what ... what the fuck do you think?' She brandished the gun.

'You won't shoot me,' John said.

'You have no idea what I'll do. What I've done. If you think I'm just going to roll over and let you play out this fucked-up game, then you clearly don't know what you've got yourself into.'

John didn't move. He was still smiling. He took a coin from his pocket. Flipped it. Caught it.

'Enough,' she said. 'John—'

'Let me ask you a question,' he said. 'Whatever it was you did, that you can't forgive yourself for. Would you be so hard on somebody else for doing the same thing?'

'It doesn't matter. It—'

'It does,' John said. 'It very much does.'

'The keys.'

No reply. Still smiling. Still waiting.

It surged through her then. The furious, hissing voice demanding that she pull the trigger and blow that smug fucking smile off this prick's face. Whoever he was, whatever he was playing at, it didn't matter. He was in her way. And the doubt that had held her back was gone.

'What you do now is up to you,' John said. 'I just want you to make the most authentic choice, Charlotte.'

Her real name hit like a punch to the gut. She staggered back. She lowered the gun. John didn't move. There was something new to that smile now. A challenge. An invitation.

Who the fuck was he?

She raised the gun again. Her finger tightened on the trigger. John stayed where he was.

Charlotte turned and ran.

She didn't look back, didn't check if John was following her. Pinpricks of cold in her hair and on her neck – for a moment she thought it was some terrified physical reaction then, seeing the flecks of white through the trees ahead, she realised it had started to snow.

She stopped and spun. The snow drifted down through the thin leaves and bent branches, settling on the path. She couldn't see John. Was he following? He would, eventually. He would pursue her back to the village, and then what?

'*Fuck*,' she whispered.

She looked at the gun in her hand. Anders would have used it in a heartbeat. And yet she could not.

Why now? Back in Melbourne she had been ready to kill her husband in cold blood. What had changed? John was just as much of a threat, maybe more.

More snow. Absolute silence. He still hadn't followed.

She would have to walk out. If she couldn't cross the line, then there was no other alternative.

She kept going. Leaving the trees and crossing the pale green slope speckled with white. In a couple of hours the lodges would look like a fairy tale come to life. Wind buffeted her – more sprays of cold across her skin.

Head down, gun still in hand, she walked down the road, heading for the door to Snowhaven. She would gather what she could and start walking. Maybe she would get lucky, maybe a car would pick her up. Maybe she'd die.

'Drop it.'

She stopped.

A heavyset man in dark clothes was approaching from the direction of the carpark, snow settling on the shoulders of his hoodie. He had a silenced pistol aimed at her.

Charlotte turned. Another armed man, similarly dressed and sized, was coming from White Republic. Another from behind. Two more joined the first man from the spaces between lodges.

The five of them surrounded her. All barrels levelled at her head.

'I said drop it,' the first man repeated.

Charlotte closed her eyes. Knelt and placed the pistol in the building snow.

She had almost believed Anders when he'd said no-one knew where he was. But of course he had called. And now they were here and now she was finished.

She stood, raising her hands. None of the men moved. She wondered if they would shoot her and bring her body back to Victor Caine. She wondered if they would torture her first.

It occurred to her that she wasn't scared anymore. Maybe she'd always known it would end like this. She'd stayed ahead of her past for months. Not a bad run, really. But it was over now and as angry as she could be at these men – and at Anders, John, Dominic, the world – in the end she had made her own choices. She'd chosen to be blind. She'd chosen to be compliant. She'd chosen to run. And now she was here.

'Where's the Swede?' one of the men demanded.

Charlotte nodded towards Snowhaven.

'Dead?'

She shook her head.

'Captive?'

She nodded.

The leader laughed. 'Impressive, skinny bitch like you.'

A quick conferral. 'They'll want him back. Want to know how he found her. Guess we should get him.'

The guns were all still trained on her.

'Right,' the leader said. 'Hands behind your back, then you're coming with us. Don't cause a fucking scene – it won't go well for you. Understand?'

Charlotte nodded.

One of the men moved for her.

Then a voice—

'Hey now, what's all this?'

The barrels swivelled away.

John, a pleasant smile on his face, was approaching from the slope with his hands up.

'Shit,' one of the men growled.

'This is all a bit unnecessary,' John went on. 'The guns and stuff. Can't we talk about this?'

'Who the fuck are you?' The leader's gun was aimed squarely at John's face.

'I'm John,' he said easily. 'I'd say I'm pleased to meet you, but I doubt that's mutual.'

Confused glances between the men.

'What are you up to with Katie here?' John asked.

'Mate, I'm gonna need you to get on your knees,' the leader said. 'Shit luck that you're here, but it is what it is.'

John stopped. He lowered his arms. 'What are you saying?'

'I'm saying, on your fucking knees.'

John didn't move.

The nearest of the men went for him.

Charlotte caught a glint of metal from John's right sleeve.

The man reached for him. The kitchen knife slid into John's hand. He never stopped smiling as he rammed it up under the hitman's jaw.

Silence. Then—

John swung the dead man in front of him. Gouts of blood from his back as the bullets hit. Charlotte crouched into the doorway of Snowhaven, hands over her head. *The gun, the gun was just there—*

John threw the spasming body hard into one of the other men. Keeping low, he launched at the leader, who was still firing but missing, always missing until John stabbed him in the chest, then again. The three remaining guns were trained on him but John had darted around the staggering leader and lunged straight for the next hitman, the knife in his ear and out before he could get off another shot. John ran, ducked, a bullet went over his head and then he was kicking the fourth man's ankle out from under him. He slipped in the snow, head cracking off exposed pavement.

The last hitman, the one John had thrown the body at, was fumbling with his pistol. Charlotte caught a glimpse of his wide eyes, of the panic as he fired and John dived for him. The man hit the ground, managed to scream '*Please!*' then the knife plunged into him again and again, blood spraying as the man gurgled and cried and went silent and the knife kept coming.

Silence.

Charlotte, stricken, could not look away from John. He sat, bloodied, on the dead hitman's chest, breathing heavily, cradling the knife like a child.

She picked up the gun. Stood.

John didn't look at her. He seemed to be in a trance.

Charlotte aimed at his head.

'Oh boy,' John said. 'Oh man. So much fun. God, I needed that.'

His blood-spattered face turned to Charlotte. He grinned.

'Come on,' he said. 'I just saved your life. You're not going to—'

She pulled the trigger.

The bullet sheared along the side of his head. John snapped back and hit the ground and Charlotte was on the bodies, grabbing at their pockets until she found keys – *keys!*

– and she had them and she was running, running from the bodies towards the carpark. She glanced over her shoulder – John had not got up – maybe he was dead, maybe not, what mattered was that the men who had come for her were dead and they must have had cars and if she could just reach one she could be gone.

The carpark was empty, turning whiter by the second. Charlotte ran across it, ran for the road. Further down, in the trees. They had to be here. *They had to be.*

She ran. Her muscles burned. Her lungs screamed. Her feet slipped out from under her. Pain didn't matter. She forced herself up, wincing and gasping, every breath scorching her throat. The cold was biting through her clothes – she hadn't dressed waterproof because she hadn't thought she would need to.

She limped on. The canopy was closing above her but the snow still fell, heavier by the second. Greens and browns and greys all consumed by the growing white and still no car. They wouldn't have parked further than Anders had, even for a silent approach. She kept going.

Charlotte.

The voice like a whisper. She turned, looking back the way she had come. Just road and snow and trees. She could no longer see the carpark.

Charlotte.

It came again. She lifted the gun. Stepped backwards.

And then, framed by the trees, a dark silhouette against the falling snow, he came. Walking, slow and steady. She couldn't see his face. But she heard his voice.

'Charlotte.'

She fired. She missed. He kept coming, without a falter or a flinch.

'Charlotte.'

She fired twice more.

He kept coming. Faster now. Too fast.

She jumped the barrier to the right and ran into the bush. Her feet sank in mud and slush. She struggled on, into the gloom and the cold, shifting around too-close trees, clambering over logs and through branches that tore at her. *Find somewhere to hide, find somewhere safe, find—*

Charlotte.

She slipped and fell into twigs and mud and water. Staggered to her feet and kept going. She was shivering. Her clothes were soaked through. The snow was still coming. It was cold. So cold.

Charlotte.

She had to find somewhere to shelter, somewhere to wait for him, to surprise him before she wasted any more bullets. She had to ...

Dominic's face, hesitant, pained.

Something you can do to help.

No, not that. Don't think about that.

She kept going. Her skin, her bones, all ice.

Anders in the boiler room.

Many deaths are unfortunate. Just as many are self-induced.

The forest ahead was blurring.

The cold. Still the cold.

John's blood-drenched grin.

Come on. I just saved your life.

She couldn't breathe. She tried to push on. *Where was the gun?*

And then the sky. The sky and the cold and *Something you can do* and—

CHAPTER TWENTY-EIGHT

And lying in the snow, Charlotte remembers. They come to her in broken fragments, the memories she wants purged from her, the things she has tried to forget.

Uncle Mac on one of those fishing trips, showing her how to cast a line under the dappled light of the fractured sun.

'Patience,' he tells her. 'Be patient. Let the fish think the hook is just part of the world it lives in. Let it take the bait then reel it in.'

She loves Uncle Mac so she does what he says.

And then Dominic, taking her hands in what had once been their bedroom.

'There might be something. Something you can do to help.'

And she asks him what because at that moment she will do anything not to lose him.

Then she's approaching a farmhouse door. She knocks. God she's scared, but it doesn't matter because fear is an obstacle she has overcome.

'What?' she asks Dominic. 'What can I do?'

He lets go of her hands. Stands and walks. She stays where she is.

'I'm going to tell you something,' he says. 'And I need you to promise me you'll listen until the end. It doesn't make me look good. I'm not proud. And I swear, none of this is how I planned it to go.' He faces her, 'Because there *was* a plan. But you, Charlotte, you being who you are, you turned it all upside down.'

As a child, she focuses as she holds the line.

Waits.

As a woman, she knocks at the door again.

And now in the snow she closes her eyes and whispers *please* because she doesn't want to remember any of this.

'Meeting you wasn't a coincidence,' Dominic says, and she doesn't know why he looks so ashamed. 'You have to understand. I was scared. Desperate. Cornered. I had no choice.'

And oh, the pain on his face, the guilt and the welling tears and she knows she will forgive him anything.

She feels a tug on the line and she looks up at Uncle Mac. His eyes are still on the water. 'Wait,' he says. 'We have to know it's on the hook. Don't move.'

She can't feel the cold anymore. It's inside her. She wants to let it claim her, but the memories, racing now through her flickering mind, will not stop. If she is going to die here, she will die remembering every second of what she did.

But she's never really forgotten, has she? There hasn't ever been a day when the memories didn't come unbidden, bursting through whatever happy moments she might have been near. A vicious paradox. Drink to forget. Wake aching and vulnerable and unable to do anything but remember. Repeat. Ad infinitum.

She never lets Dominic see what it did to her. At first it's because she wants him to believe that she is at peace with it. That she knows it had to be done.

But here in the snow, finally, there is no pretending anymore.

She knocks on the door again. Her heart is so loud. She hopes he isn't home. Looks over her shoulder, to the winding driveway and the trees. So isolated. You wouldn't know this house was here if you hadn't been told.

Silence. She could leave. She goes to turn just as she hears footsteps.

'I fell in love with you, Charlotte,' Dominic says. 'But that wasn't part of the plan.'

The door opens.

'I was supposed to get close to you. Get to know you. To *use* you.' He says the word with such self-disgust. 'But I fell in love, and everything changed and I swore I'd keep you out of it. But now ...'

And she can see that they are about to step into an unknowable void, that whatever has gone between them before now is nothing compared to what is about to happen. She senses this without knowing how and a warning voice whispers at her to shut him up and leave because once they are in that void they can never get out. But she pushes the warning away and leans forward.

Dominic faces her.

Charlotte turns towards the opening door.

'You've been part of this world a lot longer than you realise,' Dominic says.

The fishing line tugs hard, again. Uncle Mac claps. 'Got it.'

The door is open. On the other side, aged a little but still familiar, that warm, roguish smile as Uncle Mac pulls her into a hug and says, 'Charlotte? My God, look at you!'

'Did you ever wonder,' Dominic says, 'why your dad fell out with your godfather?'

Charlotte shakes her head. 'A business dispute, I don't know what ...'

Dominic smiles wryly. 'One way to put it. Your "Uncle Mac" is the biggest heroin distributor this side of South America.'

Charlotte laughs.

Dominic doesn't.

Uncle Mac leads her into his house.

Charlotte, barely hanging on to the fishing line, looks at Uncle Mac, hoping he'll help. He shakes his head but he's smiling. 'This is all you, my girl.'

'Your father has probably always known,' Dominic continues, as if Charlotte hasn't just laughed in his face. 'But people are very good at turning a blind eye. Until they can't anymore. I don't know exactly what happened, but your godfather got greedy. Tried to use your dad's import business to expand his. Your dad said no. Told your godfather to stay away from you. In maybe the only decent act of a profoundly indecent life, he agreed.'

'Wait,' Charlotte said. 'Wait, this ... *Uncle Mac*? No way. He's ... he runs a chain of pubs! He lives in the middle of nowhere, he's a hermit, he's—'

'Incredibly cautious,' Dominic says. 'He lives in the middle of nowhere so that his enemies can't find him. He has armed guards all over his property. When he has to come to the city for work, they spread out on the streets around him, dressed normally but guns at the ready.'

'Wait,' Charlotte says. 'Wait, this isn't—'

'This is *real*.' Dominic's voice is sharp, hard. 'You know how I know? Because the prick has been trying to kill me for months. I had problems with him years ago, back in Sydney. I left, figured I'd stay out of his way. I came to Melbourne. Started working with Victor and the others. Then our operation grew. And he couldn't have that. He's been hitting our shipments, killing our men. Killing *innocents*.' Dominic's voice wavers on the last word. 'Truckies, couriers, people who don't know what they're carrying. His men wipe them out. Kidnap anyone they think might be involved with me and torture them for information. Tonight ... Charlotte, I had to kill someone.' His voice cracks. 'A gunman he sent after me. Not the first. We can't hold out, Charlotte. Sooner or later he's going to get me.'

A growing pressure in her head. It's too big, too much. It isn't possible. More than that, it's absurd. Uncle Mac isn't ... He *can't* be ...

But there are glimmers of uncertainty. The hushed arguments between him and her dad. The way she was told never to speak to him if he reached out. When she'd tried to draw her dad on why, he'd refused to answer. His order made no sense, and privately she'd planned to ignore it, but Uncle Mac *had* never reached out, which stung.

'This isn't happening,' Charlotte whispers.

Uncle Mac leads her into his rustic living room. Deer antlers on wooden walls and a crackling fire casting light over a plush rug. 'Drink?' he says. 'Suppose you can now.' He stops and looks at her, smiling. 'I just can't believe you're here. I'm so sorry I haven't been in touch. Things with your dad were so messy and I was trying to do right. But I missed you real bad.'

He says all of that and Charlotte remembers the photos Dominic showed her, the stories he told. What Uncle Mac does to the men who cross him. What he does to the women. But despite all that his smile is warm and his eyes twinkle and Charlotte is a child again, holding on to the fishing line as Uncle Mac tells her to *reel it in* and she does because she doesn't want to disappoint him and Dominic is telling her it's the only way, otherwise they're all dead.

'You okay?' Uncle Mac asks her.

She's crying as she reaches for the gun.

She tries, of course, to talk Dominic out of it. Let me speak to him, she says. He'll listen to me.

Dominic's smile is so sad. 'He won't, Charlotte. You're a fool if you think he can be reasoned with. That he's anything other than a monster.'

The snow still falls. And maybe it's her broken, spiralling dreams and maybe it's death but a shadow has fallen over Charlotte. She hopes, in whatever part of her mind that remains clear enough to hope, that it is death. That this can all end. She's tired. She's so goddamn tired.

She tells Dominic, okay, if it has to be done, she can lead them to the house. But she can't be the one to do it. Even that, she thinks beneath the terror, even that is such an awful, awful thing to suggest.

But Dominic shoots that idea down as well. Mac's guards – they'll kill anyone who isn't supposed to be there. It has to be someone he trusts.

Uncle Mac is still smiling as she draws the gun.

The fish is big. It is strong. But Charlotte pulls it from the water and Uncle Mac cheers.

'He'll know,' Charlotte says. 'If he's that cautious, he'll know we're together.'

But Dominic is clever. So very clever. Uncle Mac is Charlotte's godfather in name only – he made sure no official documents ever reflected the fact. They only ever saw each other on trips to middle-of-nowhere places because Uncle Mac kept his personal connections a secret. Learning about Charlotte, commissioning private detectives to scrape together whatever intel they could, was Dominic's masterstroke. It never occurred to Uncle Mac that Dominic Ford might court the godchild nobody knew about.

Charlotte begs him, 'Don't make me do this.'

And Dominic looks at her, horrified, and says, 'Charlotte, I would never, ever force you to do anything. Ever.' He comes to her then and embraces her as she cries into his shoulder and he strokes her hair. He kisses her on the head. He tells her he will never forgive himself for asking. That he wouldn't if there was any other choice. He loves her and he wants to keep her safe, but Uncle Mac's men won't know she's anything other than their enemy's girlfriend, and they will as likely kill her as him. Of course, Charlotte doesn't have to do this. Of course, he won't make her. If she wants to leave, he'll understand. But she will be in danger and while he will do his best to defend them both, it's only a matter of time until he faces an attack he can't survive.

'But they'll know, they'll know it was me and—'

'None of them will get a good look at you. He won't want to risk you seeing them. He won't give them your name. By the time it's done,' he says, so matter of fact, so assured, 'they'll be confused, panicked, and that's when we strike. The smart operators will come to our side. The stupid ones will be no threat to you. I will keep you safe. It's the least I could do. The least I would owe you for saving my life.'

The reality, then, begins to penetrate the awful fog of doubt that has descended over her. That Dominic will die if she does not do this.

They have the fish, writhing and struggling on the line. Charlotte asks if they can let it go now. But Uncle Mac shakes his head. This is their dinner. This is the best catch of the weekend. Now Charlotte has to finish it. Take the fish and smack it on that rock. Put it out of its misery.

Uncle Mac takes a step back as she raises the gun. He gapes. Meets her eyes.

'Is it true?' she asks.

Dominic told her not to engage. *He will say anything to make you do what he wants.* But she needs to hear it.

'Charlotte,' Uncle Mac says.

'Is it true?'

He doesn't play dumb. He takes a step forward. 'It's complicated. Charlotte, please. Whatever he's said, whatever he's done to you, please. Listen to me.' He takes another step forward.

Don't forget what he is, Dominic urged her.

'You're a liar,' she tells Uncle Mac. 'A killer.'

'Don't be stupid,' he says.

She fires.

The bullet tears into his right eye. Uncle Mac staggers but doesn't fall. Blood sprays across the wooden wall. Charlotte can't breathe. Her throat has closed. Uncle Mac sways. His remaining eye blinks, locks on Charlotte. It's wide and hurt and terrified and confused.

Uncle Mac takes the struggling, slippery fish from the line. He gives it to Charlotte. She can barely hold on.

'Go on,' he says. 'Finish it.'

Then the sound. It's not a scream. It's not a growl or a cry. It's some terrible combination, this droning wail of agony and a complete lack of comprehension. He does not know what has been done to him. In that moment he is not a monster. He is her Uncle Mac and she has done this and he does not understand and the blood is still spraying and Charlotte is saying sorry again and again and she wants to go to him but Dominic's voice in her head is reminding her that the gun might be silenced but if he does not die straight away his screams will draw the men and even though she's crying and apologising she pulls the trigger again and his head kicks back and his body caves in and the wail dies and then he's on the ground and he doesn't have a face anymore and the blood is spreading and the gun is empty and Charlotte sits on the couch and looks at what she has done.

Dominic told her that she has to stay in the house for at least an hour. If she leaves too soon, the men will know something is wrong. They will not interrupt otherwise. Uncle Mac will have been clear on that, will not want his innocent goddaughter to wonder why he has armed guards. But they must have no reason to suspect anything is amiss.

So she sits there as the pooling blood reaches her feet. She sits and she shakes and she stares. She does not want to look at the mess that was her Uncle Mac. But she can't look anywhere else.

Charlotte arrives back at their house. She's not shaking anymore. She feels nothing. She gives Dominic the gun but doesn't look at him as he embraces her and kisses her and smiles and tells her she's amazing. Now they are free. Now they can be together. Their future is there for the taking.

She still sees the body. She remembers the wail, the sound burned into her memory. That hour sitting and looking at Uncle Mac in complete silence, the hour that never ended.

The little girl wants to impress Uncle Mac. She wants to smack the fish on the rock like he said. But looking at its glassy eye and its mouth opening and closing she knows she can't. The idea of disappointing him makes the tears come, but so does the idea of killing this fish. She tries not to cry. She can't help it.

And Uncle Mac, gently, takes the fish from her. With one strike, it's still. A smear of blood left on the rock.

She whispers to Uncle Mac that she is sorry.

He strokes her hair. Squeezes her shoulder. Smiles.

'It's okay, Charlotte. You're not a killer. That's something to be proud of.'

She wants to believe him. But she doesn't feel proud at all.

CHAPTER TWENTY-NINE

Now

The heat brought her back. Her eyes flickered open. Low, warm light. She tried to move. Her whole body felt weak and shaky. But not cold. The last thing she remembered was the cold.

Very slowly she sat up. She was wrapped in a blanket, on a rug in front of a roaring fire. Everything still looked a little hazy. Music was playing. The Bee Gees, 'Alone'.

She was in the living area of White Republic.

She went to stand but her legs wouldn't respond. She looked to the door. Tried to pull herself towards it.

'Whoa there, whoa there.'

Suddenly John was easing her back. She went rigid. Didn't look at him.

'Relax. You're safe. You're okay.'

The words did not sit right. Hadn't she shot him? Or had that been part of the broken, jagged dream in the snow?

She made herself meet his eyes. There was a bandage around his head, fresh and white.

He touched it with a smile. 'Don't stress, just a nick. Head wounds always bleed a lot.'

He got to his feet and, humming, went into the kitchen. Charlotte sat where she was, like a child in the blankets. With an unsteady hand she looked under them. She was wearing a thick hoodie and tracksuit pants.

'I am sorry, but I had to undress you,' John called from the kitchen. 'Couldn't have you dying of hypothermia. I didn't look, I promise.'

He was back with a steaming mug. He knelt and held it out to her. She didn't take it.

'Charlotte.' He sounded amused. 'You've been unconscious in my living room for hours. If I meant you harm, I would have harmed you already.'

She took the mug. Hot chocolate. She sipped. Her insides flared like embers.

'How do you know my name?' she asked.

'I'll answer all your questions,' John said. 'But first, tell me how you're feeling.'

She almost laughed. This man – whoever the fuck he was – had murdered five people in front of her, devised numerous twisted ways to keep her from leaving, and now he wanted to know how she was *feeling*?

She wasn't sure she had an answer. Nothing that would encapsulate the complete weariness, the sense of a mind scalded by memories she'd spent so long avoiding. At least she knew now what would flash before her eyes when she finally did die. She sipped the hot chocolate again. She said nothing.

John chuckled. Slapped his knees and raised his hands in a gesture of concession. 'Alright, alright, Little Miss One-Track-Mind. Ask away.'

'My name,' she repeated. 'How?'

John's smile was almost pitying. 'That part should be obvious. For a little while there most everyone in the country knew your name. I mean, you know how the news cycle is. Things blow up then they die off. Interest goes elsewhere. But not for me. I remember seeing your photo in the papers – I generally keep an eye on them, looking for reviews of my own work, so to speak. I know, I know, I'm vain.' He winked. 'Anyway. I remember being fascinated by you. The missing wife of the dead narcotics kingpin. Had you done it? Killed him, I mean? No, no, don't tell me.' He waved frantically. 'Don't spoil it. My theory is you hadn't. But that just made it more interesting. If you didn't kill your husband, then where were you? Had he had *you* killed? Were you on the run? It was a mystery and a half. But I didn't think I'd ever know the answers. Until.' He bounced a little in his seat. 'I was passing through Burnley. Looking for a change of scenery. Then I saw you.'

For a long moment he said nothing, just watched her with a considering smile.

'I have a good memory for faces,' he said. 'But that wasn't how I recognised you. No, I'm not *that* good. What I saw was the fear. You were trying so, so hard to look normal. Which of course was the giveaway. The determinedly looking forward, that stiffness in how you held yourself. The very slight sheen of sweat when the sun hit right. Oh, you were interesting. So, I stood outside the post office. Pretended to be on my phone. You walked out, gave me a quick look, then kept going. Into the café for your little job interview.'

Somebody *had* been on the street that day. But she'd had no reason to take note of him. He'd seemed so normal.

'That look was enough,' John said. 'It sparked the memory. And I just thought *wow*. You know, I try to do what all the books say, to manifest the things I want, but I do wonder sometimes if that *law of attraction*, *ask the universe* stuff is a load of bullhickey.' He winced a little as if he'd said something deeply offensive. 'But, well.' He gestured at her.

'But that … that was weeks ago,' Charlotte said. 'Ages before you turned up.'

'Well, you don't want to rush these things,' John said. 'You became my little project. I had to learn as much about you as possible. And, of course, figure out just where in the heck you were hiding.' He beamed. 'I've gotta say I'm proud of myself there. I did a little research on the area and found out about Mount Skillion. I looked at the maps and the accommodation websites and I thought gee, I know the other resorts have year-round residents, but somewhere this small? I mean, it would have to have at least *someone* to …' He whacked himself in the head, eyes wide and mouth gaping. 'And it hit me! If I was a mafia wife, or whatever the term is, on the run and under suspicion for murdering my husband, where would I hide out? This place … my God, perfect. You'd never be disturbed, not until winter, anyway. Make some money, free accommodation, the job is so unappealing that nobody would look too closely at your credentials.

'Have to say, I felt pretty chuffed there. But still, I wanted to know more. Did you know there are whole internet – what do you call them – message boards? Chatrooms? No idea, anyway, there are— *Forums*! That's right, forums. There are forums all about you and your husband. All these conspiracy theories about who killed him, where you might be. And man, I have to say, that was a trip. Imagine if I just told them! I never would, of course.' His expression turned suddenly serious. 'I hope you know that I respect your privacy. But still. Having a secret like that ...' He whistled. 'Anyway. The more I read about you, the more I wondered. The more interested I was. And what really drew me was seeing you that day. How scared and sad you were. How much you were trying to hide it. Whether you killed him or not, this is no way for anyone to live. And you're so young. It won't do. So I returned to Burnley. Waited. Saw you again. And here I am.'

'Here ...' Charlotte stared at him, wondering if she was still half-conscious. 'But *why*? What do you want from me?'

'Charlotte, I've *told* you,' John said. 'I want to help.'

'But you ...' She swallowed. 'Okay. John, I appreciate that. And I appreciate what you ...' She glanced in the direction of the street. 'But I just, all I want is to be left alone.'

'And keep living like this?' John said. 'Jumping at shadows, always wondering when they're going to find you?'

'It's better than dying.'

'No, it isn't.'

Silence but for the fire.

'That's my choice to make,' Charlotte said. 'Not yours.'

'Of course,' John said. 'But you're still wrong. This is worse than death. This petrified, shadow life. How could you be happy like this?'

At that, Charlotte couldn't help a strangled laugh. 'Happy? Jesus Christ, happy went out the window for me the moment I met Dominic Ford. Right now, I'm settling for alive.'

'And that,' John said, 'is precisely your problem. I know what you're thinking. I know you don't want me to help. That you'll tell me not to. But that's part of the process. I *am* going to help you, Charlotte.'

'How?' She could hear the wild confusion in her voice. 'By turning up here, stopping me from leaving, pretending to be a writer—'

'I never said I was a writer.'

'You ... *what*? Yes, yes you did, you said—'

'I said I was working on a book. It's not the same thing.'

She just stared at him.

'Tell you what.' John got to his feet. 'It might be easier if I just show you. Stay put, would you?'

He strolled out of the room.

Some strength had returned to her limbs. She could probably stand, get out of here and ...

It struck her then. *The gun*. Where was the gun?

John was bustling back into the room, holding a huge, heavy-looking scrapbook.

'Had this in my car before. Please be gentle.' He sat back down and opened the book. 'I've never shown this to anyone.'

'You took my gun,' Charlotte said.

'Obviously.' John didn't look up from the book. 'You shot me. Here. Start from here.'

He opened the book to the middle and slid it across to her, turning it as he did. With no idea of what else to do or say, Charlotte looked.

Spread across the pages in front of her were several newspaper clippings.

Insurance Salesman Murdered in Home.

Policeman Found Dead in Car on Outback Highway.

Wife of Suspected Killer Speaks Out – 'I Never Could Have Guessed.'

Charlotte turned the page. A lead-pencil sketch, surprisingly detailed, of a young man in a leather jacket with long, scraggly hair. Another, over the page, of a middle-aged, overweight policeman. She turned back. More articles. More sketches. A weedy man in a dressing gown. A sad-looking older woman. Forward again. A young woman, distinctive due to the three scars around her left eye – one above, two below.

'These …' Charlotte kept turning, transfixed.

'Told you,' John said. 'I have a good memory for faces.'

'Are these …' She swallowed. 'Are these people you've killed?'

'Some of them.' John gave a dismissive wave. 'The ones I couldn't help. But at that point, what's the difference? *Dead*-dead is less painful than *living*-dead. If you know what I mean.'

Charlotte didn't. But she knew an implicit threat when she heard one. She closed the book.

'How?' she said. 'How will you help me?'

'I already am.'

'But—'

'All good things come to those who wait,' he trilled.

It was hard to pull her brain into focus. That John was insane was obvious, just like the fact that he was not about to pack up and leave if she told him he'd succeeded, that she was now actualised or whatever. Which left her, in the immediate moment, with one option – figure out what she could about him, and then figure out how to use that information.

'You killed five men out there,' she said. 'All with guns. You had a knife. How?'

He just kept smiling. 'You saw how.'

'But how?' She leaned forward. 'How did you know what to do?'

John glanced towards the door. Cocked his head to the side. Looked back at Charlotte, one eye narrowed.

'I have a secret,' he said.

She had to keep him talking until she worked out how to play this. 'Which is?'

John shifted a little closer. Charlotte resisted the urge to scurry away.

'I'm not scared,' he said.

For an absurd moment Charlotte wondered if he meant scared of her.

'You're not—'

'Fear is a choice. Or rather, to *not* be scared is a choice. Here's the thing: in a dangerous situation, the outcome is probably going to be the same regardless of how scared you are. In fact, the more scared you are the less likely it is to go your way.'

'Fear can keep you alive.'

John shook his head. 'There's a difference between fear and caution. Fear makes you stupid. Desperate. Reckless. But if you accept the outcome, whatever it is, and take fear out of the equation, it's far more likely that you can make things go your way.'

She thought of Anders, still handcuffed in the boiler room.

'Those men out there,' John said. 'They were scared. Not of me particularly. But they were scared of the trouble they'd be in if they killed me and that caused an investigation. They were scared of what their bosses might do if they had to report killing a civilian, scared that they'd be in trouble for not checking all the lodges before bailing you up. That fear distracted them. Slowed them down. And meant that they didn't pay any attention to the very real threat in front of them. Then' – he raised a finger – 'after I got the first one, it was a different kind of fear. A better kind, for me. It was panic. It was *what the heck are we dealing with*? Their minds were reeling. They weren't shooting straight. After that' – he shrugged – 'it was pretty easy, really. And you and I are still alive.'

'More men will come,' Charlotte said. 'When the dead ones don't report back, they'll send more.'

'And they'll be more prepared,' John said. 'Except they won't know what for. Besides which, if I was the one sending them, I'd assume you'd be gone by now.'

'That won't stop them.'

'Of course it won't,' he said. 'But that's the other thing about fear – it makes people predictable. Makes it easier to work out how they'll handle things. The big bad men back in Melbourne, they're scared of you, Charlotte. You think whoever replaced your ex-husband gives a hoot if you killed him or not? You practically handed the new boss his promotion! No, they're scared of what you *know*.'

'I don't know anything.'

'Think they'll take that risk? Besides, that's not the point. Right now, you're scared of each other. And that's a balance that you can tip.'

He stood and went to the kitchen, whistling along to the

music. Charlotte managed to stand. She swayed but kept upright.

'Let me leave,' she said. 'Give me the spark plug for my car and I'll go. Give me the chance to just slip away and—'

'And what?' John leaned in the doorway, looking back at her with an almost fatherly smile. 'Keep running and hiding and being too scared to kill to defend yourself?'

Uncle Mac's horrible dying wail.

'That's not—'

'I'm sorry, but I do have to insist,' John said. 'We're not going anywhere. I'm not finished yet.'

Charlotte might have cried, if she had any capacity for tears left.

'Now, I have things to do,' John said. 'Get a good night's sleep. I'll come and get you when we're ready to start.'

'Just like that,' Charlotte said.

'Of course!' John said. 'I'm not a jailer.'

Watching him, Charlotte moved for the door, the blanket still around her. John stayed where he was, that beatific smile still in place. She reached the hall. Started backwards down it. In the shadows, she couldn't see John anymore.

'Oh, one more thing,' he called.

Charlotte stopped.

'If you try to run away, I *will* kill you.'

Outside it was freezing. Dark. It wasn't snowing anymore but the ground was pure white. The bodies were gone. There was no sign of blood.

She crossed to Snowhaven and stopped in front of the door. She looked back at White Republic. Looked down into the dark where the road led away. John had followed her. Was she willing to try again, to take the chance that he hadn't tampered with the assassins' cars, or sent them off the same way as Anders'?

She locked the front door to Snowhaven behind her. She shivered, then started up the stairs, towards her room. It would be a mistake to sleep. She had to be alert, ready. But she was so tired she could barely stand and the idea of trying to do anything to head John off now was enough to make her lie down and give up. Besides which, he had a point – he'd had plenty of opportunity to kill her and hadn't.

She stopped.

Anders had been ready to hand her over to men who would murder her. But she could at least try to bargain with him. If she took him up on his offer, let him go and sent him after John, maybe pretended somehow that she still had the gun, she could at least cause a distraction. Maybe.

She reached the door to the boiler room. She grabbed the handle but didn't open it. She closed her eyes and rested her head against the wood.

She opened the door to an empty room.

CHAPTER THIRTY

It didn't take her long to search the lodge, even moving slowly, gingerly. She ensured the doors were locked, for all the good it would do. Then she returned to the boiler room. She wasn't sure why. Maybe because it was warm down there. Maybe because she was hoping Anders might have left her a clue or a message, although there was no reason to think he would or could have. Either way, there was nothing down here except the open handcuffs, hanging from the pipe.

Had John let Anders go? Killed him? Transferred him to a different captivity in one of the other lodges? It was impossible to guess because it was impossible to work out the motives of a ...

She couldn't even bring herself to *think* the words. They were so strange, so foreign even to the complicated life Charlotte had led. And yet she had to acknowledge it. John was a serial killer.

Shocking herself, she burst out laughing. Huge, whooping, impossible-to-control laughs that made her double over. She collapsed to the floor. She kept laughing, so hard that her stomach hurt, that she was struggling to breathe. She laughed until she had nothing left and then she sat against the wall and wiped her eyes and laughed some more.

A serial killer. After everything that had happened, everything she'd done and been through, a fucking *serial killer*? She had wanted to escape her old life. She had wanted freedom but known jail or death were more likely, and equally deserved. But to end up stranded on a mountain with a serial killer ...

She wondered what Mel would think if she knew. What Dominic would. What Uncle Mac ...

Laughter died. She leaned her head back against the wall.

It was what she could never tell Anders, for all his probing about why she couldn't hurt him. An answer she probably hadn't fully understood herself until the snow. But it was the truth, laid out and undeniable. She had murdered – she swallowed, made herself say the word out loud – she had *murdered* her godfather. She had seen up close what death looked like, death that was protracted and painful and deliberate. The blood. The wail. The nightmare wrongness of what somebody looked like after another person had chosen to end their life. She had done that. Whatever Uncle Mac had been, whatever he had done, Charlotte had killed him. Many, many people would say he deserved it. He had chosen his path. But that didn't change how much Charlotte had loved him, the fact that he had been kind to her, made her feel safe and cared for.

She tapped the dangling cuffs. Looked towards the door.

Anders was gone. She no longer had any doubt about John. Did that change things? Could she, figuratively speaking, pull the trigger if the moment came?

Her fists clenched.

What she could *not* do was wait around for whatever fucked-up game John was playing. She had to get the upper hand and get clear before more men turned up. That meant using what she knew about him.

If you try to leave, I will kill you.

She tapped the cuffs again.

She slept. She didn't know how, just that she needed it. Four restless, dreamless hours and she was up, the sky still dark outside.

She got to work.

In the storage cupboard near the boiler room she found candles – long ones – and burnished brass holders. She chose a relatively small one, a shallow dish with a spike in the middle for the candle itself to be stuck on.

Near the back of the same cupboard she found a ball of string. Only one and a lot of it had clearly been used. That limited how much she could practice, but she would work with what she had. Finally, she took a half-dried old tube of superglue, then ducked out the back into the cold. There she found a couple of rocks, partly buried in wet dirt, small enough to hold and obscure in one hand, but with some weight to them.

The first couple of attempts did not work. The string was tied in the wrong place. The rock wouldn't hold. The candle was unsteady. She reappraised and tried again. She got more candles from downstairs, marked each of them in the same spot, lit them all simultaneously, and then timed how long it took them to burn down to where she had marked. She tested the whole thing again, with superglue this time.

A knock on the door. Charlotte gathered everything together and shoved it out of sight behind the kitchen counter. She looked out the window. Early afternoon, based on the light.

John was on the front doorstep, rocking back and forth on his heels as if everything was normal, as if he didn't have a bandage around his head, hadn't killed five men yesterday and threatened to kill her if she ran.

'Get some rest?' he asked.

She nodded, one hand on the door.

'Good, good. You need to take it easy after an ordeal like that. But not *too* easy. Can't get complacent!' He chuckled. 'Anyway, I'd love you to come round for dinner tonight about seven. No, no, I won't hear of a polite refusal! I promise it will be worth your while.'

After a moment, Charlotte nodded again.

'I can't wait!' John crowed. 'I mean I *will* wait, good to build some suspense. But still, oh boy. This'll be a good'un. The best'un, if I do say so myself. See you at seven!'

He practically skipped back to White Republic.

By four o'clock, she had stopped practising. With no more string to waste it was pointless. So she paced. In her head she went through the layout of Bushmill over and over again. She knew it well after all her attempts to remove the stubborn mould.

The clock ticked on. It hit five, then six. Time dragged. Fear fermented by the second. Charlotte closed her eyes and repeated her breathing exercises. Then ran through the steps again. She checked, for maybe the hundredth time, that she had everything. The candles, handcuffs and spiked holder in her jacket pockets. The two rocks and remaining string in her jeans, along with the lighter and the glue. None of it seemed enough.

It was nearly seven. She checked through the office windows. All the lights in White Republic were on. She could hear faint music. Whatever John was planning, he was going all out. With a bit – a lot – of luck, Charlotte would never know exactly what that was.

Ten to seven. A steadying breath that didn't steady her very much. Then she went to the front door. Gave herself a moment, then stepped out into the cold, the deepening dark kept at bay by the glaring lights of John's impending party.

She moved low and fast, up the road and into shadow. Every muscle in her body was tensed, ready for a bullet. She caught herself before she could look over her shoulder and see if John was following. She'd timed this. He wouldn't come yet. Nor, she was fairly sure, would he shoot her.

The dark void of the carpark and the road and trees beyond was getting closer. But Charlotte turned hard towards Bushmill. She keyed in the code, finally allowing herself a glance back towards White Republic. No opening door, no pounding footsteps. Not yet.

She stepped inside. The smell, somehow, was even stronger now, making her cough. She had to push through. She ran for the stairs. She didn't need to be light-footed, not yet.

The floor of Bushmill was tiled, making it a lot harder to set traps the way she had in White Republic. But the stairs were wooden. And it was there that she had prepared.

She remembered which ones she'd fixed. Had made herself memorise the numbers. Four, six, seven and nine. She went for four. Pressed her hand against the riser facing outwards under the lip of the step. She pushed. With a creak, it gave. She adjusted it until it sat at an angle, allowed by the removal of screws and brackets and pegs. The tread above would remain level until it was stepped on, then it would collapse, sending anyone heading up the stairs back down to the tiled floor below.

She looked over her shoulder. The front door remained closed.

Faster.

She did the same at the next step, then the next. She reached the landing. Hurried down the hall to the guest room that overlooked the street. Checked the window. The angle made it tough to see but light still came from White Republic, although she couldn't hear the music from here. She checked for moving shapes on the road below. None, yet.

Faster.

She dropped to her knees beside the stripped bed. Tied one end of the string around one of the legs, then unfurled the rest, which she had already tied multiple times around a rock. She stood and tossed it up, over one of the exposed beams in the roof. It worked. The rock swung. Charlotte listened. Still nothing.

The candle next, jammed onto the spiked holder. The remaining superglue on the floor, right next to the bed leg the string was tied to. She placed the holder on the glue, held it down, then grabbed the taut string leading up to the beam over which the rock hung. She pulled it, jerking the rock upwards. She wrapped the string around the top of the candle, less than a centimetre from the wick. Let go. The angle was right. The candle stayed where it was. The rock hung still.

She returned to the window. Nothing outside. She checked her watch. It had just passed seven. John would be expecting her, *if* he hadn't seen her head to Bushmill. She swore – she could be in for a long wait if so, and her vantage point was terrible. Had he really not been watching? Did he trust that she was so scared she—

Movement, below. A figure, approaching down the centre of the road. Slow. Easy. Ambling. Charlotte squinted. He wasn't turning towards any of the other lodges.

He slowed in front of Bushmill.

Her heart a panicked drumbeat, she dived for the candle. Lit it. Then out the door. Light-footed and careful down the stairs, skipping the trapped ones. She reached the bottom.

A beep from outside. Then another. He knew the code.

How?

She ducked right, into a locker room. The mouldy smell, pungent and oddly sweet, even stronger here, made her head swim. She wedged herself in behind one of the lockers. Took the second rock from her pocket.

She heard the front door open. Bit back a whimper.

Footsteps in the entry hall. Then silence. Charlotte held her breath.

They moved forward.

Up the stairs, go up the stairs.

Seconds ticked by. No more steps. He was staying right where he was. Unmoving. Listening.

Come on, come on, come on.

Another step. Then another. Louder. He was heading for the locker room.

Tears leaked from her eyes. She blinked them away. Lifted the rock.

Come on. Please work, please—

The steps stopped right outside the door. She heard him begin to push.

Then a thud from upstairs. It had worked – the candle had burned through the string.

The door stopped.

Take the bait. Take the fucking bait you psychopath, take it.

Footsteps receding. Heading for the stairs.

It was working. *It was working.* She took the handcuffs from her pocket. Hefted the rock. Moved out from her hiding place and—

Slipped on something slimy. Instinctively she reached out, grabbed one of the lockers, steadied herself as the door swung open and something large and heavy fell out, hitting the floor with a wet slapping sound.

The smell overwhelmed her. But not as much as the sight of the body, skin yellowed and stretched and broken in parts, viscous white liquid seeping from it, eyes sunken and empty.

She caught her scream. It escaped as a choked gasp.

The door burst inwards. Charlotte spun, raising the rock, but it was too late, far too late. John had her against the locker, something hard and biting on her wrist. She tried to hit him, tried to lash out but he shoved her and she landed on the body. Too much give, moisture through her clothes and the smell and the awful face in hers and she screamed. She screamed as whatever was on her wrist pulled hard. She lurched off the body, kicking and writhing, dragged towards the door by one arm. She caught a glimpse of the rope, of John disappearing around the corner, dragging it, dragging her. The rock was gone along with the cuffs. She scrabbled at the noose around her wrist, trying to loosen it, but then she was slamming into the wall and pulled around the corner, out the front door and down the stairs, into the cold.

CHAPTER THIRTY-ONE

She screamed for help. She screamed for John to stop. She screamed words she didn't even understand. Her hand was about to come off. Her shoulder strained in its socket. Concrete scraped at her. Still he dragged her.

Then the hard jarring stairs and light and warmth but the wooden floor like sandpaper. He stopped dragging. She tried to stand. He hit her in the face. Blackness at the edges of her vision and pounding in her head.

She was wrenched upwards. Shoved into a seat. She tried to lash out at him but her unbound wrist wasn't moving. John was shuffling around her, doing something but she couldn't see properly so she tried to kick but now her legs wouldn't move either.

She blinked hard. The image in front of her took shape.

She was sitting at the dining table in White Republic. There was a candle. A white tablecloth. Bee Gees on the stereo. A fire going. Her right wrist was zip-tied to the arm of the chair. Her ankles to the legs. But her left wrist was still stuck tight in the noose, about half a metre's slack from where John had tied the rope to the other arm.

'Now,' John said, sitting across from her. 'I am really sorry about roughing you up like that. No fun for me, I can promise you.'

Charlotte spat at him.

John chuckled. 'Alright, alright, I probably deserve that. But to be fair I did tell you not to leave.'

'Didn't leave.'

'On that.' John leaned forward, hands clasped. 'What *were* you doing? The noise upstairs – was that supposed to be a trap?'

Charlotte didn't give him the satisfaction of a nod.

John whistled. 'Very clever! It might have worked too, depending on the outcome you wanted. I'm assuming there was something to incapacitate me, then you'd pull a little ambush? I *love* that. That's what it's all about.'

'The body. Who ...'

John smiled and she knew.

He had the combinations to all the doors. Liam hadn't been answering his phone.

'Oh my God,' she breathed.

'To be fair, that man really wasn't doing a lot of living. Sitting around staring at the TV and drinking too much beer. I watched him for a few days before I decided. I needed what he had and let's be real, he wasn't a loss to anyone. If he could die so you could live, well, fair trade.'

'No,' Charlotte said. '*No*. What, how do you ... I never wanted this! How are you not grasping that? You ...'

It didn't matter. She was appealing to the logic of someone beyond logic.

'Forget about Liam.' John waved a hand. 'I'll bet the rest of the world already has. We're here to talk about you.'

Charlotte pulled at the rope.

'I've left you some reach there.' He nodded to her left arm. 'But we'll get to that. First, let me get dinner going.'

He patted the table, stood, and left the room. Charlotte lunged for the candle but it was too far. She reached across to her right hand, tried to get her fingers into the noose. It was tight and the zip tie left her without much dexterity. And then John was back, a big steaming platter in his hands. He placed it on the table.

'Hope you like fish!' he said. He took a pile of plates from the chair next to him and distributed three – one in front of Charlotte, one next to her, one in front of himself.

'Who …' Charlotte began.

John placed a fork next to her plate.

Charlotte grabbed it, lunged. John backed easily away.

'Come on, come on,' he said. 'There'll be plenty of time for that kind of thing. But first, dinner! Although …' He looked at the empty spot next to Charlotte. A mischievous smile. 'I do think I might be forgetting something …' A raised finger. 'I know!'

He left again. Charlotte reached over, getting the hand of the fork under the zip tie.

John returned. He placed the familiar gun next to his plate, winked at Charlotte and left again.

She could not reach the gun but her eyes remained locked on it as she tried to break the tie.

A trundling sound. Charlotte pulled the fork away.

'Our surprise guest!' John announced from the next room.

A hope she hadn't even realised she was feeling died as he wheeled Anders into the room, gagged and zip-tied to a wheelchair. His face was terribly bruised, one eye swollen shut. John guided him next to Charlotte. Anders did not look at her.

'You've been holding out.' John returned to his seat. 'Keeping a man in the boiler room! The scandal.' He crowed with laughter. 'Anyway, we're all here now. I thought, given the subterfuge – is that the right word, subterfuge? Anyway, doesn't matter. Given all the secrecy and mistrust and whatnot, it would be nice to air everything out. Have a bit of an open forum on our situation.'

'Hard to have an open forum when he's gagged,' Charlotte said.

John slapped himself in the forehead. 'Ah, I'm a duffer! You're completely right.'

He came around behind Anders, started to untie the gag.

Charlotte looked from the fork in her hand to where John stood. Out of reach, just. She'd likely get Anders.

John tossed the gag away.

Anders grimaced, opening and closing his mouth as if to remove a bad taste. He looked sideways at Charlotte. 'Didn't I say you should kill him?'

John applauded. 'Trust a European to cut to the chase.' He rounded the table, using a spatula to break up the fish and deposit some on everyone's plate. 'Now Anders, I will have to hand feed you, I'm sorry to say. But it's delicious, so the humiliation will be worth it.'

'I am well used to humiliation by now, thank you.'

'See?' John nodded to Anders. 'There's no need to be uptight. We can all do with a good laugh at ourselves.' He sat again, rubbing his hands. 'Dig in, please. Be good to have a full stomach for what's ahead.'

Charlotte didn't take a bite. John, meanwhile, had already started. He let out a satisfied moan. 'That, that right there, is my best work. Charlotte, please try some! Oh, and Anders – sorry! Here's me rudely starting without you!'

He stretched across the table, using the fork next to Anders to break off some of the fish and feed it to him. Charlotte eyed the hitman, wondering if he would try to bite John's hand.

John gestured to Charlotte. She took a small mouthful. It tasted like rubber.

'Good, good, we're underway.' John ate some more, smiling and nodding to the music. 'Now, seeing as Anders has set the tone, I might pick up the baton and run with it if that's all the same to everyone. Charlotte. Why *haven't* you killed me?'

Charlotte looked from John to Anders.

'Come on Charlotte, we can't move on until I get an answer,' John pushed.

'Because I'm not a fucking psychopath.'

'God, I dislike that word,' John said. 'Everyone just lobs it about without thinking.'

'Are we supposed to draw a different conclusion?' Anders said.

'Now that's a touch hypocritical,' John said, 'coming from someone who kills for money. *Money!* No deeper meaning, no purpose, nothing.' He shook his head. 'I don't want to be rude, Anders, but it's a little mercenary of you.'

Charlotte laughed before she could stop herself.

John and Anders both looked at her.

'I'm sorry,' she said, 'but what's the point of this? John, or whatever the fuck your real name is, you don't care why I've done anything I've done. That's not what any of this is about. You're looking for a reason to fuck with us. Torture us, kill us, whatever. Seeing as that's where it's going to end regardless, can you just get the fuck on with it?'

'That,' John pointed at Charlotte, 'is a very defeatist attitude.'

Charlotte shrugged.

'So, you've given up then?' John said. 'You're just going to let me kill you rather than fight back?'

Charlotte didn't reply.

'You had so many chances,' John said. 'You had me – what do the Americans say? – dead to rights, back in the trees yesterday. By that point you knew I was a threat. But you still couldn't shoot me. Now, the easy assumption there is that you were too scared to. But I've watched you for a while, Charlotte. I've paid attention. And I don't think you're a coward at all. You're scared, sure, but you're also, I hope you don't mind me saying, very courageous.'

Silence but for the warbling Bee Gees. John was watching her with a different kind of smile to what she'd seen so far. An almost gentle, coaxing one.

'If I'm right about that,' he said, 'which I think I am, then why couldn't you kill me?'

'I wasn't sure,' Charlotte said. 'I wasn't sure what you were.'

John shook his head. 'No, I don't think that's true. I don't think your instincts are so easily confused. I think you've known for a while. Will you indulge a theory?'

'Do I have a choice?'

'I don't think you killed your husband,' John said. 'But given what you were embroiled in, I do think you killed somebody.'

A sharp tug in her chest. She looked away.

'I think,' John said softly, 'you killed somebody and you never got over it.'

She knew both of them were watching her but she couldn't bring herself to look back.

'I think it destroyed you.'

She couldn't have stopped the tears if she wanted to.

'I wondered,' John went on, 'if I could piece the story together. And then I remembered an interesting report from some time ago. A suspected drug lord, known for being reclusive and cautious, shot to death in his secluded, guarded home. The rest of his operation wiped out shortly afterwards. The police were at a loss. And I thought, who could have managed that? Either a top assassin. Or someone he trusted. Someone he never could have imagined was a threat, someone—'

'Stop.' Charlotte's voice was high, breaking like a child's. 'Please stop.'

'Look at me, Charlotte.'

She shook her head.

'Charlotte.'

She looked.

John wasn't smiling anymore. He held her gaze.

'That man lived in a kill-or-be-killed world. He chose

that. And so did you. You can say you were naïve or stupid. But you were an adult and you knew what marrying Dominic Ford meant. Even if you denied it to yourself. Correct?'

She nodded without knowing why.

'Good. And that is why it's time to stop letting what happened tear you up. Killing – it's not a zero-sum game. Or a one-size-fits-all crime or whatever. What does that great old Kenny Rogers song say? The sentiment feels right. Sometimes you have to fight. And if somebody is trying to harm you – trying to, let's say, deliver you to those who would kill you without a second thought – then you'd be well within your rights to kill that person, wouldn't you?'

Charlotte did not look at Anders. A new, creeping dread churned in her gut.

John sat back with a broad smile. 'It's making those choices, doing what you need to do without giving in to fear or guilt, that will set you free. I think fear and guilt are killing you like a cancer. Not just figuratively either – they're stopping you acting to defend yourself. I could have killed you back in the bush. You knew that and you didn't act. And if you keep going like this, one day your luck will run out. So I'm going to help you turn things around.'

He walked over to the fireplace. Charlotte shot a look at Anders. His single working eye remained forward.

John turned. In his hands was a hunting knife. He approached the table. Pinched it by the point, lay it down, then slid it towards Charlotte. It came to a halt between her and Anders. Within reach of her left hand.

'Now,' John said. 'If I've worked this all out right, you have just enough slack on that rope to reach his chest or his throat.'

Charlotte didn't take the knife. She couldn't look away from John's awful smile.

'You want me to kill him,' she said.

John nodded.

'Why?'

'Because you should have done it days ago,' John said. 'But more importantly, because it's the only way I'll let you go.'

'Why would I believe that?'

'Well, I can't make you believe anything,' John said pleasantly. 'But I can give you my word that when Anders is dead, I will give you back the spark plug to your car and you can be gone before any more reinforcements arrive. Which honestly ...' He checked his watch. 'Can't be all that far away. So I'd get cracking.'

Anders was not looking at her.

Charlotte grabbed the knife. Anders flinched. She stuck the tip under the zip tie on her right wrist.

John had the gun aimed at her head before she could cut.

'Come on, Charlotte,' he said, almost lazily. 'Obviously I'm not going to let you do that.'

'Kill him yourself.' Charlotte didn't remove the knife. 'If that's what you want.'

'Oh, I will,' John said happily. 'If you don't. I'll kill him and I'll kill you and then I'll be on my merry way. But it's only fair to give you a chance. Now. Please. No more nonsense with the zip ties.'

The gun didn't waver.

Charlotte slowly removed the knife. She placed it back on the table. 'No.'

John raised an eyebrow. 'No what?'

'No, I won't kill him.'

'Why not?'

'Because I won't.'

'Because you're *not like me*?'

'No,' Charlotte said. 'It's got nothing to do with you. I just won't.'

'Even though he would have no hesitation in doing the same.'

'It's not about him either,' Charlotte said. 'I just won't.'

'But you *will*, Charlotte,' John said. 'You have to. You're as capable of murder as anyone. More so, because you've actually done it. Are you really telling me you never thought about killing your husband?'

Charlotte neither replied nor picked up the knife.

'So, what's changed?'

Still she didn't reply.

John sighed heavily. 'Alright. I was worried this might have happened. Some kind of reverse Stockholm syndrome thing.' He stood. Keeping the gun levelled at Charlotte, he returned to the mantlepiece. Patted along the top until he found a hammer. Hefted its weight then replaced it. Picked up the axe instead. A questioning look at Charlotte.

'Which one will it be?'

Anders, wary, watched John as he replaced the axe and chose the hammer. He returned to the table. Placed the gun down again. Raised the hammer.

'Whatever happens,' John said, 'he dies tonight. It's up to you how quick you want to make it.'

He brought the hammer down on Anders' knuckles.

A horrible, splintering crack. Anders screamed. Charlotte's whole body convulsed. John hit him again. Again. Anders' fingers were sticking out at wrong angles. John kept striking and Anders kept screaming until the hammer was bloody and the hand unrecognisable.

Charlotte tried to look anywhere but at the wailing Anders. Her gaze locked on the knife.

'Now,' John said over Anders' whimpers. 'How much more do you think he can take?'

'Please,' Charlotte said. 'Stop.'

'Only you can do that, Charlotte,' John said. 'End his pain, end your own. You can be gone in minutes. Just pick up the knife. That's all. Here. Let me make it easier.'

John came around behind Anders, turning the wheelchair so that Anders was angled towards her. Charlotte tried to estimate the distance to John but he still was out of reach. Anders was not screaming anymore but his breathing was heavy, agonised.

'Come on then,' John said. 'Give him a poke and let's wrap this up.'

Charlotte did not take the knife.

John stepped to the side and smashed Anders' kneecap with the hammer.

More screaming. Charlotte jerked forward, eyes closed, teeth clenched.

More hammer strikes. More screams.

Charlotte opened her eyes. The knife was there. Right there.

'I can do the other hand next,' John called over Anders. 'Then the other knee. Then the feet. At some point I'll start on his face. You know how many parts of the human body there are to break? At a certain point, Charlotte, you'll have to decide if killing him is kinder.'

She made herself look at Anders. The one eye she could see strained with agony.

'Go on,' John said softly.

Charlotte shook her head.

John crossed to the fireplace again and picked up the axe.

Charlotte held Anders' gaze. Tried to gauge if there was something he wanted to communicate through the pain.

He opened his mouth to speak just as John brought the axe down on his forearm.

Blood exploded over Charlotte. Anders' arm, still partly attached, flopped to the side. The hitman's neck was arched, every part of him struggling against the constraints, no sound escaping his wide-open mouth.

Charlotte picked up the knife.

John stood behind Anders, holding the bloody axe.

'Quick and easy, Charlotte. Then you're home free.'

Pale and panting, Anders looked at her. A very, very slight nod.

'Come on,' John whispered.

Charlotte struck.

A soft exhalation of breath from Anders. He keeled over and hung his head. Charlotte withdrew the bloody knife, her hand wet and warm.

Anders didn't move.

Charlotte heard her sobs as though they belonged to somebody else.

John stepped back, staring at Anders. Nudged him from behind with the axe.

'The heart?' John reached around to push Anders' head up, get a better look. 'Must have been! *Great* shot, I—'

Anders sank his teeth into John's wrist.

Charlotte cut her zip tie.

John was yanking at his arm. Anders bit deeper.

Charlotte swapped the knife to her right hand, cutting her ankles free.

John had dropped the axe. He was punching Anders in the head. It was impossible to tell whose blood was whose.

Charlotte stood. 'Hey.'

John looked up.

Charlotte slashed him across the face.

He reeled back. Charlotte snatched up the axe, slamming it into the rope still binding her to the chair. She faced John. He was staggering towards the fireplace. Charlotte came after him. He picked up a poker. Charlotte's gaze snapped to the gun on the table.

'Hey,' John said.

Charlotte looked.

He wedged the poker into the flaming logs and shoved.

A burning chunk of wood flew through the air, slamming into the table. The cloth went up in a blast of searing heat. The table rocked. The log hit the rug and rolled towards the curtains.

John ran for the door.

Flames, already rising, licked at Anders as he tried to lean away from them. Charlotte pulled the wheelchair clear as the curtains caught and fire spread across the rug. She cut away the zip ties, trying not to look at his mutilated hand and dangling arm, nor the point where she'd angled the knife to stab his shoulder instead of his heart.

'Get out,' Anders gasped.

The room swam in the rising heat.

Keeping hold of the axe, Charlotte worked her way under Anders' arm, the one that was still whole, and heaved upwards. He was heavy. He could barely stand and he cried out when he finally did. Charlotte tried to breathe and inhaled smoke. It was filling the room. The fire had reached the old wooden floorboards.

Slowly, far too slowly, Charlotte and Anders hobbled for the hall.

Charlotte chanced a look over her shoulder. The whole floor of the room behind them was fire now. There was no way to reach the gun.

The cold air outside was a wave of relief. Charlotte immediately had the axe up, but there was no sign of John. The street was flickering with the flames rising behind White Republic's windows.

About to collapse, Charlotte managed to get Anders across to the front steps of Snowhaven. He fell hard and heavy, yelping as he landed on his destroyed hand. Charlotte propped him up against the doorframe.

'Where is he?' Anders breathed.

'I don't know. Wait here.'

'Try and ... stop me.'

Charlotte opened the door of Snowhaven and hurried inside. She paused, axe raised. If John was inside, she would hardly hear him over the rising fire.

Keeping the axe up in both hands she ran up to her room. Found a couple of shirts and returned downstairs, waiting all the while for an attack that never came.

Anders was bone white. His eyelids fluttered as he watched the fire, bursts of heat rushing over them. White Republic was an inferno.

'Will it … spread?' Anders asked as Charlotte cut up the shirts and bound his dangling arm. Anders winced but didn't yell out.

'Too damp,' Charlotte said.

'The gun?'

'Inside.'

A crawling sensation across the back of Charlotte's neck. She spun, peered into the darkness.

There was a shape on the slope, obscured by the wafting smoke. Still. Watching.

It turned and headed for the trees.

Charlotte finished binding Anders' arm. Already, blood was seeping through the layers. He needed a hospital or he would die.

'You should … go,' Anders said. 'They will … be here.'

'I know,' Charlotte said. 'But I need to get my car working.'

'Plug probably … inside.'

She shook her head. 'I don't think so. I think he has it on him. He didn't want to risk me finding it.'

She stood. Grasped the handle tighter.

'You can't …'

Words were failing Anders.

'I have to,' Charlotte said. 'Don't die.'

Axe in hand, she walked forward through the smoke and dark, following John.

She didn't hesitate. Didn't let herself think or slow. She crossed the moonlit grey grass of the slope, nearing the dark trees, her only comfort the axe in her hand. Skyward, the clouds had cleared. A nearly full moon gave her some light, but once she was in the trees it wouldn't mean much. She didn't have a torch. She didn't have the gun. All she had was her familiarity with the bush, which, by this point, John rivalled.

I'm not scared.

She was scared, of course. Fear pulsed through her like too much electricity. She thrummed with it, like a live wire. She could not escape it. But she could choose to look past the fear, to what lay ahead.

She crossed the tree line into darkness.

She knew every rise, fall and knotted root of the path. But at night they seemed pronounced – deeper, sharper, more treacherous. Ahead her vision was all looming shapes and dangling branches. Shards of moonlight through the canopy brought slivers to brilliant life, but not enough to see where John might be waiting. And he would, of course, be waiting.

Her heart was thumping far too hard. It didn't matter. Shakes ran up and down her body. It didn't matter. Her mouth was dry and her head hurt and her hands were sweaty and none of it mattered because she would leave here tonight or die trying.

She continued onwards. Her vision was adjusting. She saw familiar trunks. Large rocks, perfect to hide behind. Her footsteps were too loud. She looked over her shoulder.

Back the way she had come, a faint red glow emanated through the trees. She could smell smoke. White Republic still burned.

She kept going.

Then—

'Are you going to kill me, Charlotte?'

She spun. The voice had come from behind her. No movement. Just the trees, the nothing between the trunks, the black furrow of the path.

She said nothing. Kept the axe raised.

I'm not scared.

She listened.

Then, from ahead.

'Have I done enough to deserve it?'

She faced forward but didn't move.

'All I've done was help you.'

She walked. Slowly. Steadily. Never lowering the axe.

She emerged into the little clearing. More moonlight here, highlighting a twisted branch, a trickle of sap, a tangle of scrub.

She came to a halt in the middle. Listened.

'You could have been gone already.'

From the left, through the trees.

She could see nothing in the shadows. She strained. Looking for any hint of movement. Listening for a cracking branch, leaf, a breath; anything. She waited.

John exploded from the trees to her side, slamming into her, sending her sprawling. The axe was gone. She rolled, desperately trying to find it. She could sense rather than see his towering figure getting closer.

There, lit by the moon, the axe handle. She grabbed it. Caught the base. Sat up and swung.

John, a faceless shape in the broken moonlight, stepped easily back.

'Could you live with it?'

'Give me the spark plug,' Charlotte said. 'And I won't have to live with anything.'

'But you already *do* have to, Charlotte. You always will. I'm trying to teach you how.'

'I survived once.'

The shape that was John shook its head.

'You haven't been listening to me. You're *not alive*. Punishing yourself is keeping you that way. You can be happy again. Free.'

Charlotte swung the axe. John caught her wrist and twisted. She felt a sharp pain and let go of the handle.

Then his face was in hers, pale in the moonlight, bloodied from the gash she'd given him but still smiling as he whispered.

'The predator never feels guilty over its prey.'

Dominic washing the blood off his hands.

John and the kitchen knife.

Anders: 'Many deaths are unfortunate. Just as many are self-induced.'

Uncle Mac's ruined face.

Charlotte dug her free fingers into the gash. John lurched back, letting go of her. Charlotte lunged for the axe again. John's boot took her in the stomach, sent her coughing and gasping into the ground.

Ahead, the gap in the trees. Her trap was right through there. If she could lure him to it, send him into the spikes ...

She crawled for it.

John stepped in front of her, smiling. He was holding the axe. 'You'll have to try harder than that,' he said.

Charlotte forced herself to her feet.

Instinct took over.

She ran.

Down the path, through the trees, never missing a step because she knew where she was going without having to think about it. She couldn't hear John over her rasping breathing and pounding feet, but she knew he was behind her. He knew this track, knew these trees.

But she knew them better.

The path rose, fell, turned. She kept running even though her throat was on fire and her legs were about to collapse. The forked path ahead, the narrower left turn. She took it. She ran. And then she was stumbling into the complete silence and pale shine of the bone forest.

The dead trees were unnaturally clear in the night. The moon illuminated them, stark and white and brilliant. She could see perfectly. She faced the way she had come, faced the darkness behind her. No movement or sound, but that didn't mean he wasn't there.

She backed up. Something slipped under her foot and before she could stop herself she was falling, twisting in mid-air to catch herself. Too late. Her head smacked off a fallen branch in the muddy ground. She groaned. Whimpered. Tried to stand.

For just a moment, a warm, comforting urge told her to not get up. To let whatever happened next happen.

You're not a killer, Charlotte. That's something to be proud of.

Her own hands under her, pushing her up to her knees, then her feet. Steps erratic, unsteady, she continued onwards.

Where are you going, Charlotte?

John's voice? Dominic's? Her own?

The skeletal trees around her. Her feet sinking into the mud left by the melted snow.

'Where are you going, Charlotte?'

John.

She couldn't run, not anymore. She half fell through the last of the trees and then she was on the slope that edged the cliff. Below and ahead she could see nothing. Even the stars didn't light up that empty black.

She moved sideways between the cliff and the white trees.

'Charlotte.'

She kept going. One tree ahead, distinct because of the way its trunk stuck out almost horizontal, reaching over the edge.

'Charlotte.'

The voice, too close behind her. The trunk overhead. She jumped a gap. Flailed through the air and landed winded in the mud. She rolled.

John was standing just metres away, the axehead glinting in the moonlight. Despite the mud and the angle of the slope he stood strong and solid, like nothing could ever shake him.

'Stop,' Charlotte said.

'What now?' John said. 'You going to plunge off that cliff? End it quick and easily? Do you really value your own life less than the scum back there?'

'Leave, John,' Charlotte said. 'Just give me the plug and leave.'

John smiled. 'You don't have the leverage here.'

'Please,' she breathed.

John laughed. Strode forward, under the jutting trunk. Strode right towards – near impossible to see in the dark – a rope stretched between half-buried sticks.

Then the axe was flying and John was falling forward, confused, trying still to walk, to stay upright despite the rope that had caught his ankles. He landed on his knees. Crawled a little. Looked up at Charlotte with an embarrassed laugh that died when he realised her eyes were not on him but on the space between the trees. On the dislodged, rope-bound boulder, large and heavy and almost round, rolling fast down the slope, towards the edge.

John looked at his feet. At the noose snagged around them, the trap he'd walked right into. At the rope trailing from it, all the way to the tumbling rock.

He met Charlotte's eyes. Smiled.

'Brilliant.'

The boulder went over the edge. With a violent tug, John was pulled after it. He didn't try to stop his fall. He didn't scream.

He just laughed. Laughed as he reached the edge. Laughed as he plunged over.

Laughed all the way down until a distant crash and finally the night was still.

CHAPTER THIRTY-TWO

By the time she arrived back at the village, White Republic was in ruins. Fires still smouldered inside the charred foundations of what had once been the oldest building on the mountain, lighting the night orange and dancing off the distant trees, but the inferno had been and gone and taken most of the lodge – and whatever was inside – with it. Charlotte took a moment to look it over, then headed back to Snowhaven.

The front door was slightly open. She found Anders inside, up against the wall. Blood dripped from the drenched red makeshift bandage around his arm.

'Is he dead?'

She nodded. 'But I didn't get the plug.'

He grunted. 'You'll probably die soon, then.'

She tried for a weak joke. 'Not before you, though.'

Anders' mouth twitched in a feeble smile. He was far too pale.

'I'm going to replace those bandages,' she said. 'I'll be right back.'

She went upstairs. Stopped in the living area, looking around at the place that had been her sanctuary, morphing fast into a trap and now, likely, a tomb. It could not be long until more men came for her. Reinforcements. Maybe she could hide out in the trees. Maybe she could scrape together a few blankets for warmth and get down the mountain by staying parallel to the road and out of sight. But none of that answered the question of what she would do next. What her future looked like. No car, barely any money, a pile of dead hitmen and no obvious culprit apart from herself. Dominic's old gang and the police would be even more interested in her than they had been before.

She was too burned out for regret. She cast an eye over the kitchen as she moved for her room.

And stopped.

John's scrapbook was sitting on the bench. Next to it was her bag, the one that had vanished when she first tried to flee.

When had he left them? How had she missed them before? Slowly, as though it was a bomb, she approached the book and opened it.

The newspaper articles. The sketches of people he'd killed or maybe hadn't. She wondered what he had really wanted. She'd assumed his claims of trying to help her were just self-aggrandising bullshit, but at the end he had seemed almost proud of her. Like that outcome was what he had been after all along.

She turned to the last filled page. There was a new illustration.

Herself. Standing alone among the snow gums. Even without colour the trees were recognisable. It was a strangely beautiful picture, faint in places and heavy in others, creating an uncertainty over where she ended and her surrounds began.

She was almost reluctant to turn the page. She did anyway. There was a smaller piece of paper in the middle of it, a note written across it. *Congratulations, Charlotte. The rest is all yours. – J*

With a trembling hand she slid the note aside. Behind it John had cut out a small, rectangular hole in the remaining pages. Lying inside was a spark plug.

She helped Anders into the car as soon as she had the plug replaced. She did one last round of Snowhaven, gathering up whatever clothes and belongings she had left. She considered going through and wiping down the surfaces, but she'd touched too much up here and something would slip through, some print they could match with the ones they'd doubtless taken from her old home. It wouldn't take the police long to work out that Katie McCauley, the off-season caretaker, was Charlotte Laurent. Her best recourse was to get the hell out before anyone realised anything was amiss up here.

The last of what she owned was in the car. She stood beside it in the cold, John's scrapbook in her hands. She opened it again to the picture of herself. Considered the sad, lost look on her face.

Heat kept her from getting too close to the still-smouldering remains of White Republic, sparks mingling with the stars in the black above. She went to toss the scrapbook into the glowing coals, then stopped. Every face in there, all these people whose murders might never have been solved. If this was evidence, she couldn't destroy it.

She tore out the picture of herself then crossed back to Snowhaven, placing the book inside the door. She went to fold up the illustration and pocket it. She stopped. Looked across at the last of the fire. Then scrunched it up, tossed it into the dying embers, and got in the car.

She drove slowly down the dark, winding road. Her headlights were on – it was a risk, but not as risky as driving without them. And if more hitmen were on the way, they'd find her, regardless of headlights.

Anders slept fitfully in the passenger seat, occasionally twitching or whimpering. She'd replaced his bandages as best she could and tried to splint his hand, but he'd lost a lot of blood and without a hospital she doubted he'd last much longer.

She passed a single, empty black SUV parked on the side of the road, which she guessed must have belonged to the hitmen. It wasn't much further than where she had turned off the road, where John found her.

She drove in silence, with the trees pressing in and the headlights turning the road washed-out and ghostly, thinking of the horror behind her and the nothing ahead. For days she'd been so focused on getting out alive that she hadn't really thought about what she would do with herself when – *if* – she made it. But as much as the empty quiet invited those thoughts, it wasn't yet the time. Once Anders was gone, once she was alone again and far away from Mount Skillion, then she could consider the rest.

So, she kept her focus on the road and concentrated on the drive and as she did she caught something out of the corner of her eye.

A trick of the light, maybe. A strange shadow cast by branches and rocks. She almost slowed the car to make sure. For one moment, she could have sworn she'd seen a figure in the trees, waving goodbye as she passed.

Anders woke as the sky outside paled and they rolled quietly through the empty streets of Burnley. She helped him drink from a bottle of water before driving the rest of the way to the small hospital on the outskirts of town, where a single light was on over the front door.

'I'd help you inside, but that's a risk too far,' Charlotte said. 'Once you're out on the lawn, I'll hit the horn then I'm gone.'

Anders eyed the hospital. 'Injuries like this will draw police.'

'They'll also draw death.'

He conceded that with a shrug.

'Where will you go?' Anders said.

'If it's all the same, I'm not going to tell you where I'm going.'

Anders nodded. Frowned. Went to speak, faltered, then pushed on. 'I would have brought you in. If John had not … I would have brought you in.'

'I know.'

'Then why help me? I can understand not killing me. But bringing me here … this was dangerous.'

Charlotte looked out the window. The first glow of sun was turning the distant paddocks golden.

'Tell you what,' she said. 'When you track me down, ask me again. Maybe by then I'll have an answer.'

Silence.

'You are dead,' Anders said.

A chill. 'What?'

'Your husband's associates will want to know what happened,' Anders continued. 'The truth will not look good for me. Or get me paid. And in my current state, I will need the money. So whatever story I come up with, that will be the ending.' He looked at her. 'You died on that mountain. Your body is in the trees somewhere. Charlotte Laurent is never coming back.' Then, a little harder: '*Is* she?'

Charlotte shook her head.

'That story will reach the police as well, knowing my employer's connections. They will investigate of course. But nothing they find up there will contradict what I say. After a few weeks, a few months' – he attempted a shrug – 'nobody will be looking for you. So wherever you go, whatever you do, please don't draw any attention to yourself.' His smile was weak but there. 'For my sake.'

She didn't know what else to say. She didn't know how to untangle the aching mess of emotions that nearly overwhelmed her. So she said nothing. She got out of the car. Took a long, deep breath. The sun was a little higher, the grey sky giving way to morning blue.

She rounded the car and helped Anders out, with some difficulty manoeuvring him into a seated position on the lawn. She stepped away. He nodded to her.

She got back in the car. Pressed down the horn. Held it for ten seconds. Then she gunned the engine and drove. She didn't look back at Anders. Didn't look in the rear-view to see if Mount Skillion had become clear in the sunrise. Her eyes were on the soaring blue and the molten glow of the rising sun.

Something was growing. A strange understanding.

Uncle Mac had been a cold-blooded killer, a willing participant in a violent world. So had Dominic. So was Anders. Two of them were now dead. But one wasn't.

What she had done to Uncle Mac had left a scar that would never heal. For the rest of her life it would be there, twinging sharp and sudden if she moved the wrong way. But there with it would be a new knowledge. That Anders was alive even though she could have killed him, maybe should have. And if he was true to his word, it was her very refusal to kill that might just have earned her freedom.

Did she deserve freedom?

She didn't know what she deserved. She didn't know how she felt about what had happened to John – although she had warned him. She didn't know what any of this made her.

But she knew, for the first time since she aimed that gun at Uncle Mac, that she could live with it.

She drove fast. Faster than she probably should have, but then nobody was on the road at this time. She passed trees and paddocks, lone farmhouses just beginning to stir. And then she started to laugh.

Loud and ragged and raw and real and alive.

EPILOGUE

And there she was. Stepping out of the car, sunglasses on, coffee in hand.

She was early. She didn't start until six. She crossed the road, entering the bar. Smiled words with her boss. Took a seat in a booth.

From his car he watched, the coin moving between his fingers. It had taken time to track her down. This town was bigger, more obvious than he would have expected, even if it was in a different state.

He got out of the car. Hands in pockets, crossed the road. Leaned against the wall, looking through the window of the bar at an angle. He raised a hand to knock. He wondered how she'd react when she saw him.

Her head was hunched over the table. He leaned a little closer.

A notebook open in front of her. She was writing something.

She looked up, biting her lip. He shrank back slightly. She nodded, grinned to herself and put pen to paper again.

He watched her a moment longer. Took a coin from his pocket and flipped it. He caught it. Opened his hand. He didn't look at it.

She was still writing.

He smiled, pocketed the coin, and returned to his car. He whistled the Bee Gees' 'Alone' as he drove into the evening.

ACKNOWLEDGEMENTS

I've been trying to tell this story, in one form or another, since 2009. Over the years, Charlotte Laurent had appeared in various drafts of various attempted manuscripts, but the entirety of her sad, complicated but ultimately hopeful story never quite became clear. She seemed destined to appear in the background of a different character's book, the perpetual supporting part.

But Charlotte's moment has finally come, and for that there are so many people who deserve the utmost gratitude. This book was not easy to write, but with the help of an amazing team we finally got there.

Firstly, to Catherine Milne, who backed a different kind of thriller about a different kind of protagonist after the hardcore action of *The Hunted* and *The Inheritance*, thank you for your support and belief. To Scott Forbes, without your careful oversight all my books would be incoherent messes. To Lachlan Jobbins, your in-depth editorial work was beyond invaluable, leaving me nodding along in embarrassed agreement as you gently identified ways to turn a messy draft into something far closer to what I had in my head. Thanks to Samantha Sainsbury for her proofreading that has saved many a book, including a couple of mine. To Rachel Dennis, for some very important last-minute catches – I owe you a lot! To Hannah Lynch for her work in getting this book out into the world. To Alex Ross for coming up with such an eerie, eye-catching cover. To John Erasmus for, completely off his own back, making the most awesome trailer imaginable for it.

To Tara Wynne and Caitlan Cooper-Trent at Curtis Brown Australia, always my biggest advocates, thank you for getting behind another big shift. Thanks to Nina Culley, who had to, first-hand, hear so much hair-pulling and agonising and misplaced optimism during the writing process and somehow put up with all of it. To Kate Murfett, a much better writer than me who always takes the time to read, guide and be a sounding board – I hope you know how much your help is appreciated, always. Thanks to April Newton, who has been there for so much of Charlotte's journey and supported me every step of the way. To my parents and brothers, and every friend who has nodded and rolled their eyes while I ramble on, thank you.

But, finally, I want to thank somebody without whom I wouldn't be here. In 2019, Tara sent *The Hunted* to Jerry Kalajian, who read it overnight and called me from his LA office, effusive and excited and ready to help represent it. It was Jerry who sold the film rights and advocated for me, who provided so much honest guidance and no-bullshit truth-telling in an industry that tends to lack both. But beyond that, Jerry was a friend, who along with Tara let me feel like I had a team to help me through a sometimes terrifying, sometimes exhilarating whirlwind.

Jerry passed away last year, only days after I finished the first draft of this book. It hit me hard. Jerry was so larger than life and so kind and so supportive that it was a struggle to imagine a career without his advice. While I'm lucky enough to have a wonderful support system, he is missed every day. And I will never, ever forget what he did for me. Jerry changed my life and helped give me the career I'd always dreamed of. I owe him so much.

Rest well, my friend. This one's for you.